Forever Falling

Book Two in the Series
Sunshine And Moonlight

Paige Randall

Photography by Paige Randall

ISBN: 978-0-9961523-2-7 (kindle)
ISBN: 978-0-9961523-3-4 (paperback)

Dedication

To the true **Paige** and **Randall**.
You are my everything.

One

He's not sure what pisses him off more, the fire searing his flesh yet again or the fact that his dick got him thrown out of his own restaurant. He flips the sea bass, ignoring the burn, and wonders who would order this shit. Who is paying forty-seven dollars for a decent piece of fish crapped up with a fucking basil infused beurre blanc. It's a shit dish. Damn her for adding it to the menu anyway. The line cooks are doing a lot of whispering tonight. *Cunts*, he thinks through his hate. He tries to breathe through it, to control his reaction, his impulse. He is successful for a count of fourteen seconds, and then he is done.

He throws the sauté pan, with the fish and shit sauce, into the sink. Metal hits metal loud enough to silence everyone in the kitchen. *Why wait until dinner service is over? They can all go straight to hell.* He might as well make a decent exit. With two hands and a big shove, he flips a silver prep cart covered in oysters. They scatter across the kitchen floor between the black rubber soled shoes of stunned, but blessedly silent, line cooks. He reaches behind the bar and grabs a bottle of McClelland's single malt scotch on his way out the front door. The London air is cold and wet and grey, at the same time a relief and oppressive. *Goodbye England, you bitch*, he thinks taking the first slug from the bottle. *I'm going to America.* He calls to book a flight on his mobile before the McClelland's takes hold.

1

Callum Townsend's plane lands in Columbia, South Carolina, before he thinks to call his sister to tell her he is coming. As the jet taxis toward the airport, he sends her a text. *Guess who's coming to dinner? If that's ok.* His sister, Anna Halloway replies in all caps. *ARE YOU JOKING? ARE YOU HERE?* Callum stands, or tries to. His nearly six foot, three inch frame isn't going vertical anywhere near his window seat. When his head clears the overhead bin, he still stoops, but reaches for his bag and shoulders the slight collection of possessions he has brought to America. A little ginger-haired boy, no more than five, leans over from the seat in front of Callum's and sticks his tongue out. Callum mouths *fuck you* silently. The little bastard was screaming and whining for half the flight and Callum wants to punch him in the face. Callum isn't as patient as he might be with poorly behaved children. The mother is a fat-faced ogre. She would probably dump the little fucker on the runway for a shot at ten minutes in the rest room alone with Callum.

Callum replies to Anna's text. *Just landed in Columbia. Spontaneous trip. Ok if I come to Osprey Island for a few days?* She replies immediately. *YES!!!YES!!!YES!!!* Well it's nice to be welcome, somewhere.

Callum just met his half-sister, Anna the previous winter. As a teenager, Callum's father got his girlfriend pregnant. Anna's mother was young and her parents coerced her to give up her baby for adoption. Callum's father never even knew he had a daughter. Finding a sister at the age of thirty was unbelievable for Callum. When he met Anna in January, she was just married and pregnant. Callum is ready to meet his niece. Actually there are two nieces. Anna is in the process of adopting her stepdaughter Clara.

Callum knows he shouldn't want to, but he is considering kicking Anna's husband's ass. Anna and John were separated when Anna came to London last winter. Even though Anna and John are together now and Anna says they are happier than ever, Callum thinks John needs a good old kick in the teeth for deserting his pregnant wife. *Who does that?* Callum rubs both hands through his short blonde hair, trying to decide who he wants to beat on more, the little ginger fuck or John. Having a sister is new to Callum and it's making him feel protective. He rubs his head harder, creating spiky points of hair. His head hurts, his hair hurts, his entire fucking being hurts. He needs a drink or a pill or something.

Callum walks while he texts and declines Anna's offer for a ride. He picks up the black Jeep Wrangler he arranged for yesterday. It feels very American. He easily navigates the Jeep toward the coastline of South Carolina. Within thirty minutes, he is speeding down an arrow straight, quiet, two-lane road, lined with tall trees. He stops at a gas station with a mini-mart, grabs a jacket from his bag and pulls the fabric shell top off the Jeep. He syncs his mobile to play through the car's Bluetooth. He picks up a six pack inside, cracks the top off a Becks and speeds along in the open air.

After years cooped up twelve hours a day, sometimes more, six or seven days a week, in hot cramped kitchens, screaming at line cooks, and taking orders, literally and figuratively, the air feels really good. Smooth music from *The Black Keys* fills the Jeep. Callum immediately likes South Carolina. The December air is cool and crisp but well warmed by the setting sun. It is a hell of a lot nicer then the dreary shit he left behind in London. He breathes in deep, tasting the sweet American air and pops open another Becks.

Ninety minutes later, Callum pulls onto a two-lane bridge for Osprey Island. Salty ocean air fills his soul. The bridge separates the mainland from a small barrier island about twenty miles north of Charleston. John and Anna live in a southern vacation paradise year round. When Callum pulls under the large ocean front house, he thinks this looks like a hell of a nice way to live. The house is large with dark rustic wood. Tall trees sway in the breeze. Callum admires hearty winter flowers still in bloom. Before he can get out of the Wrangler, Anna is in his arms.

"Callum, my darling brother. What the hell are you doing here?" Anna left England nearly twenty years ago to attend college in Maryland and she never returned. Her accent is much more prevalent when she is with her brothers. "This is the best surprise ever!"

He is happy to see her and picks her up, giving her a spin for good measure, but he doesn't have anything to say just yet. Seeing Anna is making him feel it all over again — the happiness of finding a sister, combined with the fury of knowing she grew up ten minutes away and he never knew.

After Anna came to visit, Callum tried to find her adoptive parents who were actually Anna's biological aunt and uncle. When Callum and his brother Eric learned of Anna's unhappy childhood, they wanted answers. More likely, they wanted a confrontation to defend the sister they never had an opportunity to defend. Her parents had died years before. *Lucky bastards.* Callum and Eric might have killed them. Callum realizes his brother Eric doesn't know he has left London. He should call later.

"Anna," Callum finally says, putting his sister down. They stare at each other, still learning the face of their new sibling. Their hair is nearly the same light shade of blonde and their sky blue eyes are the identical color. Both are slender, but Callum lifts a lot of weights and played nearly every sport England schools had to offer. He liked the contact of rugby, but he can play anything with a ball. "I'm not entirely sure what I'm doing here. I needed to get away," Callum says honestly. Anna accepts his indefinite answer.

"Okay then," she says and smooths his windblown hair into place. "Well come one in. There's a houseful who want to meet you and John is getting ready to cook out back." With a look of disapproval, Anna collects his six empty Beck's bottles and tosses them into the recycling bin.

"Really? You're drinking and driving during your first two hours in America? Can you imagine what prison is like down here in the south?" Anna says searching his eyes for answers that don't come out of his mouth. He just shrugs.

"*Deliverance* meets *Midnight Express* I'd imagine. You'll be getting an ass fucking in a Charleston prison, Turkish style. Behave your damn self, Callum," she scolds him and he lets her. Having someone give a shit is actually nice. He puts his arm around her shoulders, mumbles some apologies and they walk up the dark wooden stairs into the house.

John has him in a bear hug before he can get in the front door. Callum floats his hands in the air, not quite accepting John's warm embrace. "Callum, my new brother! I am so happy to know you." John's Austin drawl makes his enthusiasm damn near contagious. Near, but not quite infecting Callum. John wears his dark hair long, in waves below his collar, with a neatly trimmed beard. He is just an inch or two shorter than Callum, but much broader. John is all shoulder. John's smiling green eyes welcome Callum into his home and before Callum's bag is down, he has a McLellands in his hand. Callum is impressed, but he doesn't want to be.

"We'll move you over to bourbon, before too long. But for your first night, I wanted you to feel at home," John says rubbing Callum's shoulder. These Americans are very handsy.

Callum thanks John halfheartedly before setting down the scotch and dropping to his knees to greet Clara, John's three and a half year old daughter. Callum smiles at this long-haired beauty through dark ringlets falling over her face. He holds her curls back to get a better look and is rewarded with a smile.

Anna introduces them. "Clara luv, this is your Uncle Callum."

Callum takes Clara's hand in his for a shake. He could fit her entire arm into his hand. He might have liked to have a little girl like this one day, before he decided he is never having another relationship with a woman and, therefore, no children. Clara smiles tiny white teeth at him and sways side-to-side, but doesn't say much. Callum smooths his thumb along her silken cheek before rising to meet Lynn. Lynn sits against her mother's hip. She is just eight months old and her blue eyes are all Anna. She has John's dark hair and Clara's smile. Her lashes are a mile long.

Lynn's lashes make Callum's heart break a little. She is so tiny and so perfect. He tosses back his scotch and toasts the baby Elizabeth and Jeremy will be expecting soon back in London. They got the restaurant, a revived marriage and a new baby in the making.

"They are both beautiful," Callum tells Anna with a sullen smile. Callum glances at John lighting the grill on the deck. He feels less like kicking John's ass now that he's got the McClellands in him, and he's met John's two cute kids. Anna looks much happier than when he saw her in London. Despite the pregnancy, her face was too thin. She looked tired and drained. He thought it was exhaustion and travel, especially being pregnant. Now he can see how beautiful Anna really is. Her face is full of happiness and her smile is whole. Funny, when he saw her last winter, his smile was whole. Now his is hollow.

"Is everything all right Callum? You seem a bit sad. Is it just the travel or is something happening?" Anna asks, looking worried.

Callum shrugs and offers Anna a half smile. He shrugs a lot. Since he obviously is not interested in talking, Anna shows him to a large guest room at the end of the hall. "You'll have your privacy down here," she says. "No middle of the night baby nonsense for you."

He really is grateful. After his fall from grace, having someplace to land is a relief. "Thanks Anna, for letting me come. I am so happy to meet your family. The girls are a dream come true." He sets his bag down on the bed.

"Callum, you are my family too. Don't forget that. Absolutely anything you need, any time. That's what big sisters are for, right?" Anna asks with a worried smile.

He nods and takes another offered hug from his sister. He can't remember the last time he hugged so much. *When in Rome.*

"Just settle in then. John and I will get the girls to bed and we can have a nice quiet dinner. You have everything you need?"

"I do. Thanks Anna. I have everything I could ever want."

Lies and more lies, he thinks. *I don't have what I want at all.*

A few minutes later, Anna calls down to ask if he'd like to read a book to Clara. *Shit.* "Can I tell her a story? I'm a good story teller," he offers.

Callum sits next to Clara on her purple covered bed and tells her a story about a princess named Victoria who saves a prince from a mean cow named Moo Moo. Let the princess win this round. Little girls shouldn't grow up thinking they need saving.

"This is great John, really excellent," Callum says, pointing his fork at the perfect medium rare steak. No one grills a steak like John. Most people can't grill a steak for shit.

"I'm glad to hear it. Cooking for a chef is a little daunting," John studies Callum hard. This is his first opportunity to really look at Anna's brother. "My god you two look a lot alike. Not just look alike, but you move alike. It's pretty fucking amazing."

Anna takes Callum's hand for a squeeze. John can see she is happy to have her brother here, but she is worried about him.

"And how's Eric? And your Mum," Anna asks.

Callum tells them about Eric's latest travels. He is a surgeon and prefers to spend as much time traveling as possible. He works with a London practice when he is in town, but he is just as likely to be found in one of many African or South American counties. "Eric has more air miles than anyone I know," Callum comments and adds quickly, "Mum is well enough," without elaborating.

John can't help wondering why Callum is here. He is offering no explanations and he isn't the happy go lucky guy Anna had described.

John waits until Anna is clearing the dishes before he tries to do some digging. "So is this your first time in the states, Callum?"

"I came years ago on a school trip, New York and Washington. Lots of sightseeing and sneaking out of the hotel, chasing American girls at night. That sort of thing."

John leans back in his chair and sips his bourbon. He doesn't want to interrogate his guest, but Callum is not giving any clues to the reason for his sudden appearance on Osprey Island. Anna gives John an encouraging nod to get Callum talking.

"Callum, this might seem a strange question from one man to another, but do you want to go for a walk on the beach with me?"

Callum laughs hard. "Romance is in the air. I accept, my darling brother-in-law. On one condition."

"Anything," John says.

"Bring the bourbon." Callum says rising, pushing in his chair and kissing Anna's cheek.

They head out the back deck, down the wooden walkway and into the sand. The tide is high so they sit close to the dunes in the dry sand. They sit with the bottle between them and drink from short glasses.

"It's fucking fantastic here," Callum says, watching the ocean pound the surf.

John laughs out loud.

"What?"

"The day I met Anna, we stepped into the sand and that is exactly what she said. It stuck with me."

Callum smiles into his glass. "Let's hope things end differently for us, John."

"Agreed," John says, remembering lying Anna naked across her countertop, shortly after their first visit to the beach together. John lets Callum enjoy the calming sounds of the surf. It is every bit as intoxicating as the bourbon and John doesn't mind a little silence.

"I'm a little disappointed in you John," Callum says finally.

John is surprised. "You are?"

Callum takes his time before explaining. "I had planned on hating you. I was going to beat you senseless, actually."

John gives him a slight nod and a *Hmmm*.

"How the fuck did you leave my sister when she was pregnant with your baby?" Callum doesn't really ask. It is more of an indictment.

John hasn't had to answer this question at all. Everyone in their lives understood the complications of his relationship with Anna in those early days. Their rocky start is behind them now and John isn't really interested in apologizing for it. Still, Callum is Anna's brother and he does have certain rights.

"What do you know about us Callum?" John realizes he has no idea what Anna has shared with her brothers.

"I know that Anna's first husband died of a brain tumor. She lost her baby too, before you met. And you are a widower. After all that, you still left her?"

John is a little surprised that Callum doesn't know more. He would never describe Anna as an open book though.

"There was a little more to it than that," John says. He decides if he wants Callum to trust him and open up, he has to open up a little too. "My wife committed suicide. It was post-partum depression, maybe psychosis. Clara was just a baby. I left her with my brother and his wife, and I ran off for a year and a half. I was in pretty bad shape. Guilt and grief and a lot of anger. I met Anna here when I started putting the pieces back together last summer." John leaves it there. He still struggles with how much detail to share with new people. Finding the right balance between shocking and understating when he's trying to be honest is difficult. He looks as Callum's eyes go wide and knows that was enough detail.

"Jesus I'm so fucking sorry mate." Callum says, staring at the ocean and tipping back his bourbon.

John runs a hand through his hair and shrugs it off. "I'll let Anna tell you her bit, but I will say one thing. Her husband was abusive. She had a lot of shit to work out, so did I. And we needed to do it apart." A cold wind blows off the water and John fills their glasses. "You like the bourbon?"

"I do," Callum says draining his glass again. "I am so fucking sorry John. I had no idea."

"You were dreaming, thinking you could kick my ass anyway." John says with a sideways smile. He is starting to like Callum.

"Bullshit. I box. I play rugby. I could absolutely kick your ass."

"You probably played soccer too," John says with a smirk.

"Soccer," Callum says through his nose, imitating the American pronunciation. "No such sport."

"I figured the football versus American football debate was coming, but this is faster than expected," John's smile makes his green eyes shine. "So what are you doing here, Callum? International travel isn't usually so spur of the moment."

"Oh shit, I did sort of pop in. I didn't mean to be an imposition." Callum says, regretfully.

"No way, man. No imposition at all. You can stay all winter. See that house there," John points over his shoulder to the blue house they call

517. It is next door to his own house, numbered 516. "That is ours too. It's empty until summer. Want it?"

"Jesus that is a generous offer, John," Callum says, surprised.

"Are you here to stay?" John asks.

Callum shrugs. "I seem to be without plans at the moment."

"I have to be honest with you Callum. You look a lot like I did when I ran off to South America for all that time. It's your business, but I'm asking anyway. Are you running?"

Callum looks out over the ocean for a long time. Again John is taken aback by how much he is like Anna.

"I fucked my partner's wife. We owned the restaurant together. I'm saying I fucked her, but I was really completely in love with her. I don't really do love. I'm more of the one and done sort. In a nutshell, I lost her and I'm fucking gutted."

"He find out?" John asks without judgment.

"I told him," Callum says and shares an ironic smile.

John knows enough. The whys and whens are Callum's business. John rubs Callum's shoulder and feels a lot like he's sitting with his own brother, Brian.

The next morning Callum wakes up early to run. He is surprised to find John lacing his shoes on the front steps.

"Beach or streets?" John asks.

"Both. Let's make it a long one," Callum is sure he can beat whatever miles John can do.

They run four miles north on the beach, cut back to the streets and run another six. Their stride is about the same and they both go two or three miles longer than they would have gone if they were running alone. They are quiet, but their unspoken competition is a little fierce. They finish, exhausted, panting, covered in sweat and fall onto John's front steps. Anna opens the door and leans against the door jamb with a proud smile, observing her men.

"Breakfast, my darling boys?" she asks.

"You cooking?" John asks. Anna doesn't cook, but she bakes.

"Of course not. I did bake scones though. Callum will you cook for us?"

Callum is happy to cook as long as it isn't in that damn kitchen he left behind. After a quick shower, he walks into John's kitchen. John is an avid cook and gives Callum a tour of his well-stocked kitchen. Callum is impressed with the selection of professional grade knives, cutting boards, as well as fresh herbs and spices.

While John feeds Lynn in her high chair, Anna sits at the table watching her brother move masterfully through the kitchen. He chooses pans, checks the weight of a knife, and pulls what he wants from the refrigerator. He smells and tastes herbs before they warrant a spot on his cutting board. He dampens a towel and sets it under a silver mixing bowl to prevent sliding.

"I want to thank you for offering your house John. It is very generous." Callum cracks eggs with his left hand and whisks with his right. "But I've decided to travel around a bit. I'd like to see some mountains and ski. I want to get to know America beyond the big east coast cities. I'm going west."

"How long are you able to stay?" Anna asks.

Callum knows he should be honest with her. He feels like such an ass though. "I'm not going back for the immediate future Anna. I left the restaurant. I have some money put away, and Jeremy and Elizabeth are buying me out of the restaurant so I'll have that check in a few weeks. I'm going to stay in the states for now. I don't want to think about the future just yet."

Anna smiles. "John and I have some experience with living in the present tense, Callum. We get it. What can we do for you?" Anna asks.

"I'd like to visit here for another few days and then I'll head west. I'd like to take my time. I want to see St. Louis and Nashville and do some skiing. Maybe get to Salt Lake City."

"Salt Lake?" Anna asks, enunciating the words more than necessary. "Where the Mormons live?"

"There's a lot more than Mormons in Salt Lake City. Utah hosted the Olympics in 2002. It was really beautiful." Callum says defensively, even though he makes this declaration completely on the spot. This plan is forming in his mind even as it flows from his mouth.

"All right then. It sounds wonderful," Anna bites into the offered omelet. "This is fantastic," she says, pointing her fork at the eggs.

"Will you consider coming to Austin for Christmas?" John asks. "My family is there and they'd love to meet you. Austin, Texas." John says in case the location of Austin isn't known the world over. "We'll fly out there a few days before Christmas."

That gives Callum almost four weeks to explore before he gets to Texas. He can fly from wherever he ends up if he doesn't want to drive. "Sounds like a perfect plan. I'd enjoy meeting more Texans." Callum laughs and feels better with a plan in place. *My first Christmas with my sister.*

Callum's visit extends longer than he initially planned. He likes the pace of Anna and John's Osprey Island life. They work, spend time with their kids and friends. They cook and play a lot of music. Callum thinks he needs to learn to play guitar to spend time with John and his friends. They are all musicians and good ones. Callum adores his nieces too. Every day Clara insists on a story from "Uncle Callie" and walks the beach with him, digging for shells. He finds this uncle thing to be surprisingly enjoyable.

Spending time with Clara, Lynn is still a little unresponsive, makes Callum think about all he is missing and all that he is going to miss. Every time he thinks about Elizabeth, which is all of the time, the hole through him is so big that he can only feel regret and pain. He questions every decision. He wonders why he got involved with her in the first place. She isn't the most beautiful woman he's ever known. She is lovely, but that is about it. Her body is definitely top notch, though. She was always in charge which he detested before he was fucking her. She was a bit of a know-it-all too. He didn't really like how she ran the restaurant.

Still one day, almost a year ago, he held her against the wall in dry storage and wall fucked her brains out. *Why?* He wasn't in love with her or pining after her, but after he wall fucked her, he couldn't get enough of her.

Walking the beach alone one evening, Callum really tries to be honest with himself about why he started it. *Was I just bored?* The bloom had rather faded from the rose of having a successful restaurant. Initially the satisfaction alone fed him. For years it fed him. The minor celebrity status he enjoyed in London was fantastic, but the hours and commitment were enormous. He had a selection of numbers to call day or night for a quick lay. He prowled the bars after closing a few times a week when he wanted to meet someone new, but that was it.

Fucking is fantastic but approaching thirty, suddenly everyone is getting married and there are babies everywhere. It can start to feel, not so much hollow as, less fulfilling. Elizabeth made everything come alive for Callum. Colors were brighter, food tasted more intense. Coming to work, meant coming at work. The lying and hiding. It was exciting as hell. And then the excitement and the game became more. He didn't want to share her with Jeremy any more.

Callum suddenly imagined a different life for himself. Instead of a bed in a room in a flat he didn't own, maybe a house. He shared a place with Jeremy and Elizabeth. It made sense when they were just starting out, but it never seemed the right time to leave... until he wanted his own home, with Elizabeth. There could be curtains and a garden. He could plant herbs and Elizabeth could grow roses. They could light a fire in a fireplace, the wood kind, no remote controlled gas thingy. They could make babies. He could be a daddy. He would be a wonderful daddy.

But Elizabeth enjoyed the sharing. She didn't want to give up Jeremy. So Callum finally told Jeremy one day over a scotch at the bar of their restaurant after closing. Callum said his piece very matter of fact and he gave Jeremy one free punch. Callum took a decent hit to the jaw. Callum isn't entirely sure how, but it all fucking backfired. Now Jeremy and Elizabeth are happier than ever and Callum is an outcast.

After four days, he realizes he needs to move on. He's having trouble stifling his anger and depression. His stiff upper lip is going soft, with too much drink and not enough activity. Idle hands make for... whatever. He wonders if Elizabeth is pregnant already. She and Jeremy will be quick to make their marriage-saving baby. The thought of Jeremy's hands on her makes Callum want to scream and then it makes him want to touch himself.

On the last morning, Callum loads his bag into the Jeep and says goodbyes in the driveway.

"John, I've decided that I'll love you like a brother," Callum says and John picks him up for a very unmanly hug. Callum feels that John is the perfect match for Anna and his initial reservations are all gone.

When John finally sets him down, Callum says, "I've also decided not to shave or cut my hair because I like your look, John. You define forty-year-old American cool."

"Go fuck yourself," John says with a smile. "I define cool at any age. I guess we'll see you at Christmas with a beard and a little more hair. We'll look like brothers," John rubs Callum's short spikes and Callum kisses John's checks only because John doesn't see it coming.

"No surprise that John has another fan. He has that effect on people," Anna hugs her brother tight. "My god, spending time with you has been wonderful. Just wonderful."

Callum just smiles at Anna because he is feeling those emotions he isn't used to feeling. She smiles back and smooths his check with her hand. Words aren't always necessary.

Callum takes Clara into one arm and Lynn into the other, doing that fake I'm going to drop you thing to Clara that moms hate. Anna just laughs.

"Again Uncle Callie, again!" Clara screeches and Callum complies.

"I have never been called Callie in my life. Less than a week in America and I have a nickname and I like it, too." He kisses cheeks again, climbs into the Wrangler and drives off, watching John pull Anna close to his side, wondering if he could have had that with Elizabeth if he'd kept his fucking mouth shut.

Two

Callum spends exactly three minutes familiarizing himself with Utah using Google on his mobile. He decides to head toward Park City instead of Salt Lake. Park City because it looks cooler and the webpage shows Aaron Paul eating in a restaurant there during the Sundance Film Festival. The only television show Callum has watched in the last six years is Breaking Bad. One night he was up late recovering from a marvelous blow job. After Callum shooed the waitress out the door, he flipped around the channels and landed on a season one, episode one, late night re-broadcast. The characters' misuse of the concept of cooking fascinated him. He bookmarks the photo to make sure he sits in the same seat as Aaron Paul.

With the Expedia app, he finds a resort called Red Canyons that sits on the side of a mountain. Nice but not extravagant. He hates the assholes at extravagant resorts. Google Maps tells him the drive is 2,203 miles and should take about thirty-two hours of driving. He maps out a rough schedule and chooses fun cities to visit along a mostly direct route — Asheville, Nashville, St. Louis, Kansas City, Denver and Cheyenne. He plans for six to eight hours of driving a day.

The Wrangler has a good heater and he is glad for it. Despite the cold, he wants some damn fresh air and drives most of the time with the windows

17

open. Driving west to Asheville through the mountains, the sky is so blue that it looks fake after years of living in the city. The evergreens make a colorful tree line despite the time of the year. A light dusting of snow coats the grass. White clouds circle the mountain tops.

When Callum drives into the city, he circles around until he finds a nice looking hotel with a bar and then he moves on to the next hotel where he parks, unloads his bag, and checks in for one night. A hot, long shower soothes his stiff muscles and he regrets not taking a run before the shower. A good run would help take this edge off. Instead, he lets the water run and uses his hand to take the edge off.

Remembering the top of Elizabeth's head as she sat between his knees gets him started. She could do wonderful things with her mouth. She would spread her hair over his thighs before she devoured him. After the shower, he is more frustrated than before. He decides to run in the morning but now is time to tend to other needs.

He dresses in straight black jeans, a surprisingly crisp white shirt (he packs well) and a gray jacket. He slips on black shoes and his Tag Heurer watch before checking himself in the mirror. His blue eyes pass over his reflection with a look of approval and more than a touch of arrogance. He looks good and he knows it. His skin is unmarred by any imperfection. Cheek bones are high and help him exude an air of confidence that men of less height and looks cannot achieve. He slides a wallet, mobile and key into his pocket and heads to the hotel next door.

The walk is less than a block, uphill, past an alley with extraordinary paintings covering the brick. Callum stops and stares, wondering where the difference lies between graffiti and art. Are paintings like this a menace or a welcome contribution to the local color of Asheville?

The block gives him some distance, some privacy. He isn't interested in an overnighter. Callum finds the hotel lounge easily and takes a seat at the bar. He orders a double McClellands, straight up. These Americans and their ice. The bar is modern, lots of grays and metal accented with dark woods and lime yellows, hot pinks and rich teals. A denim dressed woman strums an acoustic guitar and sings an old James Taylor song. Callum sits comfortably in a tall chair and surveys the other patrons at the bar.

Married woman, who want to fuck strangers, sit at the bar not at tables with their girlfriends. He isn't interested in single women. He'll take an attractive, married, older, even slightly heavier woman, over a single, young hottie every time. Married woman are a fuckload more enthusiastic with their mouths and don't act like you owe them something for getting a glimpse at their pert young tits. They are also less complicated. There is no *What's your phone number? Follow me on Twitter*, bullshit. Just a fuck. All he wants is a damn fuck.

He downs the scotch and thinks he probably should have eaten something. He'll get this going quick and then grab a burger back at the hotel. A cheeseburger and fries. Simple American food will be just the thing. He taps the rim of his glass with his index finger and the bartender fills it immediately. Tall, handsome men get better service than the rest of the world. He surveys his options. There are six women sitting at the large bar. Two are together so he counts them out. Four are alone. Two are within his preferred age range, attractive and wearing wedding rings. One is texting and seems to be watching the door so he sets his eyes on the other. Sipping dark red wine, she is more than adequately attractive. Dark hair is piled on top of her head with strategically placed curls hanging down in front of her ears and framing both sides of her face. Dark eyes are lined in brown but not heavily. Her dark lipstick will look good on his dick. He guesses her age to be early to mid-forties. No crow's feet or laugh lines show, but there is a confidence to her that doesn't come for most women until after forty. He likes confident woman but not for too long. Sitting back, relaxing in his seat, Callum decides she is the one.

Before the minute Callum takes to assess her has passed, she seems to feel his eyes on her. She has done this before and points to the empty

19

seat next to hers with mascaraed lashes. He picks up his drink but not the napkin under it and makes his way around the bar. Callum sits at her side and the bartender lies a clean cocktail napkin as Callum places his drink on the bar, on the fresh white napkin. It is almost a well-rehearsed dance.

"Hello," is all Callum says. She uncrosses slender but shapely legs, turning to face him. She lets her knees fall to either side of his.

She says nothing in return. She sips her wine and appraises him, silently approving with a smile. Callum knows women like her have a lot to lose from evenings like these, even if she is far from home. He lets her assess his worth silently, knowing he'll come out on top of any equation.

"I'm…" he starts.

"No need," she stops him.

All the better. "Very well then," Callum drains his second double and turns to his new, nameless friend. She has a great mouth. She looks like a woman up for a challenge. She leans in to hear his low voice and to give him a glimpse down her shirt. Bras are for less determined women.

"I'll tell you what, luv, I'm going to let you blow me. If I like it, I'll give you the best fuck of your life. If not, we'll say goodnight." Nothing like a little motivation to get things going. He figures he has a fifty-fifty shot she'll slap him and move on. There are other fish.

She continues to study him with a savvy smile. "You are a bad one, aren't you? You have a room here?" He shakes his head. "Mine then." She places a key in his lap, taking a feel of the merchandise he is offering. "Give me ten minutes." She leaves him to pay her tab and walks straight to the elevator, no looking back.

When he knocks, she answers by cracking the door and walking into the room. He walks in and sits in a soft, brown chair by the bed. The chair isn't for hours of lounging, the arms are low and the back is narrow, but it is wide and will suit his needs just fine. She sits on the edge of the bed in a white hotel robe. She manages to make it look sexy, draping the center low. Her toes are tipped in red and they remind him of Elizabeth's toes. This makes him angry.

"I won't kiss you. Your kiss is for your husband," He unbuckles his pants but leaves the rest for her. He hears a shower turn on in the next room. *Oh good, thin walls.* He likes thin walls.

She moves across the room and kneels between his legs. He appreciates her silence. Her robe intentionally drapes lower. He wants to touch her, to move the robe off her but doesn't. First things first. She unfastens his pants and he lifts himself so she can slide them to his ankles. There is no place he would rather be on the planet, than sitting with his pants around his ankles and an eager woman between his knees, deciding best how to please him. And please him she does. She uses her mouth with the aggression of a woman who is confident in her skills. She uses her hand creatively to support the work of her mouth.

Twelve minutes later, he does pull the robe from her and give her the fuck of her life. He leans her over the back of the same chair and wraps his hand around her neck. He applies enough pressure to make her feel controlled but not raped, a little choke fuck. She is too wild and he can tell she desperately wants to be controlled. He could tell before he moved across the bar. He isn't a hitter, but he knows when someone wants a little discomfort to move things forward and heighten the experience.

After he comes a second time, he pulls up his pants and buckles his belt and asks, "Are you satisfied?"

Tying the robe around her waist, she nods without looking at him and he walks out the door.

Back at his hotel, he strips, showers and calls down for a burger, fries and chocolate shake. He flips through channels, and finds Julie Andrews singing, *How Do You Solve A Problem Like Maria.* He turns the TV to face the table and bites into the burger humming along to the tune.

The next morning, Callum feels refreshed. The lay served its purpose. Thoughts of Elizabeth and London are more distant, not at the front of his brain tormenting him with regret. Running the streets of Asheville, early before foot and car traffic can impede his speed, he feels better than he has felt since the plane landed. Even elated. The beauty of the low morning sun over the mountains catches his eye. He scopes out a place to stop for breakfast on his way out of town. The city is full of head shops and art galleries, restaurant after restaurant. Construction cranes reach toward the sky and a reversing trash truck sounds in the distance. Bronze art lines the town square and, even this early, an old bearded man with a guitar stands on a corner singing a song Callum doesn't know about lost love. Callum shakes his head at the cliché and runs faster, pulling a sprint until he is well winded.

Asheville is like a pill. A happy pill. It is the furthest thing he can imagine from London. For a city, the pace is much calmer, the buildings are low, the mountains, the art, the casually dressed people walking dogs. Dogs are everywhere. He could get a dog. A big white dog with blue eyes. Maybe a Husky. Not a little shitty lap dog. A man's dog. He could move to Asheville, open a restaurant, get an apartment over a head shop and walk his dog in the mountains. It sounds like a good life plan. He feels good, energetic.

Back at the hotel, he decides not to live in Asheville. There is a lot more to see in American. He can't choose the first city he sees as his new home. Callum grabs a quick shower, skips the shave, packs and checks out before heading to Tupelo Honey for a big breakfast. He eats biscuits, over easy eggs, smoky sausage gravy, bacon and a bowl of berries. The food is well prepared and he is pleased, satisfied.

Callum drives out of the city thinking it was a good night in Asheville. He will come back here someday. It feels very American and he likes it. He likes the women here too. He remembers the feel of her neck under one hand while making her come with the other hand. And how he filled her. It was a good night in Asheville indeed.

The rest of the drive is more of the same. Callum falls in love with each of the cities he visits. Driving six to eight hours a day, sometimes more, sometimes less, depending on the traffic, he works up a variety of appetites. He samples the cuisine and the women at every stop. The stretch between Kanas City and Denver is toughest. An overturned tractor-trailer turned an eight hour drive into a fourteen hour drive. He didn't mind too much though. It was still better than being stuck in that fucking kitchen watching Jeremy with his hands on his wife while she still had some of Callum in between her legs.

Callum samples a lot of local flavors. In Nashville, he spends time with a buxom, redheaded country singer after her set at the Mercy Lounge. Callum sits a few rows back while she belts out tunes about love and pain and finding Jesus. Eventually, she finds Callum and she sings his praises too. Callum doesn't really enjoy her singing, but he enjoys her tits. She is eager, pulling him into her dressing room with her mouth on his and her hands down his pants. She does exceptional work with her mouth before he bends her over a chipped Formica dressing table circled with light bulbs, half of them are out. Lifting her turquoise sequined dress, he takes her from behind so he can watch himself come in the mirror. He likes the stubble. After, he finds some Memphis style barbeque.

In St. Louis, Callum enjoys seeing the sights aboard a river boat cruise along the Mississippi. The tour guide is cute with short blonde hair but a little young. After she does her bit, she seeks Callum out on a bench on the back of the boat. She claims to be a writer, but she is probably more of a fantasizer. She takes the tiniest bit of convincing. She has never been with a man like Callum, that much is obvious, but she wants something to write about on her blog. He pulls her into the men's room. She isn't that great with her mouth, but Callum gives her points for enthusiasm. After the passengers disembark, he bends her over the railing of the riverboat, lifts her navy blue tour guide skirt, and comes while looking at

The Gateway Arch. It is cold, but he doesn't mind. He gives her a good enough lay to provide material for many future blog posts. On her recommendation, he finds a gooey butter cake and toasted ravioli for dinner. It is a little heavy and over the top but still nice enough.

Kansas City, Denver and Cheyenne. Another blonde, a brunette and a black haired woman who claims to be of the Cheyenne nation, but Callum thinks she is lying and is really Mexican. He isn't that good with accents though so he isn't sure. Kansas City is in the dry storage of an outstanding steak restaurant. He nearly closes his eyes passing through the kitchen because he can't bear to look at it. The steak is first rate. He opts for the porterhouse with a potato and broccoli. Very traditional. The steak is more memorable than the lay.

In Denver, he meets a woman in a hotel bar and fucks her high as a kite on the roof of her hotel. He bends his rules in Denver for a young single model type. The sex is extraordinarily athletic. There is a wall fuck against brick, a stair fuck on the way back down, and finally a bed fuck that gets a little too touchy and looky. Callum pretends to fall asleep after the third round until she falls asleep and then he slides into his pants, grabs the rest of his clothes and slips out the door. He doesn't bother putting his shirt on through the hallway. The patrons of the hotel seem to enjoy the show. He does slide on his shoes and gray jacket for the walk to his hotel next door. He likes Denver more than anyplace else so far.

And finally he drives the rest of the way and into Park City, Utah. The pot and the sport fucking had him sleeping in, so he arrives in town later than intended. He parks in the historic downtown district to stretch his legs before checking into Red Canyons. Walking the streets he thinks Park City looks more like a movie set than a town. The streets are built into a steep incline. Block after colorful block of old west architecture mixed with the modern sensibilities of capitalism. Theaters, galleries, lots of retail and restaurants. The feel is all west. A street musician, with a hat as large as Callum has ever seem, strums a guitar and sings in a tone

Callum can't even understand. Country music is not for him. The hat is interesting though.

The Stearns Cowboy Shop catches his eye and he goes in, walking the rows of leather boots, hats and bags in every color, breathing in deep the smells of the Wild West. He likes it here. Christmas presents! He chooses four cowboy hats in varying sizes for John, Anna, Clara and Lynn. Callum asks another shopper who looks about Anna's size to try on the hat intended for Anna. This leads to a brief conversation and a quick fuck in her car at the back of a parking garage with the bag full of boxed hats resting on the cement outside the car. Callum just gives her the easy fuck. He is tired, hungry and anxious to explore Utah.

After reconsidering carrying four hats around the country, Callum goes back to the shop and asks the girl at the counter to ship the hats to the address Callum has for John's family in Austin. The girl is pretty with long dark hair and light blue eyes. She reminds him of that actress from Transformers who married that guy from 90210. He can't remember her name. She offers him some shipping forms and he flips her a twenty for filling them out for him. As she self-consciously tucks her hair behind her ear, smiling expectantly, Callum wonders if he should reconsider his policy against young, single woman for a second time. Fresh from the car fuck, he decides against it. No need to get greedy. He thanks her and ignores her pout when he exits the store before going down the block to 350 Main Cafe.

Callum sits at the bar in the seat he thinks Aaron Paul sat when he came for Sundance. Feeling very American, Callum orders a double bourbon, buttermilk fried chicken, garlic red skinned mashed potatoes, red eye gravy and braised kale with house-made bacon.

"What kind of bourbon can I get you?" the bartender asks, pointing to the bourbon bottles on a high shelf.

Callum realizes he doesn't know a thing about bourbon and tries to remember what John was drinking. He surveys the shape of the bottles and the color of the labels. One of them has a red waxy top. It wasn't that one. A few are very square in shape with long necks. Callum visualizes John pouring to fill his glass on the beach. The bottle was rectangular, with rounded shoulders and a short neck.

"That one, two from the left," Callum says pointing.

"Woodford Reserve? Good Kentucky bourbon. An excellent choice," the bartender pours one for Callum and one for himself. "You new in town? First one's on the house."

Callum laughs and they both tip back their shots. "I always wanted to say that. It just felt right." The bartender introduces himself as Derrick. He is a native Floridian and arrived in Park City a year ago to ski, fuck and generally have a good time for a year before heading east for law school. He is a good looking guy with long blonde hair pulled tight into a man bun. His skin is dark, reddened by hours in the sun on skis and in the surf.

Callum inhales the dinner, it is good, while Derrick gives him the rundown on the area, the best bars, restaurants, places to meet the right women. He tells Callum to ski his resort until he gets bored with it and then to come back in for suggestions on other areas. Derrick reminds Callum what he liked about working in restaurants. The camaraderie and lifestyle are like no other. Callum tips him heavily and promises to come back soon. As an afterthought, Callum asks Derrick about Aaron Paul. This in fact is the stool where Aaron Paul sat, or so Derrick says.

Red Canyons sits at the top of a hill. The lobby is very western in style with wooden carvings, Native American tapestries and lots of leather furniture. Callum decides to stay away from the staff. You don't shit where you eat. He learned that lesson the hard way in London. He checks in and is pleased to find his room has a nice balcony facing the mountains and a gas fireplace. Despite the cold, he opens with door wide and watches hundreds of skiers descending the mountain and red gondolas climbing up. Bright lights illuminate the slopes. He leaves the door open, points the remote at the fireplace to get it rolling, strips and gets into bed.

As an afterthought, he wraps a towel around his waist, gathers most of his clothes and sets them in the hall for laundry service. He gets back into bed, feeling a little charged up from just being here and kicks off the blankets to feel the cold air and the warm fire on his skin. With an elbow under his head, he slides a thumb along his mobile photo gallery to look at Elizabeth. Callum is quite the photographer when the subject is naked and prefers to be headless. The photos are filtered into black and white. Elizabeth's hips and the curve of her ass, just one nipple, his tongue encircling her clitoris (that one took some doing to get right), dark hair spread over a pillow, and his favorite, a shot from behind of her head with her mouth wrapped around him, sucking him in deep. Elizabeth gave glorious head. He can't look at that without rubbing one off. The cold air, the warm fire, the anticipation of getting back on skis. It is intoxicating. He comes hard and then falls into a peaceful sleep.

The next morning, he hits the gym hard. He hasn't touched a weight all week and he's feeling it. Might as well set up a good routine right off. Doing curls he faces the mirror and evaluates his changing face. He likes the short beard that is filling out, but his hair looks like shit. *Biceps look good though.* After breakfast, he stops in at the salon and gets his hair shaped up but leaves it longer than he wore it in London. An attractive woman having her toes polished watches him from across the room. Her eyes bat slowly in his direction. She reminds him of someone, but he can't identify who right off. *Not this morning*, he thinks and heads off to the ski shop.

He buys everything, jacket, pants, goggles, gloves, even skis and rods, in black. He likes the Darth Vadar feels. No hat. He could have rented the equipment, but he doesn't like to share. It is an investment anyway. He'll be here for a long time.

When he steps out of the ski shop, there is the same woman again. She looks a little dikey but hot. Dark short hair, too much make-up, blue liner, tight jean and high heeled boots, a sheer top with a dark bra. He gives her a glance and keeps walking. *Laila.* She looks just like Laila. It is her mouth he remembers first, of course. Wrapped around his cock.

One of the few benefits of growing up with a nearly perfect older brother, was the access to good parties with lots of liquor and some drugs. Another was the incorrect assumption by all adults, their mother included, that Eric could do no wrong. Callum's fourteenth summer, the summer after his father died, he dreaded coming home. Boarding school offered distance from his mother's crying jags and her days spent in a housecoat. Ten weeks seemed a lifetime. Callum's best friend, Jeremy was traveling with his family overseas for most of the summer so he wouldn't be around. The thought was torture.

When Callum arrived home, he was pleasantly surprised to see his mother had taken a job. She seemed to be trying to regain her stiff upper lip, dressing dutifully in bright suits with brass buttons and scarves for her work as a secretary in a law firm.

Callum found himself on his own a lot. He looked older than his fourteen years. Eric didn't mind having him around and offered to take him out. It was the first weekend of the summer that they ended up at some house passing around joint after joint and bottles of scotch. Parents were away and their kids didn't mind draining the stash of liquor or fucking in their house. Eric quickly disappeared with some girl from the neighborhood, winking at his little brother.

Hendrix's guitar spilled out of large, ashtray covered, speakers. Callum passed a joint to a redhead curled up in an easy chair with her brunette friend. They looked quite cozy. When the redhead blew her smoke into the brunette's mouth, Callum figured they were worth watching. Short spiky hair on Brunette. Red's was long. A few tattoos, lots of black eye liner and about a dozen piercings between them. Mostly ear, nose and Brunette had an eyebrow.

When they noticed Callum noticing, there was some whispering and giggling before Brunette slipped a hand up Red's shirt and massaged her breast for Callum to watch. Red licked her lips with desire and put Brunette's index finger into her mouth all the way before she pulled it out slowly. Callum felt like an asshole because he could not take his eyes off them, but he knew they were fucking with him. Even at fourteen, he knew he didn't need to chase. He was the chased.

Fuck them. He got up and walked toward the door. Before he made it to the hallway, they each locked an arm through his.

"Hi," Red said. Her voice was low and throaty.

"Want to hang out?" Brunette said. It wasn't a question though.

He didn't bother answering. They walked him up a wide staircase to a large bedroom. The bed was big and Red pulled off all the bedding except for a bottom sheet. She left a few pillows.

"How old are you? And don't fucking lie?" Brunette asked.

"Fifteen in another few months."

"You look at least seventeen, maybe eighteen." Brunette was the talker. "Virgin?"

He shrugged at the question. An all-boys school made that more challenging.

Brunette looked at Redhead and Redhead shrugged too. "He's young, but I like the looks of him. We can consider it community service. Right?"

Their accents were strange, definitely American, but strange American.

Brunette pulled off his shirt and smoothed her hands on his already well-developed pecs. He stood a head taller than her and looked down into her upturned face. Her eyes were icy blue and she was much prettier than the make-up and hair first let on.

"Nice." She tasted his nipple. "Very nice."

If he could get a blow job out of this, his summer was made.

"Sit," she said and pushed him into a chair. "You like to watch?"

He shrugged. "Sure. As long as I can get in on it too." Might as well give it a go.

Brunette sat on the edge of the bed and Red came over and sat between his knees, pushing them apart wide. She licked his balls through his pants. "You'll leave this room the happiest fourteen year old in the fucking country," she assured him.

They undressed and started kissing. They put on quite a show for Callum. They were natural born performers. Red watched Callum while Brunette went down on her. She told Callum he should undress. He did. Brunette watched Callum while Red went down on her. She pulled her tongue out of Brunette to tell Callum they didn't mind if her jerked off. He did.

After they all came, they sent Callum downstairs for beers. He pulled on his jeans, made his way through the thick cloud of smoke in the living room, found a bathroom and pissed. He spent a moment with his refection realizing he was about to fuck two girls, not one, for his first time. In the kitchen, he pulled three beers from the fridge, then took the stairs two at a time.

The bed was made, pillows were plumped and they were gone.

Callum arranges for a week-long lift ticket. That should be enough time to sharpen his skills on the slopes and to ski the resort a few times over. He thinks he'll ski for the afternoon, enjoy a few cocktails in the hot tub and find a companion before dinner. He can work fast in a bathing suit. He realizes he doesn't have a suit and goes back to the shops to pick one up. Black. There is a nine o'clock show at a comedy club in Park City he'll get to later. Maybe he'll stop by that hat store and visit the girl who looked like Megan Fox. *That's her name Megan Fox.*

After a short wait, he boards a gondola with a young couple who immediately share that they just got engaged. *Fuckers.* Callum is almost tempted to see how fast he can break that up. He can and he knows it. Ring or no ring, she looks at him like she'd enjoy a taste. He leaves it alone. She isn't bad, but he'd rather ski today. Callum reaches the top of the mountain and takes a few minutes to survey the trails before he points his skis downward and lets himself go. And he does fly. Despite feeling a little rusty, he takes the hills at top speeds. The air rushing at his face gives him a feeling of freedom he has felt few places other than on slopes like these. He loves to ski.

By Callum's third run, he is completely confident, like he has been skiing every day of his life. As he sails down the mountain, the air screams past his ears. This is why he is here, not giving a shit about anything but getting to the bottom of the mountain. This is about the journey, not the destination.

He can ski and forget what Elizabeth's dark hair looks like spread over his white sheets and how she would run her tongue along his lips when she wanted him to go down on her. He forgets how she holds his face when she comes to look straight into his eyes. He forgets how she laughs with her eyes closed and the sound of her voice. It all goes away as he glides down the mountain.

On the fourth run he hits new speeds. The slopes are a little crowed, but he can make his way. Most skiers here are fairly advanced, traveling along at speeds comparable to Callum's. After his fifth run he goes in for a cocktail, then another and buys a set of head phones. He listens to AC/DC loud on his sixth run. *Back in Black* is perfect ski music. Until the lights go out.

Three

When he comes to, he is in some type of cart, being pulled by a four-wheeled something or other and all he can hear is the screech of the engine and *I'm sorry, I'm so sorry. Mister I am so fucking sorry. I'm sorry. I'm sorry* coming from someone, somewhere, like a gnat buzzing in his ear. He is in extraordinary pain.

"Will you shut the fuck up," he whispers to the air hissing past his face. His head explodes in pain at those six words and then everything goes black again.

The next times he opens his eyes, white walls surround him. Bright lights sear his corneas and pain throbs in his leg. The pain in his head is nothing short of agony. Through blurred vision, he can makes out a girl in the corner. She sits in a low chair, hugging her knees, wearing a hideous hat with two strings hanging down the sides of her face all the way to her shoulders. The unzipped bib of dark blue ski pants, hangs around her waist. This must be the owner of the voice from before.

"Get your fucking feet off the furniture," he says, before realizing the volume of his own voice is the greatest torture of all.

She stares at him silently afraid and slowly slides her feet to meet the floor.

An intercom system pages some fucker, STAT, and a nearby machine flashes lights and sounds that feel like they'll put him into a seizure.

"Who the fuck are you?" he whispers, with as much anger as he can muster.

She stiffens at the tone of his voice but starts to move toward the bed. When a physician enters the room, she cowers back to her seat.

"My uncle's up," the girl tells the woman with a stethoscope and long white coat. The presumed doctor might be hot, but he can't tell with his vision all fucked up. Blonde. Tall. Slim. In charge. Glasses. He likes glasses. He likes removing glasses.

"I'm not your..." he starts but the maybe hot physician interrupts him.

"Hello Mr..." She searches his chart for a name. "What's your Uncle's name?" she asks the girl.

"Callum Townsend," says girl with ugly hat and she tucks his wallet behind her back.

The fucking little thief!

"He's visiting from England."

"Mr. Townsend, how are you feeling? You had a bad fall."

"I feel like shit and I did not fucking fall," he growls.

"You and your niece had a collision on the mountain. A bad one. You've suffered a fairly severe concussion. Do you remember the incident?" She asks, taking his pulse.

"I remember enough," he says. She has nice hands.

"We'd like to do an MRI to be sure there it isn't anything more going on."

She stares at Callum to make sure he is absorbing her words, so he nods to move things along. The nod hurts like a motherfucker.

"Also, your femur is broken and will require surgery. We need to insert screws here and here." She holds up an x-ray and points to the break with a pen like he might give a single shit about a word she is saying. He is done.

"I'm sorry to say it is a nasty break and you've got a long road to recovery. We'll schedule you for surgery as soon as possible. You'll be here two or three days and then you'll need to follow up with an orthopedist."

"Jesus Fucking Christ," is all he manages.

The physician excuses herself and he is left staring at the kid with the fucked up hat.

"Who the fuck are you and why did you tell her I'm your uncle?" He whispers in a very quiet rage.

She pulls her chair closer to the bed, quietly. "I did this to you. I am so sorry. They only let family in. Uncle seemed better than daughter since you have the accent and I don't."

"A tiny little shit like you did not take me out on the slopes. Utter bullshit." She's about half his height and a third of his weight. She finally pulls off the hat. Light brown hair piles atop her head, tied in great disarray. Blue, he thinks, evil looking eyes pierce from a serious face with a smattering of freckles across a small nose. His vision is clearing, but focus is painful. He closes his eyes, disgusted with her. *Why am I even communicating with a fucking child?*

"I did hurt you." She does not elaborate further which is fine because he isn't exactly up for conversation.

34

"Run along then," he instructs, but she doesn't move.

He dozes and when he wakes, he feels slightly better. Or higher. He looks at the bag hanging above and dripping into his vein and wonders what he is on but not enough to bother asking. A side effect of the drugs perhaps. Whatever it is, he'll take it. Now a woman, a mother maybe, is standing next to the girl, who still sits in the chair in the corner with the fucking ugly hat in her lap. When he opens his eyes, the woman moves to the bed and takes his hand in hers like she knows him. *Who the fuck are these people?*

"Mr. Townsend?" she asks him.

"Ask your daughter. She's quite a little pick-pocket," he says and turns to face the wall hoping they'll both go away.

"Listen, Mr. Townsend. I am so sorry to bother you, but Marina feels responsible for what happened today and we'd like to help you."

"Who the fuck is Marina?"

Whoever she is takes a deep breath and stands tall with her hands on her hips. "I'm going to assume you are high as a kite and you did not just use that word as a precursor to my daughter's name on purpose."

She has an accent, but he doesn't recognize it. It is a little like John's Austin drawl but different. He can't distinguish the subtleties between regional American accents anyway.

He shrugs, facing the wall. Yes he is pretty damn high, but he can still shrug with the best of them.

"Do you have any people we can call?" she asks.

People. Well there is his ex-girlfriend who is in London making a baby with her husband who used to be Callum's best friend. But he isn't really spending much time with his best friend anymore since he learned how Callum had been fucking his wife for the past year. There is a mother who isn't speaking to him because he is a destructive asshole, and he threw away his restaurant and his self-respect. There is a brother, Eric, who is somewhere on a different continent, but Callum doesn't even know which one at the moment. And there is Anna. And there is John. And their two babies. He is in no way going to ask them to rescue him. He can get by on his own.

"I don't have any people currently. Thanks. I'll be fine." He can't remember why he is even talking to her. *Who the fuck are these people?*

The girl gives her mother a powerful look with sad puppy eyes and her hands held together. The gesture is somewhere between praying and begging. The mother turns slowly to face Callum. He checks her over. Red hair but not bright red. Sort of darker reddish. Blue eyes with very long lashes, maybe a few freckles. Good nose, not small, not big, just strong. Impressive cheek bones and jaw line. Tiny waist, but she fills out her jeans nicely. The sweater makes it impossible to get a feeling for the tits. She is sexy almost but trying not to be. No makeup. Ponytail. She is a strange combination of contradictions. She could be hot with some makeup and a good haircut.

"Mr. Townsend…" she starts slowly. "Marina, my daughter, feels responsible for your fall and we'd like to offer to care for you until you get back on your feet. You'll need help after surgery and some supervision after that concussion…" She doesn't sound done, but he is.

"No."

"No, what?" she asks, not understanding.

"No. I don't need any help. Go away. Take your kid with you. And take that ugly fucking hat before it makes me throw up. And where the fuck is my wallet, Brat?"

The mother eases her daughter toward the door with a whisper he can't hear. Marina lays the wallet at his feet on her way out. She looks like

Charlie leaving a stolen everlasting gobstopper for that sadistic bastard Wonka. *Good.*

He thinks he is in for some kind of lecture, but she sits in the chair vacated by Marina, raises her feet to the cushion and hugs her knees. Not a words passes between them. He falls asleep within a minute.

Later he signs forms and they take him for the MRI. She is still there. Eventually, there is a surgery. It is all blurry, but when he opens his eyes, she is there. He is moved to a room and there she is. He isn't sure it is the same day or if he lost one. Maybe two. He doesn't know and he doesn't care. He falls into yet another deep, dream-filled sleep.

The next party was Eric's own. Their mother went out of town to visit an old friend, and she had no problem leaving a seventeen year old at home alone with a fourteen year old for three days. And there they were again. Red and Brunette kissed Callum hello, each taking a cheek at the same time.

Before he could get the "Go fuck yourselves" out of his mouth, Red slid her hand into the back of his pants and squeezed his ass.

"More?" she breathed. "Please say yes."

He brought a joint, a bottle of scotch and took them to his room. Red tried to push him into a chair

"Fuck that," he said. "Do you like dick or don't you?"

"We do," Red said. "But we like when you watch, too."

Ever the diplomat, Brunette negotiated. "First a watch then a fuck, okay?"

"No thanks," Callum said. "I've seen how that goes."

Brunette tried again. "First the fuck and then the watch?"

"No. Same time," Red interrupted. She had a good sense of logistics.

And that is how Callum lost his virginity at the tender age of fourteen. First Red slid a pill into her mouth, then Brunette's, then his. He didn't question her, he just swallowed, tasting her finger. They lay down on the bed, shoulder to shoulder, Callum in the center, waiting for the Ecstasy to take effect. When it did, he knew this would be the greatest day of his life, but he was wrong. It was the first of many such days.

Red finally climbed on top of him, pulled off his shirt and kissed him like he had never been kissed. Brunette took his pants from him and took him into her mouth for just a moment before moving onto her back. Callum fucked her while Red sat on her face, cupping her own breasts, watching Callum watching them both. Watching and fucking. Everyone was happy.

After, Red climbed onto his chest and played with his hand. Brunette curled into his side and nuzzled close into his neck, clasping his other hand. They encompassed him completely. His brain sailed to places he wasn't sure were real or imagined and his body fell in love.

"You are so beautiful," Red observed.

"Will you be ours?" Brunette asked.

At that point he probably would have committed mass murder on their behalf. If they asked him to jump off London Bridge, he just might have done it. He might have cut off his own pinky to be theirs for the summer.

"We could love you, you know." Red added to sweeten the deal. "Would you love us?"

Their question suddenly seemed serious. "Yes," he said very emphatically. "I will love you. I will love you both. What are your names?"

Their names were Laila and Daisy, or so they said. He thought Red, or Daisy, took her name from the Gatsby book and Laila, Brunette, took hers from the Eric Clapton song. They were Americans from Boston, spending a year abroad. The important part of that was they had an apartment to themselves. They were nineteen.

Callum spent every day of that summer at their apartment. His mother worked enough that she hardly noticed and he made sure to be home when she got home at the end of the day. No questions were asked as long as the dishes were washed, his room was neat, and he didn't cause any trouble.

"Where are you off to in such a rush?" Eric asked.

"See a friend," Callum answered. That was usually enough. Eric was a lifeguard and worked long hours.

Callum was too young to work so he just fucked all summer. Fucked and cooked. Laila's family owned an Italian restaurant in Boston and she taught him to appreciate Italian food beyond the bland spaghetti and meatballs he was used to.

The sex was constant and they liked to play. They would tie him up and suck him off and then feed him Spaghetti Bolognese in bed. They would stick a dildo into his ass and fuck him in the shower and then teach him to make risotto with seared scallops. One day Daisy dripped hot wax onto his back while he fucked Laila in the ass and then he made them linguine with clam sauce.

"This is fanfuckingtastic," Laila said, sucking long strands of pasta with her mouth shaped for a kiss.

"Callum we love the way you fuck and we love the way you cook." Daisy said.

Laila simplified it. "Callum. We just love you."

They left the linguine on the table. He tucked each of them under an arm and took them back to bed.

No one in England fucked more or ate better that magical summer.

When Callum awakes, he sits up and immediately vomits between his legs.

And there she is. "That's just the anesthesia, not a problem at all." She pulls the blanket off and replaces it with a clean one.

"Why isn't the bedding soiled?" he asks.

She lays another waterproof pad across his lap. "Everyone throws up after surgery. We were ready for it."

He lays back and closes his eyes, trying to decide if he is going to vomit again. "Are you my nurse?"

"I'm sort of your private nurse," she says and he falls back asleep, not understanding.

The next time he wakes, a woman with long braids and a thick accent he can't identify is taking blood from the port in his hand. She is gentle and quick.

"How are you feeling darling?" She loads the dark red tubes into her cart.

"I feel like I've the worst hangover of my life."

She rubs his arm supportively, wishes him well and pushes her cart out the door. The headache has abated some, but the fog around him is thick and the drugs are strong. After a moment he notices her sleeping in a recliner in the corner. Red curls spills around her face and her shirt is buttoned wrong, revealing a pink lacey bra. Pink and lacey is unexpected and makes her a bit more interesting. He lets her sleep and she stirs after an hour.

40

"Who are you?' he asks with his stern voice before her eyes are open. She startles wide awake and jumps to her feet. Watching her confusion is entertaining.

"Don't you remember me from the ER? I'm Marina's mom," Her hands rest on her hips. They are indeed nice hips.

"I remember. Do you have a name?" He feels unreasonably angry, but he can't remember why. He's hungry, too.

"I do have a name." She doesn't seem to respond well to anger.

"May I know it, please?" He accentuates the British in his tone, faking good manners.

Her face softens. He is so doped up, he isn't in his right mind. She should be patient with him, he thinks.

"I'm Victoria," she says, taking his pulse.

He laughs out loud.

"What's so funny? My name?"

"No, your name is fine, just ironic. I was telling my niece a story about a princess named Victoria just days ago."

Talk of a niece and stories of princesses softens him immediately. She smiles like she approves of him telling stories to a little girl.

"Victoria. Or shall I call you Vicky?" He can guess the answer before it is offered.

"Not if you want to survive your injuries." She moves a bag of his clothes from a chair into the shelf by the window for no reason. "Your accent is wonderful. I love England."

"You've been?" He is surprised. She sounds like she should have a few missing teeth and live in the woods. She sounds a bit raspy, like a smoker,

41

but he thinks she probably is not. She sounds like she has just a few marbles in her mouth.

"I visited England years and years ago. When I was a teenager." Her tone is dry. The memory obviously isn't bringing a warmth to her heart.

He looks her over closer now. She does possess a natural sort of beauty, like she could model in soap commercials. Her light blue eyes are less piercing than her daughter's, friendlier, more inquisitive. She has full, pink lips and if he felt better, he might have something to think about regarding those lips. He's not even up for thinking about that though. He knows he's been an unforgiving asshole. Her skin is like cream.

"I'm confused. Are you my nurse?" he asks.

"No. I'm just here to help. But I am a nurse. Talk about ironic."

"But you have just been here watching over me?"

She shrugs. That is a language he speaks. He can't help but be touched. "All along?"

She shrugs again.

"That is really very lovely of you. Can we start again? I may have been a bit of an asshole to you. Hi Victoria. I'm Callum," he says.

She takes his cue and moves to the bed, and shakes his offered hand. Her hand in his is soft and small with no ring. She is lovely but too young and probably too single. Definitely not for him.

"Where does your niece live? Back in England?" She sits on the edge of his bed and tries to make small talk. Even in this post-surgical state, he looks damn good.

"I have a sister in South Carolina on Osprey Island. My two nieces are there."

"I should call her. She would want to know," Victoria says and reaches for her mobile.

"Please don't." He needs to explain or she is going to track down his sister and Anna will leave her kids and take the first plane across the country and upset her entire life for him and he's having no part of it.

"I've only just met her. It seems we had some skeletons in our family closet. She is the greatest thing to happen to me in my life, but she's got a husband and two little girls. One is just a baby, and I don't want her to feel responsible for me."

The fluorescent lights overhead flicker and buzz. Victoria frowns at this information, and he hopes she isn't going to track Anna down even though he doesn't want her to. Google is a powerful tool and she seems just nosy enough to do it. She finally nods, acquiescing to his demands.

"I understand Callum. I do. Responsibility can be a complicated thing." Her comment is a little loaded. He waits for more. She pats his good leg and chooses not to elaborate further about her feelings of responsibility.

He thinks she may have a skeleton or two of her own. He doesn't mind her hand on his arm. It is not sexual in any way, yet it is still nice.

"Callum, let me help you. Like I said, I am a nurse. Not here in Salt Lake but back in Park City. I work for an internist."

He is surprised but shakes his head. "No. But truly thank you. If you can just get me back to my hotel when I am released, I'll be fine." He tries to imagine the hotel and can't. "Shit, where am I staying?" slips out of his mouth.

"You were staying at Red Canyons, but Callum, you can't go back there. You need some care. You can't be on your own after a surgery like that. There is a rehab center in Salt Lake but trust me, you don't want to go to a rehab center. We'll take good care of you." Her blue eyes are very serious. Her eyebrows are neatly plucked into shapely arches. They curve at her disapproval. "I have a house."

His head falls back onto rough, under-filled, hospital pillows, and he misses the pillows on his bed back home. They are marvelous pillows, full and soft. Maybe he never should have left England. If he had stayed, where would he be now? *Drunk. Alone. Homeless. Jobless. Motherless. But with plenty of money.* Not the worst existence. No, he needed some distance. This is still better in every way.

"Victoria, you don't even know me," he protests.

"I can tell you're a good guy," she says.

He rolls his eyes. "I am not a good guy." Fucking his way across American disqualifies him from good guy status. He is fairly sure that knowledge of his adventures might alter her assessment of him.

"I can see you're a good guy, Callum," she repeats, convincing herself or him, he wonders.

"Why? Because I'm weak and broken and you pity me?"

"Well yes," she laughs.

"You can't bring a strange man into your home, Victoria. You have a daughter." He is actually appalled that she would even consider it. "Men are perverts and predators and rapists and most of the other horrid things on this planet are devised by men."

"Are you a pervert?" she asks.

"No."

"A serial killer? Rage problems? Drug dealer? Thief?"

"No."

"Well okay then. I think we're getting somewhere," she smiles. "Have you ever forced a woman to have sex with you who didn't want to have sex with you?" she asks more seriously.

"Everyone wants to have sex with me. Man, woman and beast." He replies with perfect seriousness. Her small smile lets him know he isn't wrong. She is joining the ranks of man, woman and beast.

"Let me rephrase. Have you ever tied a woman up?"

"Yes."

"Have you ever pinned a woman down?"

"Yes."

"Have you ever ripped a woman's clothes?"

"Yes."

"Have you ever wrapped your hands around a woman's throat," she says getting frustrated.

"Yes. But all in good fun."

She stands silently with her hands at her sides, beaten.

"You are asking the wrong question. So far you are running through a typical Wednesday night in London."

"Not the London I remember," she frowns.

"You were young. Ask me if I am a rapist."

"Well are you?" she asks.

"Not lately," he tries to joke, but she doesn't laugh. "I am a perfect gentleman when the situation requires. But it still isn't safe to bring strange men into your home." He'd never let a strange man near his daughter if he had one. He thinks about Clara. If he had a daughter, she'd be like Clara, sweet and giggling all the time, eating grapes with tiny fingers, climbing onto his lap and petting his face, listening to a story. He's never having any kids though.

"Thanks for the parenting advice. You have kids of your own?" She doesn't wait for his answer. "No, I didn't think so. Let me tell you what I know, Callum. Number one, I can take you. You are in bad shape and I am pretty sure I could take you out with a feather right now."

He nods because she is probably right. "Fuck with me or with my daughter and I will go all Kathy Bates in *Misery* on you and you'll lose that other leg. All I'd need is a couple of two by fours and a sledge hammer which I'll make sure to have in the garage just in case."

"Point well made." She probably would, too.

She smiles a sweet smile before continuing with her dark persuasion. "Number two, my daughter did this to you. I'm not sure how or why, but she did. She has been on skis since she was three years old, but she's been going through some stuff and I think you might be a victim of some serious teen angst. I can't turn my back on you, on all that." She picks at her cuticle while talking about her daughter.

"So what you're telling me is that I'm the one in danger? Between your lovely daughter and this Kathy Bates threat, I am really dying to come with you."

She ignores him. "Number three, I don't bring strange men into my house. I'm a nurse not a hooker. I'm a single mom, raising a kid and working full time, plus overtime, and that doesn't leave time for much else. Which brings me to number four."

He nods to encourage her on. This is more fun than expected.

"No hanky panky."

"You just said I am in bad shape," he says innocently.

"Look Callum, you seem like a nice guy, but you are clearly trouble with that face and that accent and well… that body." She averts her eyes from his well-defined, exposed chest. He notices the hospital gown is askew and he doesn't bother fixing it.

He tries to manage a dashing smile, regardless of the previous vomit episode. He doesn't do a terrible job. That smile has dropped a lot of panties in London. "Maybe I should be lecturing you about hanky panky." He pulls the hospital gown tighter, killing her view.

"I'm serious Callum. No bullshit in front of my daughter. Things are complicated enough right now. I don't want to make it worse."

He briefly wonders what she means by complicated, but he doesn't really care.

"I'm glad you swear. I was worried you were Mormon." He says getting back to a little flirty flirty.

It is her turn to laugh out loud. "Far from it. Can we be like brother and sister?"

He thinks a moment and shakes his head. "No. This has been a big sister year for me with meeting Anna. I can't have another sister. And we will probably eventually sleep together so that is very wrong. How about, how do Americans say it? Some absurd word for best friends?"

"Are you actually looking for the word *besties?*"

He finds the fact that she doesn't deny the inevitable sex to be promising. "Yes, besties. Let's be besties." He can think of a thousand reasons why this is a bad idea, but he is intrigued and rather situationally screwed. "Jesus fuck." He wonders aloud just how fucked he is.

"Excuse me?" she asks, obviously disapproving of his unique selection of words."

"How fucked up am I? I can take care of my own washing and such, right?

"By *and such* I think you mean using the ..."

"Jesus Christ, I'm English. There is no need to speak of it." He is disgusted she would even consider voicing such things.

"You will be fine handling everything alone in the loo."

"Christ!" he says too loudly and it shoots a rod of pain through his head. "Fuck!"

Victoria laughs at his embarrassment. "You can't shower for five days though."

"Might a sponge bath be in order?" he whispers with eyes closed tight, hopeful.

"This isn't *Penthouse Forum*. This is serious Callum."

She sounds exasperated, but he takes a peek at her smiling face and is assured that she still finds him to be adorable. Maybe it is the talk of sponge baths or maybe he is too high to argue effectively, but he feels himself giving into it. And he can't help imagining her in a short, white nurse's uniform with that little cap, straddling him for a wash.

"I appreciate your offer, Victoria, but just two or three days at most. Until the concussion clears." That straddle does have a lovely appeal but no. You don't shit where you eat. It does depend on what you are eating perhaps.

"You'd better bump that up to a week or two. It is a bad concussion and we have a long list of post-surgical instructions."

"Are you sure you are comfortable with this?" If he agrees to it, he thinks he really will have to be a gentleman, a platonic bestie. He shouldn't screw with motherhood. Mothers aren't like the rest. There is something sacred about mothers with children present to Callum.

"I am absolutely comfortable with this. Are we good?" She raises her hand into the air.

He stares at it for a moment. "Are you wanting a high five?"

"Would you prefer a handshake? I'm flexible?"

He gives her hand a gentle slap. "Truly Victoria. Thank you."

She shakes off his gratitude. It isn't necessary. "I'm going to Red Canyons to get your stuff and check you out. I'll come back for you in the morning. They'll release you about ten o'clock."

"I'd like to pay you. You are a professional nurse after all."

"No. Thank you Callum, but this is me, one human being doing something for you, another human being, because this is what people do. You wouldn't be in this mess without my daughter's help anyway, so we are even. Okay?"

He nods, but he isn't so sure this is what people do for each other. He thinks Elizabeth would have dropped him at the rehab facility under similar circumstances.

Victoria programs her number into his mobile in case he needs her. She takes his keys and goes.

He calls after her in the hall. "Vicky?"

She comes back around the corner. "Do. Not."

He decides he'll call her Vicky when she displeases him. "My cleaning was with the laundry service." The thought of her packing his underwear is unappealing but seems unavoidable. "Can you track it down for me please?"

Victoria Bradley calls her daughter on the way out of the hospital and tells her Callum finally agreed to come home with them. She gives Marina instructions to change the sheets in the guest room and to clean up the bathroom. Usually, Marina would argue with the given instructions but not today. She rushes off the phone to get to work.

The insanity of this plan is not lost on Victoria. He is right. Bringing a strange man into her house is ludicrous but, under the circumstances, a little pro-active kindness might dissuade that gorgeous trust-fund, playboy from a lawsuit. She visited the rehab center and she wasn't impressed. All she needs is an overworked, under-aged tech to forget his meds, let him fall, speak to him in a snappy voice and he'd be calling a lawyer in no time. No, she can care for him infinitely better in her own house. She decides to pick up a few canisters of pepper spray just in case.

Slipping into a small white SUV, Victoria forgets about Callum momentarily and her thoughts turn back to her father. All that time sitting in the chair by Callum's bedside was good think time, but she still has no answers. She wonders what he looks like now. It has been fourteen years since she laid eyes on her own Dad.

Victoria wonders for the millionth time how she is going to tell Marina about George's offer. *Is it possible?* Could she actually take Marina back home to Asheville? Marina has never met her grandfather. Victoria tries to assess if she even misses him anymore. In the beginning, she was so angry at him, but she missed him every day. Then, as the years passed, the anger dissipated somewhat and so did the need to see him. She got used to being without him.

When she left Asheville, her mother had just died. George wasn't happy about his baby becoming a momma at such an early age. The pregnancy wasn't exactly Victoria's choice, but she decided to make the best of her circumstances. Not that she was against options, she wasn't and still isn't against choices for women. But she had just lost her mom and she couldn't cope with another loss. George didn't share her perspective, to put it mildly.

Victoria drives the highways winding though the Wasatch Mountains. Even now, after fourteen years in Park City, she can still see them. They don't just blend into the background of her daily grind. The snow covers most of the mountain's face but evergreens still show through. There is a golden glow from the warm sunshine and clouds encircle the peaks like crowns. Even though the day is cold, a high of fifteen, she wears just jeans and a buttoned sweater. She doesn't like the bulk. She keeps a parka in her back seat with a hat and gloves in case of car trouble, but she prefers to feel unencumbered.

These mountains remind Victoria of the mountains surrounding Asheville. It is different here, higher, drier with more Mormons and fewer Hippies. But there are similarities between the hearty people of these regions. A surprising number of comparisons can be drawn between the Mormons and the Hippies. Both are tight knit groups of very happy people who share a kindness in their everyday attitudes. Victoria is neither a Mormon nor a Hippie. Even as an outsider, she has been happy in Park City, but Asheville will always be home.

She parks at Red Canyons and sits with the engine running, remembering her dad. They have spoken here and there and Victoria sends photos from time to time, but that has been the extent of their communication since Victoria left. Without her mom to bring them back together, they just stayed apart. Stubborn runs in the family and Victoria knows she has been stubborn. That awful day in the driveway, she was screaming and he was pleading. She took nothing more than clothes and $12,000 she had acquired from a lifetime of cash giving grandparents, all dead by then. She crushed her cell phone under her boot heel because she saw someone do it in a movie and she didn't want anyone following her.

Her best friend Mindy came from next door, hearing the yelling. She thought Victoria was just going to cool her head. She tried to calm George. "She just lost her mother, she needs to run. Let her go." Mindy didn't know about the rape or the pregnancy. If George had his way, no one would ever have known. Victoria drove west and she never looked back. She refused to look back. She doesn't know if she can look back, even now.

She goes over the plans in her head and knows she might be crazy for taking Callum. Marina did something. Marina isn't talking, but Victoria knows she did something bad. She is too good a skier and too guilty for this to have been an accident. Victoria laughs to herself at the irony that the first man to stay overnight in their home, ever, is a man that her daughter nearly killed on the slopes. It is pretty damn ironic. Not a husband, or a boyfriend or even a relative, but some stranger that Marina knocked out. Well if this is how she is looking for a Daddy figure, she is probably a sociopath, but she certainly chose a cute one.

Damn he is good looking, Victoria thinks. She can admire him from across the room, but that is it. Her daughter is her first and only priority and something is going wrong. If she is being honest with herself and she isn't entirely, she'd think that a lot of things are going wrong. Marina's grades are bottoming out. She is moody, uncommunicative, angry, secretive. Victoria reads the parenting books, but she isn't sure where the line falls between normal teenager and fucked up teenager. Being a single Mom makes it all the more complicated.

The next morning, Callum is released from the hospital and wheeled to the front entrance where Victoria gets him into the car with some difficulty. He is tall, unsteady and still fairly doped up. He isn't used to the crutches and the concussion is screwing up his balance. When he gets settled in the seat, he stops her before she closes the door. "Wait," he says, taking her hand in his. "Thank you. From my heart. The bottom of it. Thank you for this."

She ignores the intimate gesture, chalking it up to pain meds and points the car to Park City. She has never had a man in her car before. Sure she has given a co-worker a ride home on occasion but not a man like this. Tall, gorgeous, British. She points out different sights and mountains she thinks he would find interesting. Playing tour guide helps her pretend this is normal.

Victoria hasn't dated much. *Who has the time?* But she has enjoyed a friend or two over the years who have helped keep certain needs in check. There is a bartender she used to work with and they still get together from time to time, always at his place, when Marina is on a sleepover or once in a while during the school day. She is a busy single mom, but she isn't dead for goodness sake. At thirty-one, these needs call loudly from time to time. If she does sleep with Callum, she decides it should just be once or twice on his way out the door. She smiles at that him sitting in the car at her side.

"What?" he asks. "You look like the damn cat that ate that poor canary."

"Nothing," she protests.

"Sure nothing. Remember, no funny business," he says as Victoria pulls into the little neighborhood of dark wooden houses that are so common here. Hers is set on the sharp incline, backing up to a snow covered mountain. She is pretty damn proud of this three bedroom house. The rooms are large and bright with lots of windows and mountain views. This house is the result of years and years of bartending, living in a tiny apartment spending too little time with her daughter, and a hard fought for nursing degree, one class at a time. Her house has a garage which bring her endless joy. She pushes the button and the large wooden door rises at her command. Heaven!

"Nice," Callum says.

Marina runs out the door in a tee shirt, sweat pants and bare feet, despite the snow. "Marina, shoes!" Victoria demands.

Marina doesn't even bother responding to her mother. She opens the door for Callum and helps guide him from the car. He can't put any weight on her, but she helps with the balance. "I made some soup if you are hungry, Mr. Townsend."

"Callum please. No soup now. Just sleep."

Marina leads him into what is his bedroom for the next days or weeks. Victoria watches from the doorway as Marina eases him to the bed and shows him how she unpacked his clothes and which drawers to find which items. She lined his shoes in the closet and arranged his toiletries on the dresser below the mirror. The blue quilt is folded down to the bottom of the bed in thirds and she has turned down the corner of the gray sheets. Three water bottles line the end table within easy reach. He sits on the bed and opens a brown bottle of pain killers, shaking one free and swallowing the pill dry.

"I moved my stuff into Victoria's bathroom so you can have this one all to yourself." She points out the bathroom that connects to his room and her room. "Mine's locked and I locked this side for you so you don't have to be weirded out about it."

"You call your mom Victoria?" is his only comment and it is steeped in disapproval.

She shrugs off his comment and Victoria intercedes. "Come on honey. Let's get out of Callum's hair so he can get some sleep."

Victoria shuts the door and drives Marina to school late so she can finish out the day.

Four

The room is pitch black when Callum awakes and he has no idea where he is. After getting his bearings, he assesses the pain and decides to forgo the pill. The leg is manageable enough and he is getting used to the low throb of the headache. Tylenol will do the trick. He's ready to start feeling like himself not like he's moving under water.

It takes a moment to find the switch on the cord and turn on the lamp. When the room is illuminated, he surveys his temporary home. The walls are painted stark white, but they are covered with seemingly local, western inspired oil paintings, mostly landscapes, with lots of earth tones. The furniture is simple and inexpensive. A light wooden dresser with a mirror faces the bed and two matching bedside tables with black wrought iron lamps and white square shades sit on either side of the large bed. Overall, the look is inviting without being fussy and he likes it. Nice enough digs. No TV though.

He throws off the blankets and hops his way to the bathroom, double checking that the door is locked on Marina's side. This Brady Bunch bathroom doesn't inspire feelings of confidence for privacy. He pulls on a tee shirt and shorts, opens his bedroom door and peeks into the hallway. Marina and Victoria are arguing in the kitchen.

"We need to talk about this Marina. Cutting school is bad enough but what the hell happened at Red Canyons with Callum?" Victoria demands, not for the first time.

"Nothing." Callum can't see Marina, but he imagines her shrugging with a shitty, disrespectful facial expression. *Brat.*

"*Nothing* is not good enough Marina," Victoria tries to keep her voice calm, but Callum can hear the struggle in it. "We have that poor man in our guest room. Why Marina?"

Callum decides she isn't talking anyway and he really wants a Tylenol or four, so he inadvertently rescues Marina by crutching his way to the kitchen. He has to practice this crutch thing.

"Good morning," he says despite the blackness outside the windows.

"Well for you it is." Victoria pulls a chair out for him. "How are you feeling?"

"Sleep was good. It was nice to be out of that fucking hospital." He glances at Marina. "Sorry. Damn hospital?"

"Fucking hospital is fine," Marina ladles soup into a blue bowl.

Callum looks to Victoria for confirmation. It is her house. She offers a sideways smile and a nod, acquiescing.

Marina watches the exchange and gives him a snotty *I told you so* grin before setting down a bowl of soup and a plate with a thick slice of bread. She has laid a blue ironed, folded cloth napkin with silverware on a green placemat in front of him. Butter and a tall glass of ice water are within reach. This gesture of food warms his heart. He knows he is still coming down from the drugs, but if he let himself, he could cry. He can't even remember the last time someone made him a meal like this. He doesn't let on that he is overwhelmed by their kindness but just tastes the soup. "Thank you Marina. This is simply lovely," is all he says.

"I figured we'd start you off slowly on food and we need to hydrate you. How many pain pills have you had today?" Victoria asks.

"Two. I'd like to try to stop them though. I need to get back to my own head. Do you have Tylenol?"

She opens a cabinet and pulls out a small bottle handing it to him. He takes three and then digs into the soup. It is better than he expected with onions, carrots, potatoes, broccoli, tomatoes, cannellini beans and chicken. He would have added chorizo and some fresh herbs, but it is a good balance of flavors and textures. This soup was finished with lemon juice. Very few people know to finish a soup with acid to make the flavors brighter. The bread is full of nuts and whole grains and the butter is sweet. This is the best meal he has had in days. He nearly starved to death in the hospital.

"So Callum, what do you do? Professionally, I mean." Victoria asks. She truly doesn't know a thing about him.

He doesn't really want to get into it. *I was a chef until I fucked my partners wife and told him about it so he'd leave her and she'd run off with me. But it all blew up in my face when they rededicated themselves to each other, threw me out and decided to have a baby.*

"I worked in restaurants back in England, but I'm taking a sort of sabbatical. I was pretty burned out. I've been visiting my sister and traveling the states." He sits back in his chair, crossing his arms across his chest defensively, awaiting interrogation. Marina offers him more soup, but he declines. His appetite isn't there yet.

"Marina," he says, turning his attention to the little girl who makes good soup but apparently beat him to shit on the slopes. She squirms in her seat under his gaze. She manages to keeps her eyes to his and holds her defiant chin high. He realizes she looks a lot like her mom.

"What happened at Red Canyons?" He uses in the same voice and deep tone he uses with the line cooks. It is a telling tone not an asking tone. It doesn't leave much room for bullshit. He taps the passing seconds off with his index finger on the table.

Marina looks to her mother as if waiting for Victoria to intercede. She does not but squares her eyes on Marina. She and Callum share a patiently awaiting united front.

"I cut school," Marina says.

"Alone or with others?" Callum figures Victoria would want to know. He has years of experience with being questioned by adults in power for his bad behavior. Being on this side of the table for a change is actually quite satisfying.

Victoria tries to sink into her seat. She doesn't get far into the wood though.

"Answer my question Marina," Callum wonders if he is pushing too far, but he doesn't give a shit. He remembers his last headmaster at boarding school, his favorite. The name is escaping him now.

"I cut with a few other girls," she looks towards her mother, "Rebecca, Lindsay and Alyssa. And some guys."

"What happened?" he asks.

"We were buying lift tickets and the guy asked if we were cutting school. You were ahead of me in line so I said you were my Dad and we were here on vacation from Delaware."

"Why Delaware?" he asks even though it isn't important. But he is curious. *Where the hell is Delaware anyway?* He might need to learn a thing or two about American geography.

"I didn't think it had a recognizable accent like New York, New Jersey, Texas or whatever," she explains.

"Good thinking," he agrees. "Marina, how did lying to buy a lift ticket translate into me flat on my back with a broken leg and a concussion?"

She winces at his words and the guilt is all over her face, but she does start talking. "The guys have this club."

"A gang?" he asks and Victoria gasps.

"This is Park City Utah for Christ's sake. We don't have gangs here!"

"Actually, Mom, there are a lot of gangs around Salt Lake."

Callum is happy to hear her use the word Mom. "So?"

"So these guys have been messing around, talking about starting a gang at our school," Marina explains.

Victoria leans forward ready to jump in and Callum places a hand on her knee under the table to stop her. It is a subtle message, but she takes the hint. Marina is talking, let her.

"They decided to have an initiation. You had to hurt someone bad enough to leave a mark. Most of the kids, even the girls were picking fights at school. I'm too small to fight, but I'm a good skier. I decided to knock someone over, but I didn't really want to hurt anyone, like a kid or an old person or something. Callum is big and a good skier. I just meant to knock him over and then the kids would leave me alone and let me in."

"Where did they go after we collided?" he asks.

"They left me there."

"Even Lindsay and the other girls?" Victoria asks and Marina nods.

Now that it is out, she seems to want to finish it. "So I cut into Callum's path he was going fast and he tried to avoid me." Her blue eyes fill with tears. "If he'd just hit me, he would have been okay, but he didn't want to hurt me. He cut hard and his ski popped and hit him in the back of the head. Then he went down and his leg snapped. It was so loud. It was so horrible." The memory of the sound of the break stops her from talking. She cries quietly. After a moment he lifts her chin with his index finger and looks into her eyes. Her eyes aren't as sinister as he thought. But he always was a sucker for a few tears.

"Callum, I am really sorry," she says and just like that, his anger goes. He isn't much of a grudge holder and he has a lot of shit to be sorry about too. He's sorry about fucking his best friend's wife. He's sorry about letting himself love her. He's sorry about telling her husband even though she begged him not to. He's sorry she told his mother to get back at him. He's sorry he has no job and the best part of his day has been shaming women into giving him blow jobs.

"I forgive you Marina," he says. "I understand the pressure of the assholes at school. I was one of those assholes."

She was not expecting that. She leans in and hugs him hard. He was not expecting that. He manages to lift a hand to give her a *there there* pat on the back. It seems the right thing to do.

Victoria hugs Marina too and thanks her daughter for being honest, finally. She says something about punishments being forthcoming, after some consideration. Then Victoria sends Marina off with instruction for homework and no texting.

"You make good soup," Callum calls to her as an afterthought.

When Marina is clear of the kitchen, Victoria falls heavily into the kitchen chair, folds her arms on the table to cradle her head and sobs as silently as she can manage. Callum isn't sure what to do so he reaches a hand over to pat her shoulder for more *there there*. She puts a hand up in protest, palm out, letting him know *no thanks*.

So he waits it out and resists the temptation to check game scores on his mobile. Within two minutes, she sits up and wipes her face with a napkin and tops it off with a good nose blow. He notices that she missed a button on her shirt again and decides not to mention it. This bra is just as frilly but black. *Lovely.*

"Jesus Callum I am so sorry," she says.

"Don't be." He can't believe he is defending her, but the apology was sincere. "She's just a kid."

"I'm a shit mother," she says and dabs her eyes again with the napkin.

"No you aren't," he says with fake confidence. For all he knows she is a shit mother.

"And how would you know?" she asks.

"The same way you knew I was a good guy."

"Oh. It's total bullshit then," she says with a snorty laugh.

"Exactly," he agrees.

She pulls a Ben & Jerry's carton from the fridge and offers him a spoon. "New York Super Fudge Chunk. Want a bowl?"

"Besties don't need bowls." He dips his spoon into the carton and wonders what she looks like naked. When she leans forward, the missed button gap shows more creamy fair skin and soft curves around the black lace. She is so much more than he expected.

After the kitchen drama, he goes back to bed and sleeps another three hours, waking after midnight. The Tylenol is managing the pain well enough, so he pops another three and then he's up. He walks the house quietly while Marina and Victoria sleep, learning the lay of the place. A TV with three remotes is daunting so he decides not to bother. American TV doesn't really work for him anyway. He reviews titles in a bookcase. Lots of nursing books, parenting books, and a plethora of young adult fiction series: *Twilight, Hunger Games, Divergent, Uglies, Pendragon, Maze*

Runner, and a few classics, presumable assigned reading. At least she is well read.

He pulls out the first *Hunger Games* book. Jennifer Lawrence is hot and he can fantasize about her while reading it. That is about the best he is getting for the immediate future.

He sits on the brown, leather couch and with a little effort, elevates his leg onto the coffee table, carefully hanging his foot over the side. It is one of those tables that looks like the slab of a big tree but shellacked and glossy. He pulls a soft, blue blanket from a basket nearby and covers up.

He wishes he had a cup of tea and tries to remember the last time he had a cup of tea. On Anna's porch swing. John was taking the girls for a walk with his neighbor Joe. Two big men and two little baby girls in strollers. You have to respect a man who can look manly pushing a stroller. For a quick, lonely, up in the middle of the night moment, he regrets his decision not to call Anna. He knows she'd come, but it would be a hardship. They are too new for him to be a hardship to her.

He reads about Katniss Everdeen and District 12. He tries to read anyway. He is a terrible reader.

Marina wakes early, before seven o'clock. She walks by Callum's door and leans her ear against the wood to hear if he is up. She can't hear anything so she tiptoes toward the kitchen to make coffee and finds him asleep on the couch. He is slumped down into the cushions with his arms crossed over his chest and the bad leg hanging over the table.

Callum startles awake when she enters the room. He stretches painful kinks from his back.

"Sorry, I woke you up," she says. "You didn't look very comfortable though."

He rubs his eyes with his fists like a five year old and groans at his back. "No problem. The pills have my days and nights all turned around."

"Do you drink coffee? We have tea too." She adds since he is from England.

"Mornings are coffee. Afternoons are tea for me. Thanks. Can you grab the Tylenol from my bedside?" Callum asks.

Marina is happy for a task. She gets his Tylenol, a sweatshirt, fresh water and makes good strong coffee. She brings him a mug full and sits in a burnt orange chair, crisscrossing her legs.

"Do you have kids?" she asks, "or a wife?"

"Neither."

"Ex-wife?"

"No."

"Girlfriend?"

"No." She wonders how long he'll let her go on.

"Ex-girlfriend?"

"Not worth mentioning."

"Brothers and sisters?"

"One of each."

"Mom and Dad?"

"Mom yes, Dad dead. Are you getting bored yet?" he asks.

"Not yet. You like movies?"

"Yes."

"Do you like to read?" She gestures to the book on the table. "I love that one."

"Some."

"Music?"

"I love music. My turn," he says. "Where's your Dad?"

"You really went there?" She is a little shocked but still laughs.

He shrugs.

"My Dad isn't." she says without elaborating.

"What does that mean, your dad *isn't?*"

"He just isn't," she says.

"I don't understand," he says. "You are a bit of a wise ass, aren't you?"

She ignores the insult. "As far as I can tell, Victoria never got married. She never dates. She never brings guys home. She won't tell me anything about my Dad."

"That must be hard," Callum says to this little girl who is a stranger to him. All little girls are strangers really.

"Why does your mom have an accent and you don't?"

"She used to live in Asheville." She adds "North Carolina" in case he doesn't know United States geography. "She moved here before I was born."

"I was just in Asheville. I couldn't understand half the people. There were a lot of men with very long beards and no teeth. Some of the woman weren't much better. Nice city though. I liked it there a lot. Good music, good food. Beautiful mountains."

"Yeah, I've never been there. Mom never went back after she left."
Marina doesn't explain.

"How old are you?" he asks.

"Thirteen."

"Do you get in a lot of trouble?"

She skips that one, just stares at him, and he stares back. Why do you call
your Mom, Victoria?"

"Because she doesn't care," Marina says with no emotion.

"She cares," Callum defends Victoria.

"How would you know? You've been here for five minutes? For all you
know she burns me with an iron when I don't do my homework."

"Good point. I have no idea if she cares about you. It seems like what
house guests do though," he says looking slightly pensive.

"Whatever. Do you want pancakes?" Marina asks. He does so they move
into the kitchen. She pulls together the ingredients and starts dumping
everything into a bowl.

"Hold on a moment there. First combine your dry ingredients with a
whisk."

She does.

"Now add your milk but not the eggs, yet."

She does.

"Now the eggs, but don't over mix it. You're not baking a cake."

She does.

"Does your batter usually lump?" he asks and she nods. He pulls the whisk high into the air and silky batter ribbons its way back into the bowl. "See?"

She smiles at the perfect batter. He ends up taking the spatula and eventually the ladle too, and by the time Victoria walks into the kitchen, Marina is sitting at the table munching on pancakes and Callum is flipping golden disks of deliciousness. He hands her an oven warmed plate with three large, perfectly symmetrical, stacked pancakes.

Marina watches her mother watching Callum. He is old, but for old he is probably handsome. Victoria obviously thinks so. She fluffed the back of her hair walking into the kitchen and she practically fell over watching Callum flip a pancake.

Callum joins them at the table and loads maple syrup over his pancakes. Marina watches as he dives in. Having a man at their table is weird. She has never really had an opportunity to study a grown up man. He is really big and takes enormous bites. He doesn't talk much. He doesn't smile much either. *Hunger Games* is a weird book choice for an adult male.

"Marina, I have been thinking about your punishment," Victoria says suddenly pulling Marina out of her thoughts. "Grounded for a month. No cell phone, no TV. Straight home after school. You'll get home two hours before me every day and you can start dinner and take care of anything Callum needs."

Marina slams her fork to her plate, shoves her chair from the table, stomps into her room and slams the door.

"So, how's your day going?" Victoria jokes, ignoring her daughter's outburst.

"Better than yours," Callum returns, stuffing a big bite into his mouth.

"Glad to see you've got your appetite back."

As if to prove her point, Callum stabs another two pancakes and makes quick work of them. When he is done, Victoria brings a basin of hot soapy water to his room so he can wash.

"You need some help? I'm a professional. No sponge bath jokes though."

He checks to see if Marina is within earshot. She is not, still he whispers. "It would be impossible to enjoy my first sponge bath without a joke or two. It will be far more interesting in my imagination anyway."

He reaches to button the missed button near her belly button, but before he does, an index finger slides in, only for a moment, brushing the soft skin of her belly.

"If you keep missing buttons, I'll think you're flirting with me." Then he gives her a tap on the nose and closes the door with a smirk.

Victoria takes a deep breath and smooths her shirt to center herself before getting down to more serious business. Having a gorgeous, flirtatious man in the house is more challenging than she expected and more delightful. She wonders how the simple brush of a finger on her bare skin can be so arousing. Forget the skin, the spatula alone was arousing. He handles himself with complete confidence in the kitchen and it is extremely attractive.

She catches herself humming an old Police song while she puts in a load of laundry. After folding some towels, she takes her laptop to the sofa and checks her email even though she already knows what is waiting in her inbox. Again, she looks at the email from her father.

Victoria, it's time for you to come home. We've let this go on long enough. I don't have much time left. I want to know my granddaughter. I miss you. The house and everything I have are yours. Please come home.

The email is dated four days ago and she has still not replied. She leans her head into her hands and contemplates the pros and cons yet again.

Pros – Victoria misses her home, her mountains, her city, her world. Park City has been a nice place to live, but it isn't home. She can also settle things once and for all. She has been carrying this grudge against her father and it is wearing her down. Marina can get to know her grandfather. Marina can get away from these kids and getting away from these kids seems more and more important.

Cons – Uprooting their lives. New home, new job, new school, new friends, everything they have known for the last thirteen years. Truly, there aren't many friends to give up. Victoria has grown comfortable with being a loner.

Friendships are a lot of work and she doesn't have time. Lacey lives next door with her two little boys. Her husband is in the service and usually overseas. They help each other out with their kids, but Lacey is only twenty-three and Victoria's thirty-one feels ancient next to her. Religion isn't Victoria's thing so there is a deep void between her and a lot of the community. Marina is doing terribly in school and a fresh start might not be a bad thing. She has done some research and there were plenty of jobs for her in the city.

Another Con… dealing with it all. Again. Christopher. How can she possibly deal with Christopher? She hasn't seen him since that night fourteen years ago. She has resisted the temptation to track him down and kill him all these years. In her more violent fantasies, she goes back and forth between collapsing his skull with a baseball bat and a shovel. She is pretty sure he is still living in Asheville. Google tells all. She decides not to think about him for now. Wherever she is, he is going to be a problem and she won't let him keep her from anything she wants or anywhere she wants to be. He had six minutes of power over her life and she won't allow him a single moment of power over her, ever again.

She leans into the keyboard willing her fingers to make the decision for her.

Dad.

That's as far as she gets before Marina comes in and hands over her cell phone.

"Thanks. Can we talk?" Victoria asks.

"More?" Marina whines.

"Not about Callum, something else," Victoria smooths Marina's long bangs and pulls her to sit down on the couch. Victoria resists the temptation to pull her baby girl into her lap. Thirteen is a funny age, still her little girl but almost a woman. Marina has been less and less affectionate these last months. The good night snuggle has become a perfunctory hug and a "close my door." And that hurts.

The older Marina gets, the more Victoria feels a void growing between them. Secrets start as little seeds and then grow like cancer. There is so much Victoria never wants Marina to know. Going to Asheville won't make that any better.

"This is going to sound a little odd, but I got an email from my father."

Marina sits up straight, her full attention on her mother. Victoria looks into her beautiful girl's face, she has her grandfather's eyes. They should probably go. She can't keep Marina from him any longer. Victoria suddenly questions her decision to keep them apart all these years, but she isn't apologizing for it. He wanted her to have an abortion. He wanted her to let Christopher get away with it. Her father got half of his wishes. Christopher got away free and clear. Victoria wanted to have his ass hauled off to prison.

"My grandfather?" Marina asks, wide-eyed with shock. Her face is changing, thinning out. She is losing her little girl face so fast.

"Yeah. He wants us to come to Asheville. To live with him."

Marina is confused. "I thought you hated your family."

Victoria feels a sharp stab of regret for how she has talked about her family over the years. "Hate is a strong word. I was really angry for a long time. Maybe too long. I'm not angry anymore."

"Why?" Marina asks.

"You know all of this." Victoria has dodged this question again and again.

Marina frowns. "I don't really know anything."

Victoria gives her the same abridged version she has been giving for years. "After my Mother died, my Dad and I didn't get along. At all. It was really, really bad. I had you and then I left."

"Was he mad you had me?" Marina asks, looking young and vulnerable and Victoria just wants to protect her from the world and everyone in it.

"No, no no," Victoria protests. "It was other things. None of which matter a lick now. He is getting older and his heart is failing. He wants to see us. He really wants to get to know you."

"Do you talk to him?" Marina asks.

"Not really. We email occasionally and I send him pictures of you. He has been wanting to see us for a long time."

"Why didn't we see him before?" Marina asks.

Victoria has no good answer. "I've been stubborn Marina. I don't think I did the right thing keeping him out of our lives. It's time to change that."

"Is he mean? Did he like beat you?" Marina asks with wide eyes.

Victoria does pull her daughter into her lap then. "No Marina! It was nothing like that. He is a good man. He was a wonderful father to me. He never laid a hand on me. He coached my soccer team. He taught me how to read the stars like a sailor. He took me camping. I can start a fire with sticks. Did you know that? He gave me everything. He did

70

everything for me." Victoria hears the unspoken *then why did you leave him?* "After my mom died… it was so sudden. Things went bad."

"Can't we just visit him?" Marina asks.

"We can do whatever we want. Or nothing at all," Victoria pulls her daughter close. All this remembering opens old wounds.

Marina finally says "He's sick. He needs you."

Victoria feels the tears sting behind her eyes. She won't let them go though, not in front of Marina anyway. "What about your school? Your friends? Park City? And Marina, we don't have to decide right now. We can take some time on this."

Marina's twists her mouth side to side while she considers her answer. "I think we should go soon. We could both use a new place."

"Are you sure? Tell me why."

Marina shrugs, tears filling her blue eyes.

"Marina you don't have to punish yourself for what happened with Callum. Punishment is my responsibility, not yours."

"I want to go Mom. It will be good for me. For you too."

"Why me?"

"Well he is your Dad."

"Okay, why else," Victoria asks.

"Mom aren't you a little lonely?" Marina's words makes Victoria's breath catch. You never think your kids are emotionally evaluating you, even judging you, until it's too late.

"I have you sweetie," Victoria says slowly. "I'm not lonely at all."

"A man Mom. Lonely for a man?"

71

"Oh shush, you don't know a thing about anything." Victoria laughs awkwardly

"Mom, I'm going away to college in four and a half years," Marina tries to reason.

Victoria bites back the words that Marina is going nowhere past the local community college with her current grades.

"I don't really want to leave my mommy alone," Marina says with a sad puppy, pouty face.

"You think about these things?" Victoria similes, but she is shocked, and not in a good way. Marina feels needed and that can't be good for a kid. Victoria is providing no healthy example of a male/female relationship. Marina has nothing to model. How is Marina ever going to have a healthy relationship of her own?

"Callum." Marina says simply.

"On no you don't, young lady," Victoria says to end the conversation. This is going nowhere fast. If and when she does bring a man into their lives, it won't be some over the top, hot, British, unemployed playboy. He's a terrific bestie and a lot of fun to look at, but she can't imagine there is a lot of substance there.

"Marina, if you are absolutely sure, I'll send your Granddad a note. He'll be lucky to have you," Victoria hesitates voicing her next thought. "Marina, I want you to do something else for me. Call Lacey and offer to babysit for free tonight. She does a lot of nice for us and you can use your time to help others. Give her a night out with her girlfriends."

Marina starts to argue but doesn't bother.

"How about I make some dinner for you and Callum before I go? I saw a good recipe for a Barefoot Contessa stew that looks pretty easy. We still have some of that nice bread?"

"Marina, I'm not kicking you out so I can have a quiet evening alone with Callum. This isn't a damn date! Marina that is not happening." Even as she says it, Victoria knows it probably is happening but very short term. She just might treat herself to a quickie or two on his way out the door.

Marina shrugs and goes to call Lacey.

After the lonely sponge bath, Callum falls asleep. He startles awake to a knock at his door. The evening sun is deserting his room and darkness is taking over. As always, he takes a moment to remember where he is.

"Come in," he finally says and Victoria ducks her head in the door.

"You up? I was afraid you'd be up all night if I let you sleep any later." She comes in and feels his head for a fever. He is sleeping a lot, but his head is cool. Can I change your bandage? I want to check your incision."

He points to the bandages and tape in the bathroom and pushes off the blankets. He is almost regretful that he is wearing shorts as opposed to his usual nothing for sleepy time, but he can't be in a house with a young girl, sleeping in the buff. Disappointingly professional in manner, Victoria removes the bandages and examines his wound.

"It looks good. You heal quickly." She points her index finger high on his thigh. "What's this?"

He glances at the faint, old scar at the top of his inner thigh. There are three parallel lines, the center is about an inch long and jagged, the outer two are longer and straight. Jesus he had almost forgotten.

"If you shrug, I think I might just punch you," she says.

He smiles at her. She is pretty. "Just old scars. Nothing interesting."

"You're a little quiet. Feeling okay?" Victoria asks, letting the scars drop.

He isn't entirely okay. "I'm dreaming a lot. I feel like I'm remembering everything that has ever happened to me," he says joylessly. "Things I haven't thought of in years." Suddenly the scars itch.

"Anesthesia can do strange things to your head. Not to mention the pain and the meds. And the laying here. You are usually a fairly active guy, I'd imagine. Anything you want to talk about?" she asks.

"God no." The smile he shares is forced. Daisy and Laila have invaded his thoughts and he doesn't understand why. He'd rather forget that time in his life. That summer changed him and he was never like other boys his own age again. Other boys had first kisses and first loves. They went to dances and movies and got to first base and then second base and eventually had sex. It was never like that for Callum. He spent his life trying to recreate what he had with Daisy and Laila. Marina is just a year younger than he was when that all started. She is nothing more than a child.

"Want some dinner?" Victoria asks. "It's just you and me tonight, Marina is next door babysitting."

Interesting, he thinks, pleased for a diversion from his thoughts.

"Not just yet. I need to wake up for a moment. Sit and tell me about yourself."

She sits, a little reluctantly, at his side on the bed.

"Who are you Victoria?" He leans back into the pillows and studies her hard. Now that he is more clearheaded, he can judge her better. She crosses her legs, resting a thigh against his good leg. She says a few sentences. Something about nursing school at The University of Utah and a physician's office and bartending. He doesn't hear much of it because he is enjoying the weight of her thigh on his leg. That slight pressure is very enticing. While he isn't up for any actual activities of a sexual sort, a little pet and flirt keeps things interesting.

74

At this point in his life, he can get most any woman into bed. When he told Victoria that everyone wanted to sleep with him, he wasn't being facetious. But the fun has been going out of it as of late. He remembers to interject an, "Interesting," as Victoria explains her life and then he starts to wonder if that is why he let himself love Elizabeth. Was he just getting bored with the capture and the kill? Was it just the timing? Is he just aging out of banging strangers? Is he wanting more out of life, something meaningful? *Bullshit*, he tells himself and gives Victoria a sympathetic nod. Or is it more about Daisy and Laila? Did they curse him to only care for women he can never have?

"That's about it," she says. "What about you?"

"I am boring as hell," he tries. It fails, of course.

"I doubt that. Men like you don't lead boring lives. I am as sure of that as I am sure that the sky is blue and the day is long."

"Men like me?" he asks, fishing for it.

"Oh come on. Movie star good looks. Trust fund babies." She frowns as if disapproving of his movie star good looks and his trust fund.

"Is that what you think of me?" He smiles for the cameras but tries not to pose.

"I'm sure this is all a big shocker to you. Do you actually have product in your hair right now?" she asks, leaning forward to rub her hand across his very styled hair.

"Whatever, moving on," but he could talk about this topic until the sun sets, rises and sets again.

"What makes you think I'm wealthy?" He is genuinely surprised by that one.

"Trust fund baby," she adds. "Not your own money. Inherited, not earned."

75

"Ouch. Why on earth do you think that?"

"What are you doing Callum? Not everyone can afford to take a, what did you call it? Sabbatical?

"Ah that. You are so very wrong about me, my love. I have been working since I was fifteen. This is the first time I have had a break for more than three consecutive days in almost twelve years."

"Really?" she asks, dubious of his words.

"Really. I am starting to understand your face," he says. "You are actually quite lovely."

"What in the hell is that supposed to mean?" Her hand instinctively goes to protect her cheek.

He laughs because she is easy to irritate. "It means you need no adornment. You require no make-up. You have fantastic bone structure. You freckles give you the slightest contrast in skin tone. Those lashes are extraordinary against your blue eyes. You are really lovely."

"Fuck you," she says.

"Fuck me?" he asks, not sure if she is mad or happy.

"I have been thinking we were flirting a little, but you are gay. I am so mad you didn't tell me."

"I'm not gay," he says. He reaches for her foot, holding it firmly in his hand. "Metrosexual maybe but very hetero."

Her toes are soft but cold. He warms them with the heat from his hand. She tenses but lets him keep her foot. "I'm having thoughts of pulling you closer and doing things to you with my mouth. I could do wonderful things to you with my mouth. I promised no hanky panky though, so off with you," he jokes holding her foot tight. Her breathing deepens just a little.

"Behaving well isn't one of my better qualities. You had better scram for your own good." His voice is low and intoxicating, like a siren drawing sailors into the water. But his lure is all sex.

Still she doesn't move. Her mouth moves like she is trying to decide what to say. She wets full lips with the tip of her tongue. She has a lovely mouth. The glimpse of her tongue breeches his resolve to behave and he pulls her foot closer to his side. His fingertips dance across her calf. "I'm not going to kiss you. The moment I kiss you, it is all over. I'm just going to touch you a little."

She closes her eyes at his words. He sits up so he can reach higher and grazes her thigh with his thumb. Her breathing deepens and he is sure he has just seconds before her panties are off or she runs out the door. Discerning the subtleties of these situations is Callum's specialty. And then she smiles. He thought he was playing with her, but she is really playing with him. She is going to be a no. Not yet anyway. She is laden with traits like self-respect and dignity.

He debates going for it anyway. Her shorts are loose. He could glide his thumb over her clitoris and have her coming in his hand within moments. Her face would relax and her head would fall back, spreading curls along her back. Her first moan would get him hard. And then he would... but that is certainly not behaving like a gentleman and a promise is a promise. He lays his palm over her thigh and slides it back down to her calf. He holds her calf like he owns it.

Her eyes open. Does he detect disappointment or is that just his own ego imagining it?

"You are so lovely Victoria," he says and the words snap her out of it.

"And so are you." She says very matter-of-fact and tosses a nearby sweatshirt at him before walking to the door. "But you know that already, don't you?"

Ouch again.

"Come and get it. Dinner I mean," she calls over her shoulder from the hallway.

Five

Callum's head clears over the next few days and he starts sleeping through most of his nights. He decides reading isn't helping his headaches so he sets *Hunger Games* aside for a few days, but he wants to keep the TV off after school since Marina is banned from TV for the month, so he just watches while she is at school. He learns to work the remotes and flips channels all day long. He watches old Seinfeld episodes, but he doesn't get the humor. He tries to watch Food Network, but he can't stand it for two consecutive minutes. American soap operas are hard to follow and the women are so so. No porn or pay channels of course. He ends up flipping around and not really committing to anything. Marina reads to Callum after she does her homework.

"I'll read Hunger Games myself later," he says, to keep Jennifer Lawrence to himself. "You pick another. Not Twilight though. No romance please."

She chooses *The Maze Runner.* A perfectly unromantic but very interesting story about a colony of young people trapped in a bizarre reality complete with an endless maze. It ends in a cliffhanger so after a few afternoons of reading, she continues with book two.

"I'm hungry," she says laying the book across her lap.

Callum and Marina go into the kitchen. Rummaging through the cabinets and refrigerator has become a daily afternoon activity. She has good instincts as a cook and he likes teaching her.

"I want to make this," she holds up a page pulled from a magazine. The photo shows a pot of stew, beef presumably, being stirred by a dark haired woman, smiling with her arm around a seemingly good friend.

"Barefoot Contessa," she says and gets no reaction. "Ina Garten?" still nothing. She pulls a recipe book off the counter and hands it to him. It is a nice enough book.

"Why do you need a recipe book?" Callum asks her.

"To learn to cook, duh," Marina responds with the requisite eye roll.

"Oh bullshit. You just need to understand the basics and then you know what you like and you go from there. You already have a good grasp of the fundamentals." Callum places the torn magazine page and the book back down on the counter and pulls a pot from the cabinet.

"Callum, can you read?" Marina asks simply.

Callum sets the pot down and exhales deeply to manage his irritation and impatience at this child.

"Yes I can read," he says.

"But you don't like to, do you?" Marina asks.

He grips both handles at the sides of the pot while carefully choosing his words. "I do, in fact, like to read very much. I just so happen to suck at it."

"Are you dyslexic?"

For a precocious little brat, she is very intuitive.

80

"I am." He pulls stew beef, vegetables and butter from the refrigerator. She gets stock from the cabinet.

"Beans. Tomatoes. Garlic." He demands tersely.

"Are you mad at me for guessing? You shouldn't be ashamed of it," she says "It is a medical condition."

Little shit.

"I'm not mad. I just hate talking about it and it is a huge pain in my ass." He pulls a knife from the drawers and starts chopping onions on a large cutting board. "Flour, salt and pepper. Where are those herbs your mom bought?"

"There is a kid in my class and he's dyslexic too. What's it like?" she asks.

He decides to let go of his ego momentarily and educate a single human being on dyslexia. "Words on a page tend to shift around for me. I have to focus incredibly hard to get the basic meaning. I might be reading *Hunger Games* for 6 months."

"I can read it to you," she offers.

"No, I have set that goal for myself and I'll read it." *As least until I can find a Playboy or get laid*, he thinks.

"Everyone thinks dyslexia is just about numbers and letters reversing on the page. It isn't just about what is happening with your eyes. It's also what happens in your brain. I am atrocious with numbers. I can't follow a recipe. I didn't finish school, if you must know. I can't follow a fucking map, thank god for GPS."

"Really?" she asks.

He chops and adds onions to the sizzling oil. She stirs the pot and the aroma fills the kitchen quickly.

"Really. I worked my way up in restaurants and learned the business through experience and hard work. The moral of the story is do your fucking homework. With a less complicated brain I'd be running the damned world by now. Use yours well."

Together they make a stew that Ina Garten herself would approve. An hour later, Victoria gets home from work and Callum and Marina sit at a decorated table, complete with candlelight and the good placemats. Victoria shoots Marina a look that Callum thinks he might understand. Marina is determined to create an atmosphere of romance for Callum and Victoria. That's okay, Callum likes romance. Marina eats quickly and then begs out for some fabricated homework she forgot about.

"I'm sorry about that. She seems to have plans for us beyond besties," Victoria says because she seems to like keeping everything out in the open.

He leans back in his chair and she pulls his leg onto another chair. "You've been upright too long today. Elevate."

She sips her wine and watches him over the rim of her glass. "You look better. How are the headaches?"

"Much better, thank you. I should probably be about ready to drink a little wine." He gestures to the bottle.

"How about a half?" She reaches for another glass. "Don't forget your follow-up appointment at the ortho in Salt Lake tomorrow. Hopefully, they'll move you to a less restrictive cast."

He nods and gratefully sips the offered Cabernet. She takes good care of him considering they are strangers. Actually, she takes good care of him, period. His mother wasn't much of a caregiver. Getting sick at boarding school meant a few days in a cold, antiseptic smelling infirmary. The time he hurt himself with Laila and Daisy, they wrapped him up with a towel and dropped him off a block from his house.

He doesn't want to overstay his welcome though. "Victoria, I want to thank you again for taking me in. Your care and hospitality will never be forgotten. I will go on to Osprey Island in a few days to my sister. I called the leasing company to take my car and I'll fly out of Salt Lake. I have been a burden to you long enough."

"You are not a burden at all Callum. I am getting used to having you around." She smiles over her wine. *A little flirty* he wonders.

"Your sister will be happy to see you."

"They have an empty house next door to theirs. I can hole up there for a few months and heal."

"This is weird," she says shaking her head. "In a few weeks, Marina and I are packing it up and going to try out living with my Dad in Asheville. We'll be just a couple of hundred miles away. It is kind of ironic."

"Seriously? When are you leaving?" he asks.

"In a week or two. I want to get there before Christmas, but I don't want to rush it. I'm going to rent this place out furnished and just pack us and our clothes. I need to be sure I can go back there before I actually sell my house."

"Isn't Thomas Wolfe from Asheville?

"Yeah, thanks for the reminder," she says referring to the title and subject matter of Wolfe's novel *You Can't Go Home Again*.

"You're driving?" Callum asks.

"To Asheville? Of course."

"Alone?" He doesn't like the sound of that.

"No, me and Marina," she says, not liking that he is obviously not liking the sound of that. "Why?"

He looks at her like she is crazy. "There are predators out there looking to prey on women like you." He doesn't mention that he might just be one of those predators, non-violently of course.

"Is that how you see me, Callum? Do you see me as a victim?" She is angrier than she should be.

"No, of course not. But there are a lot of assholes out there. Turn on the damn news."

"Oh for God's sake. We'll be fine, Callum. I can take care of myself and my daughter." She stacks his dishes and Marina's onto her own.

"And the weather. And the car. And who knows what else." He is not expecting this flow of words out of his mouth. They have taken good care of him and he is truly grateful, but he is starting to sound like he cares.

"I have been handling weather and the car and the who knows what else for thirteen years."

He isn't sure why she is speaking like she is ready to punch him. So he asks the question that he thinks will piss her off the most. She's mad anyway. "Why?"

"What do you mean *why*?" she nearly spits.

"Why are you alone?" It is a simple question, but she doesn't answer it. She stares at him with angry, wide eyes, breathing shallow breaths.

"I just am," comes finally and she gets up to clear the table.

"My being here requires a lot of trust on your part."

She loads the dishwasher loudly, carelessly slamming dishes onto the rack.

"Mine too. For all I knew you could've been Kathy whatever her name is in *Misery*. You already got one of my legs."

84

She can't help but smile at this.

"What do you want to know Callum? Why I have no husband?" She folds her arms defensively across her chest.

He doesn't want to demand information from her, but he is curious. "You are a beautiful woman, Victoria."

"And that's enough? My beauty has all the perfect, single, men dropping at my feet, ready to care for me and my daughter and protect me and change my oil and shovel my driveway?" She mocks him.

"You are a nice person, too," he concedes.

"Ah, the true value of all women is unleashed right here in my very own kitchen."

"Okay you don't want to talk about it, I get the fucking point. Forget it."

He rises quickly, annoyed, and knocks his crutches to the floor. Victoria reaches for them and hands them back to Callum before she leans up and lays her lips on his. She doesn't touch her hand to his chest. She doesn't grab his head and pull him close. She doesn't let her tongue touch into his mouth. She doesn't make it any more than it is. She just rises to her toes, his head naturally lowers to the necessary height and she lays her lips on his just for a moment. She doesn't even look into his eyes to share her desire through thick, fluttering, eyelashes. *Still…* She just touches his lips with her own, for a moment, maybe two. A low sound of surprised pleasure escapes Callum's throat.

Without warning, Victoria pulls her lips from his and leaves the kitchen silently. He hears the bedroom door close gently behind her. Callum is left standing in the kitchen with his jaw low. A woman hasn't lowered his jaw in a very long time.

Victoria leans against her bedroom door, trying not to regret that kiss. *It shut him up is all.* Her hand moves to her lower lip, touching where she touched him. She hasn't kissed a man in a long time. Oh a few have kissed her, but that is different. She hasn't wanted to be the one to do the kissing in a long, long time.

Dating in Park City is interesting. Truly her interest in dating is slim to none. Working, studying, caring for her daughter and all of the day-to-day crap that makes up a life have really filled her days quite adequately. Her nights, well that is another story. She has a friend she can call. He is sweet enough, but there are no fireworks. She also has the necessary apparatus to make a boyfriend less relevant.

She sits on her bed and tries to decide what she wants from Callum. Sex? So much for no hanky-panky. The thought of sex with an actual man like Callum has her digging for the lockbox at the back of her linen closet. Despite the kiss and the desire that are flooding her senses right now, she really doesn't want to blur the lines.

Marina seems hell-bent on pushing a romance here. Well, what is the point of that? Another few days and he'll be on his way. Still the thought of a few good rolls in the hay while Marina is in school is well within the realm of possibility. All she needs is to fall in love with this gorgeous, underemployed Playboy, and then say good-bye and then she will be a mess before she even gets to Asheville. A recipe for failure. Forget it.

Still, she thinks about it, over and over and over again.

Six

The next morning, Callum and Victoria make the thirty minute drive into Salt Lake City for the ortho follow up. Callum is overjoyed at the smaller leg brace. Victoria has a few hours before she needs to get to work, so they find a diner for a late breakfast in the city. They order omelets, bacon and sausage, fruit, toast, biscuits, juice and coffee. Callum has a good appetite and enjoys the big breakfast.

"I think there is a shower in your future," Victoria says. No word of the kiss has passed between them.

"Thank god."

"You're telling me," she laughs.

"Oh shit, do I fucking smell?" he asks, sniffing himself wherever he can reach.

She smiles because she can get him going so effortlessly. "No, but you look a bit scruffy." She scratches his new beard. "Is this intentional? I can shave you."

"It is very intentional. I'm updating my look." He tells her about John being the inspiration for the longer hair and the new beard.

"Do you have a man crush on your new brother-in-law?" She stuffs a piece of bacon into her mouth.

"So what if I do?" He stuffs his own bacon in.

"Show me a picture. My guess is you have more than a few selfies in there." She points to his mobile. Beautiful, arrogant men pose for a lot of photos.

"Are you bloody mocking me?" His voice is higher than usual. He stops chewing his mouthful of eggs and waits for an answer.

She shrugs. "You do though, don't you? I bet you have over thirty selfies from your visit with your sister."

"My god you are a vile bitch." Even though the words are harsh, their tone isn't.

He hands her the phone and she scrolls through countless photos of his nieces, three sunrises, a table laden with shellfish and a crowd of people around it laughing and drinking (tilted sideways), a boat, six of John and Anna (she looks at those for a long time), and exactly four selfies -- one with Callum and Anna, one of Callum and John fishing, two of Callum with John, Anna and their girls.

"Okay I was off by 26."

"Bitch," he says tucking the phone back into his pocket.

"You just found them?" she asks. "You look like you have known each other for years. I can see the love between you in every picture. Your sister is beautiful. John's not too bad either. Definitely a bromance there."

Callum tells Victoria about that day when he got the call from his mother. Facebook changed his life. Anna's birth mother, Ellen, had been looking for her daughter for years. Anna's best friend, Pemberley, found Ellen. Ellen and Callum's mother were old friends from their childhood days in England and had connected on Facebook years before. When Callum got the call that he had a sister, he almost dropped dead on the spot. He was in bed with Elizabeth at the time, trying to talk her into running off with him. The more she resisted, the more he pleaded.

"What a blessing Callum. I can see how much they all mean to you. You are very lucky."

"Am I? I think my life would have been very different with a sister. Hers certainly would have been better with us. Her parents were monsters." He tosses his fork onto the plate. This subject always gets him angry. "Sometimes all I can think about is the time I missed with her. She is six years older than me. I missed my whole life with her"

"No Callum. You have your whole life ahead of you." She lays her hand over his and he pulls his back fast.

"Jesus Christ, Callum. I wasn't making a pass at you," she says indignantly.

He doesn't bother to answer, just frowns in her direction.

"Oh that." She keeps her eyes on her plate. "Good eggs."

"Fuck the eggs. Are you tossing me about, Victoria?" he asks.

"I don't even know what that means. You know sometimes you speak much more English than others. You accent isn't very balanced."

"Oh shut it about my accent," he tries to get the conversation back on track.

"See?" she says determined to keep the conversation off track.

"Are you wanting to get me in the sack or not? Just out with it. Don't play the kissy in the kitchen game with me."

Her face goes six shades of red. "No."

89

"Just a bit of a flirt then?"

She nods, then shakes her head. "I'm lying. Yes. Wait a second. Why am I being defensive? Weren't you the one fondling my leg just a few days ago? That felt pretty flirty." She deepens her voice and fakes his British accent, "I'm thinking about doing things to you with my mouth."

He smiles. "So no or yes. I'm confused."

"You are too scruffy. No."

"What if I shower? You might find me irresistible then."

She takes an unnecessarily large bite of sausage, "I'll let you know."

Because she is funny, he lets her off the hook.

Driving back to Park City, Callum can't help but fixate on the time he missed with Anna. As the mountains pass by the car window he thinks about those lost years. Everything would have been different with a sister in his life. Laila and Daisy would never have happened. He isn't sure why, but he thinks Anna could have saved him from that. Especially the end. It ended badly.

One day they were gone. It was a Tuesday, not even a Saturday or Sunday when events of note typically occur. Callum rode his bike over as he did every morning when his mother left for work. They always left the door ajar for him. They liked him to find them in interesting predicaments. Showering together, tied to the bed, dressed up as vampires (there was a lot of biting that day). Just once, with two other men. That day was the worst day, the day he hurt himself.

On this day, the door was locked and there was no response to his knocking or his fist banging the wood. He jumped off the step, walked around to the back, climbed the red wooden fence into the garden. He knocked a window out with his elbow and turned the lock on the back door.

Dresser drawers hung open as empty as his heart. Closets held nothing more than hangers and lies. The bed was stripped as bare as his soul. In the kitchen, only his apron remained. It was carefully laid over a kitchen chair, striped in blue and white. Callum searched the apartment. He opened every closet, every cabinet, overturned every lamp, every table. He pulled every painting off the wall and put his knee through each canvas. Surely they left him a clue, some way to find them. There was nothing. He folded the apron and tied it into a neat package and took it with him.

He pretended to be sick for the next few days to avoid facing his mother and Eric. Finally, he went back to school.

Before classes started, Callum got caught drinking scotch alone in an empty classroom. Headmaster Lester had been supervising young boys for most of his career. He was most disturbed that Callum was alone, isolating himself. Callum sat by a shuttered window in headmaster's office fiddling with the heel of his shoe.

"Mr. Townsend, you know we do not tolerate this type of behavior on campus. This is grounds for expulsion. But I think you know that and expulsion seems a rather simplistic solution."

Callum opened and closed his mouth making a lip smacking sound which Mr. Lister chose to ignore.

"Answer me a question, Mr. Townsend. Why were you drinking alone?"

Callum of course shrugged.

"That is not an answer, Mr. Townsend. Vocalize a response immediately."

Headmaster knew how to use a tone to elicit action. "I wanted to be alone. These guys are all assholes."

91

"I struggle to disagree, but you enjoyed those assholes very much last year."

Callum shrugged again.

"Very well. I will not expel you because that would be a punishment more to your poor mother than to you. But your punishment will be severe."

"What is it?" Callum asked. "Headmaster Lister," he added as an afterthought.

"If you don't want to spend time with the boys, we'll eliminate your participation in all fall programs, athletic and otherwise. You'll work outside of class time."

"The kitchen," Callum volunteered.

"You are volunteering to work in the kitchen?" This surprised Mr. Lester. He could see a tiny spark in Callum's eyes at the thought of working in the kitchen. Heaven knew this poor boy didn't have much of an academic career ahead. And with no father to guide him, Lister could not send him home. Kitchen work would be good for him.

The hole in Callum's heart filled a little when he cooked. There wasn't a lot of actual cooking, but the chef let him do prep. Peeling five hundred potatoes was mind numbing and comforting at the same time. The work offered him freedoms the other boys didn't have. He traveled into town on the bus every week for one supply or another.

He met a girl at the grocery with short blonde hair and a nose ring. On his second visit, he talked her into the alley behind the store. When she tried to kiss him, he turned his face from hers. She tasted like an ashtray. But he fingered her and as soon as she came, he pushed her to her knees. She blew him while a trash truck backed into the top of the alley. When she used an index finger to wipe the overflow from the side of her mouth, he thought she was the most beautiful girl he had ever seen. For the first time, he knew that he could live without Daisy and Laila.

Victoria drops him off at the house and heads to work. He takes a long hot shower, washing his incision with care, feeling like shit. *My god, I'm a fuck of a mess.* He leans against the shower wall and tries not to think about how he got here. He is suddenly drowning in self-pity, ruminating over the lost years with Anna and the years he would rather were lost with Laila, Daisy and Elizabeth.

He tries to avoid the regret. He fucking hates regret. *Make your decision and live with the consequences.* But he does have regrets about Elizabeth. He was so sure telling Jeremy would solve all of his problems. Jeremy, ever the gentleman, would bow out, and Elizabeth and Callum would live happily ever after.

Callum knew Jeremy his whole life. They were side by side for season after season of every sport. Their families were best friends. They travelled together, touring Europe through their teen years. After school, Jeremy went on to university and Callum worked his way through restaurants. He left Manchester and found good work in London, apprenticing wherever he could. Callum learned cooking through and through, but his lack of schooling was going to hold him back. He couldn't manage the business end, but he was extraordinary in the kitchen. In the four years Jeremy was mostly away earning a Finance degree, Callum made a good name for himself as an innovator in some of the best kitchens in London.

When Jeremy moved to London after graduation, suddenly there was Elizabeth. They had met in school. When Callum first met her, he didn't think much of her. She was attractive but bitchy. Long dark hair, usually piled on her head. Her eyes were dark and a little mean, often covered in horn rimmed glasses. Her skin was fair and the contrast gave her a slight vulnerability that was interesting. She smiled all the time, but she wasn't funny and she always seemed a little detached. She had a lot of confidence for a woman her age. She acted like she could do anything and do it very well. She was usually right.

Before long there was a wedding and then they were the three fucking Muskateers, opening a restaurant together. Elizabeth had her hand in every pot. She designed the restaurant and managed the business end while Callum ran the kitchen. Jeremy worked a more traditional banking job to keep the rent paid. They all shared an apartment to save money since they were never home anyway.

It took four years, but *Mise En Place* took off. The name is a French term for organization in the kitchen. Callum's dyslexia made kitchen organization his highest priority. This was the place where he could finally see everything he needed to see, how he needed to see it. He had complete control and designed a world where he could create magic. And he did. There were Michelin stars and press and *Mise* had a month long waiting list and celebrities clamoring their way in.

The water runs cold and Callum gets out of the shower gingerly, wrapping himself in a soft, white towel. He uses his forearm to clear the mirror of steam, rubs his hand over his face and decides the beard is working for him. The beard makes him think of John and Anna and brings him back to the present and then he is grateful. A more likely scenario would have been never finding his sister. Finding her at thirty is far better than never. He feels better.

He dresses in jeans and a collared shirt, then puts on his ski jacket and very slowly makes his way down Victoria's driveway, one house over and up Lacey's driveway. They met this morning on the way to the ortho. Lacey gave Callum an enthusiastic *anything you need*.

Lacey opens the door before he knocks.

"Hey." She stretches the three letter word into three syllables.

"Hi Lacey."

She swings a little boy on her hip.

"I was wondering if you might possibly be going anywhere near a grocery today?"

"I sure am. Can I pick up a few things for you?" she offers.

He has a brief thought about lonely women with husbands overseas, but dismisses it before it even fully forms in his brain.

"Could I ride along with you?" He is ready to cook and he can't just hand over an ingredient list.

"Sure Callum. Give me an hour and I'll pick you up?" She doesn't seem to mind the idea of spending the afternoon with him. "I just need to be back by three-thirty to meet the bus."

He thanks her profusely and tries not to slide back down her driveway.

"Be careful! Can I drive you back?"

He waves, indicating he is good and she picks him up an hour later.

Walking the aisles of an American grocery store is a bizarre experience for Callum. He has hardly grocery shopped in years. He has eaten most of his meals in restaurants, his own or friend's, since he can remember. Selecting food for a restaurant isn't anything like this. There are more choices than he expected. He pushes a small cart along while he crutches through the store. He and Lacey go their own ways. She spends more time with cereals and canned food. He is drawn to produce and meats. There is a lot of meat here.

When Lacey drops him off, he thanks her and pats the boy's head for good measure. After putting away his groceries, he pushes Victoria's laundry through so he can do his own. He wants to close his eyes when he moves her laundry from the washer to the dryer, but he doesn't. He hangs anything he finds questionable for the dryer on a garment rack lined with wooden hangers and he borrows the lacy white bra that was already hung and is dry. He loads the washer with his own things. He'll need to get more clothes eventually. Marina will be home in thirty minutes. He takes *Hunger Games* to his bedroom along with the white lacy bra. He really does feel better.

When Marina gets home, he tells her to get her homework done, so they can cook a special dinner for her Mom. By the time she is finished, he has the table set. He bought long blue candles and found a table cloth in the linen closet in Victoria's bedroom. He has suddenly become a snooper. There was a locked box on the top shelf in the back. He considers picking the lock another day but is pretty sure he knows the contents already. *Way to go Victoria!* The thought alone has his mind in the gutter. He did replace the white bra with Victoria's other unmentionables.

Marina walks into the kitchen and admires the table. "Looks nice in here." She smooths a wrinkle from the edge of the blue and green floral cloth. She looks a little downtrodden.

"Tough day?" he asks.

She shrugs off the question and asks what they are cooking. He shows her two large, still kicking, lobsters that they are going to use to top off a penne. She has never done this before, but she is game. They set out vegetables and start preparing the sauce.

He shows her how to hold the knife properly and, after a little practice, she slices the onions and garlic paper thin.

"You are a good cook Marina. You learn fast."

She smiles, but not many words are coming out of her today. "You okay," he asks wondering when he started caring. "And don't shrug please. Chefs never shrug."

She has tears in her eyes, but they might be from the onions. He's not sure and he can't get her to say anything.

"What is it Marina?" he asks more insistently. When she still doesn't answer, he takes the knife from her hand, sets it down on the cutting board, and pulls her to sit down next to him at the table.

He waits. She covers her face with her hands and her tears flow silently.

"My God did something happen today?" He has no idea what to do. "Should I call your mother?"

"No!" That gets her going. "Don't tell her anything about this!" She is overly emphatic, but at least she is talking.

He hands her a clean dish towel to wipe her face.

"Then tell me."

She takes a deep breath and what she says next stops his own breath. "Callum, I think I'm a rape baby."

"What does that even mean?" he asks, understanding perfectly what that means. He is buying time.

"I think my mother was raped and she got pregnant with me. I think my father was a rapist." Tears roll down her face and he pulls her onto his knee, trying to decide if this is what people do. She weeps into his shirt and he has no idea what to say.

"Marina, why would you think that?" seems like a start.

She tells him about sex ed at school today. They covered a "No Means No" segment and there was a speaker from a rape crisis center. She shared statistics about date rape.

"Callum, my mother has literally never told me a thing about my father. I have never seen a single picture. I don't know his name. She left

97

Asheville before she had me and never went back. She tells me she fought with her Dad, but there is more. I know there is."

"Maybe she loved your father so much that it hurts her to remember. Maybe he was in the service and died in Afghanistan or maybe it was a one night stand and she didn't know him." He stops talking. A daughter shouldn't be thinking about her mother having a one night stand.

"She would tell me that. She is really open. And Callum she never ever dates. She pretends to, but she doesn't go near men."

"Maybe she is a lesbian." He's not sure he is helping.

"She's not a lesbian. Callum, I just know this is it. I'm a rape baby."

He smooths his hand on her back while she cries and thinks what she is saying might not be wrong. "You should talk to her about it."

"No Callum. Not now. We're going to Asheville. So much has happened with me and then you. I don't want to do this to her. If she was raped…" She can't go on talking through the tears.

"Listen Marina. Worst case scenario is that you are right."

"And?" she asks.

"I don't know. I thought more would come to me as I said it, but it didn't," he says honestly. He's got nothing.

She smiles despite his less than satisfying soothing. "Yeah I know, it sucks right? Please don't say anything to her Callum."

"I won't, but I'm not sure you shouldn't. You're a kid. You shouldn't have to worry about shit like this. Your life should be all ponies and rainbows."

"And killing lobsters?" she asks to change the subject.

They cook together and this secret between them connects them more than the shared collision, the shared house, the books or the passion for cooking and food. Somehow there is a genuine friendship growing between them.

When Victoria walks through the door, the lights in the house are low but a glowing candlelight comes from the kitchen. Her favorite Mumford and Sons CD plays low and Callum is pouring wine into stemless glasses.

"Surprise!" Callum looks freshly showered and disgustingly handsome. "Can Marina drink a little wine? Just a bit, watered down?"

Victoria stands in the doorway in her dirty blue scrubs and messy ponytail. "Yes, of course. You two did all this?"

Marina added two low vases of dried flowers to Callum's candles and tablecloth. The table is set with folded napkins and perfectly aligned silverware. Sliced bread rests on a board next to some type of a dipping oil with herbs. Marina is grating fresh cheese into a bowl.

"This is so sweet. And something smells good. Can I change? I feel so underdressed."

Callum checks the pasta. "Six minutes."

Victoria dashes to her room and finds a pile of freshly folded laundry. *Marina did laundry?* She is in awe. Callum is a good influence on her. She changes quickly into blue jeans and boots with a white sweater. It is a little tight and flattering. There is nothing wrong with a little flirty. She adds a light spray of perfume, earrings, some eyeliner, mascara and lip gloss before letting her hair out of the tie. She fluffs it and lets it roll loose down her back. *Not bad for six minutes*, she thinks, and walks to the kitchen.

Callum holds her chair out and she can feel him leaning in to smell her. He goes a step further and blows on her neck, just slightly, sending a chill down her spine. Maybe she imagined it. By the time she turns her head, he is back at the counter pouring wine.

"You look better," she says. "You clean up nicely."

"A shower does wonders. You don't look so bad yourself. You have hair. I don't think I've seen it loose before. It is lovely."

She smiles in appreciation as he hands her the glass of wine. "Come on Marina. Make a toast." Marina leaves the spoon she is using to stir the sauce and picks up her own glass.

"Um okay. Callum I'm sorry I broke your leg, but I'm not sorry you're staying here with us."

They raise their glasses and drink. Victoria notices that Marina looks a lot happier than she did a week ago. Callum is good with her. He doesn't take any crap, but he listens to her too.

"Can I add to that?" Callum asks. "I just want to say thank you. You have both been very kind to me and I am awfully glad I didn't have to hire some Nurse Rachet to care for me. I am forever in your debt." This time they clink glasses the American way and drink. When in Rome.

Marina serves the penne in a lightly herbed sauce topped with lobster and fresh peas.

"My God this is unbelievable," Victoria says with her mouth full of food. "Amazing." Because Victoria is human, she takes a moment to imagine they are a family. Callum isn't as void of substance as she thought. In the romance story version of her life, she would be jumping his bones about now. She is very tempted. Marina doesn't need it though. Victoria can tell she is getting attached and their time together is nearing an end.

"Marina, Thank you for doing the laundry. What a sweet surprise."

"Sorry Mom, I didn't do any laundry."

"That would be me," Callum says casually, passing the bread.

"Oh my god you folded my underwear?" Her cheeks fill with color.

"When you packed me up from Red Canyons, you folded my underwear so I decided that boundary had already been crossed. It goes both ways and it's just underwear." He says it nonchalantly, but he is sending her a very penetrating stare. That stare about melts her insides.

After dinner, Marina volunteers to do the dishes and sends them into the other room with their wine. They settle onto opposite sides of the couch. There is too much space between them so she turns her legs onto the cushion to be closer to him.

"This is almost too nice Callum," Victoria says. "I think we could get used to having you around."

He smiles and reaches for her foot. She has nice feet. He holds her toe in a way that could not be construed as sexual. More like a piggy going market. There is a child in the next room.

"Was that too much? I'm not proposing. I'm not even flirting. The food is good, the laundry is done. There are groceries in the fridge. My kid is happier than she's been in months. You are a damn good Manny."

"What's a Manny?" he asks bewildered.

"Male nanny. New line of work? I'll hire you in a second."

"Ah, another American colloquialism. There are so many. Tempting but no thanks. I did have a thought though. I was thinking that maybe I could hitch a ride with you as far as Asheville and I can fly to Charleston from there."

"Why Callum? We'll be fine. I don't want you worrying about us." She gets immediately frustrated because she can handle herself. She hates being thought of as weak or incapable or worst of all, a victim.

"I know you will be fine. I really do."

"Then what?" she asks.

"I care what happens to you two. But more than that I think going back to Asheville is a big deal for you. I think maybe you could use a bestie."

When he says it, she almost bursts into tears. There are no words he could say, that would be more true. He has no idea how much she needs a friend for her re-entry to Asheville. She wills her eyes not to tear, but they do a little.

"Don't you need to get to Austin for Christmas?" she whispers, forcing the tears away.

"I'll get there. Or I won't. I'm not worried about it. Anna will understand either way."

"Why Callum? This is a really nice offer, but I don't want you to think you owe us anything. If anything, I still feel like we owe you."

"Can't we call it even? I am just one human who wants to do something for you, another human," he pauses to sip his wine. "Well if I'm honest and I want to be honest, there is a little more to it than that."

She waits to see if he'll continue on his own. He hasn't shared much about himself.

"I was a really terrible friend back in London. I mean a first class asshole." He swirls the wine in his glass. He says nothing more.

"Are you going to tell me or make me guess? My guess will probably be worse than your reality." She takes her foot back and leans in to listen.

He stalls, giving his beard a good rub. "I fell in love with my best friend's wife. I pursued her, even when she tried to stop it. We owned a restaurant together. We all lived together. She and I ran the restaurant. At one point we were friends and then it all changed. I'm not even sure what happened. I try to trace it back and I don't know. I had to have her. I was relentless. I wanted her to leave him. She wouldn't. They are back in England making a baby together now."

"That was all about her. What about him?" she asks, keeping the judgment out of her voice.

"Jeremy."

"What about Jeremy?"

"He was like my brother. Truly. I have a brother and Jeremy and I were closer. I don't know what happened. It was like I was there and then I wasn't. My mother is absolutely furious with me. Our families are close. Were close anyway. Now they aren't even speaking. I have brought great shame to the Townsend name, to hear her tell it."

Victoria lays a hand on his good knee. "Warning, this is not a pass. I am just giving you a supportive rub on the knee. If it was a pass, it would be higher."

"Understood." He lets her share the supportive rub. "I want to be a better friend."

"To me?" she asks. She doesn't want any misunderstandings. No bullshit.

"And to Marina. She's gotten under my skin a bit." He looks surprised at the words as they come out of his own mouth.

She can't hold it back. The tears well up and he pulls her to his side with an arm around her shoulder.

"I'm not going to lie," he says, "I really want to get you into bed."

She sniffs a response. She knows. The feeling is mutual. It is all in that sniff.

"I am typically sort of a one and done kind of guy."

"Yeah I kind of got that from you," she laughs.

"That isn't what you need though. And I'm not playing games with you. I'm still turned a bit upside down from Elizabeth. Jeremy too."

"I hate games."

"Let me be a friend to you. Let me help you get settled in Asheville. It is a selfish request really. I want to feel like less of a shit," he says honestly.

"We are probably going to screw," she says with equal honesty.

"Agreed. But let's not lead with that. Let me be your friend first."

Seven

By the next week, Lacey has found a friend to rent Victoria's house. Personal items are packed into boxes and put into storage. Victoria trades in her small SUV for a slightly used larger model. Victoria and Marina load up clothes, books, CDs, electronics and mementoes they can't live without. They leave for Asheville ten days before Christmas. Callum packs the same bag for the drive back east that he packed for the drive west. Victoria calls her father to tell him when they are coming and to let him know she has a friend traveling with them who is probably staying for Christmas.

Callum calls Anna to tell him about his weeks in Utah. She is furious he didn't call her to come to his rescue, but she is intrigued to hear about Victoria and Marina. She is understanding about him missing Christmas in Austin, she tells him, because he sounds much better than when he came to Osprey Island. She pretends to cover the phone and yells to John that love is in the air for Callum. Callum doesn't bother denying it. They agree to spend Easter together no matter what.

Callum's right leg is braced so he is no help with the driving, but he is good company. He manages the GPS, the hotel reservations, and finds interesting restaurants along their route. They drive for hours and hours on end. Marina reads, talks, sleeps, listens to music. Callum avoids destinations from his previous trip through these same towns, lest he run into old friends. He confesses about his dyslexia to Victoria since Marina knows anyway. The shame he usually feels is a non-issue with them. Marina continues to read the *Maze Runner* series aloud after they give Victoria an unnecessarily detailed summary. It is a very long drive.

Ever since their talk in the kitchen, Callum feels responsible for keeping a close eye on Marina. He isn't entirely comfortable knowing that she thinks her father is a rapist since Victoria has no idea. He is tempted to tell Victoria about it since Marina is determined not to, but he doesn't want to rock the boat this close to Asheville.

Somewhere around Missouri, Victoria looks back at Marina, well engaged with headphones at the back of the truck, before saying, "Tell me more about you Callum. I feel like you know my whole life and I don't know much of anything about you."

Dangerous territory, but he is curious too. "Fact for a fact?"

"No," she counters. "Question for a question."

"Fair enough. You first," he agrees. The windshield wipers rock back and forth clearing a light rain from the glass.

She wrinkles her nose in thought. Her freckles are cute as hell and then she tops it off by nibbling on her index finger. Cute and sexy mix into a dangerous cocktail.

"Okay. First question." She checks Marina again in the mirror. Her eyes are closed and her head is back on a travel pillow. Earbuds are firmly in place. "Tell me about your first love."

"So this isn't a one word answer game? You want editorializing?"

"I do."

"Pass."

"Pass?"

"I would hate to bore you with tales of my first loves," he says dodging that very loaded question.

"Loves?" she asks.

"Forget it. I'm digging a hole. I meant love. Give me an easier one to start."

"What are those scars on your leg?" she asks, innocent as a butterfly on a sunny day.

"Jesus Christ," he says. "Pass."

"What? Why?" she nearly shrieks.

"Tell me about when you lost your virginity," he says and immediately feels like an asshole.

"Pass," she says, gripping the steering wheel tighter.

"This game is crap," Callum puts in ear buds and the Arctic Monkeys go on loudly, singing about *Arabella*.

The one and only time Callum told anyone about Laila and Daisy, it was a school therapist. After Callum was caught with his dick in the mouth of a shopkeeper's daughter, he took a few good hits to the face and headmaster forced him into therapy. Session after session Callum refused to cooperate. When that became unbearably boring, Callum found that the shock value of honesty was at least interesting.

This friendship business is complicated though. Talking seems required. He chose to be in this car, driving across this damn enormous country, yet again, because he committed to being a friend to Victoria. What does that really mean? You have to give trust to get trust or some such bullshit. He pulls the earbuds from his ears and starts talking with no preamble.

"I thought I was in love when I was fourteen. I spent a very secret, very sexual summer with two nineteen year old, bisexual girls. They pretended to love me and made me feel like the luckiest kid in the world, but they also brutalized me and in the end, deserted me without a word. They were quite sadistic. The entire entanglement fucked me up for a long time." *Maybe still*, he thinks silently.

He follows droplets of rain with his finger on the glass. He doesn't want to look at her, but he tells her more.

"One day their antics were too much for me. I carved three lines into my thigh with a butcher knife. The outer two were meant to be Laila and Daisy. The smaller jagged line caught in between them was me. It bled a lot. They thought I'd cut my femoral artery. I didn't, but I was damaged just the same. And yes, I kept going back for more until one day they were gone."

The rain tapping the windshield won't permit silence.

"They abused you." Victoria says. "I'm so sorr…"

"Oh no, is that how this works?" he interrupts. "I emote and then you feel pity and say things."

"Typically, yes."

"Can't we just both know? Does there have to be chatter about it?" The raindrop on the window could probably hold his gaze all the way to Asheville.

"Is that better for you, Callum?" she asks. There is no right way to handle these things.

"It is."

They drive on with only the patter of rain for a few minutes.

"My first time," she says after a while. "It is something I'd rather forget."

He lets the questions lie unasked and unanswered.

On their last night before reaching Asheville, they detour to Memphis. Callum books a suite at an extravagant hotel celebrating the near end of their journey. They walk the city, visit Graceland and stuff their faces with barbeque. Marina has been noticeably quiet all afternoon and falls into bed as soon as they get back to the suite.

"I wonder what is going on with her. Do you think it is all the traveling or is she regretting leaving Utah? She seems like something is bothering her."

Callum thinks Victoria is just talking out loud to herself and not really asking for his advice, so he just grunts a noncommittal "I dunno."

"Do you know something Callum?" she asks.

"Why would you say that? No, of course not." He lies poorly, his eyes avoiding hers.

"Jesus Christ you do too know something. What is going on?" she demands, temper rising.

He has no choice but to tell her and he is truly relieved. Secrets fester. "Close that," he says, pointing to the door that separates the bedrooms from the rest of the suite.

Using a remote, he lights the gas fireplace and pours two bourbons, neat. He hands her one and sits on the sofa. She stands looking at him, frozen, expecting the worst. He pats the sofa and she finally sits, curling her legs under her, facing him, ready to pounce, but waiting. The fireplace hisses and sends out a glowing light. He turns off the lamp at his side, preferring the firelight. The atmosphere is exceedingly romantic, but he is really just trying to create a calm.

He watches the flames dance on the manufactured log. The effect is artificial but still nice.

"Callum, I have no idea what you are going to tell me, but please don't bother with the *I don't know how to tell you this*, or whatever kind of bullshit. Fucking tell me."

So he does. He tells her fast and straight. "Marina thinks your pregnancy with her was the result of a rape. She thinks you were raped in Asheville."

The way her face goes slack, he knows it is true. He catches her bourbon before she drops it to the floor. Palms press against her forehead in a futile effort to control the thoughts contained within. He reaches a hand to her back, but it never gets there. She flees to the balcony, holding the railing with both hands, breathing and breathing through her pain. He can see she is saying something under her breath. Her lips are moving. When he finally crutches to the door he hears her.

"Fuck. Fuck. Fuck. Fuck…" she repeats in a monotone. He is stunned that Marina was right. How on earth did she guess this? Victoria's eyes are free of tears and he isn't sure that is a good thing. Sadness and rage are two options for dealing with pain. Rage often blocks the sadness, but it blocks the reason too. He did learn a thing or two from that school therapist.

"Victoria?" He isn't sure what he is asking. *Are you okay?* No, she is not okay. *Can I help you?* No, he cannot help her. There isn't a good enough question to ask.

"Victoria?" he repeats, because she needs know she isn't alone.

Finally, she hears him and looks into his face with fear in her eyes. It is the first sign of fear he has seen from her since the day they met.

"Callum, we have to go back. I'll call Lacey. I want my house back. This was a mistake. I thought I could do it, but I can't. I'll wake Marina. You get the car out of the valet." She walks inside toward the bedroom and she almost reaches the door before he can stop her.

He tosses the crutches aside and silently lifts Victoria off her feet into his arms before she can wake her daughter. It is awkward and there is some hopping involved, but he carries her back to the sofa and sits with her across his lap. She curls into him and cries thirteen years of tears for the night that changed her life forever.

Her mother had died three months before. The aneurysm took her suddenly, and Victoria and her father were reeling from the shock and grief. He tried to pretend everything was fine. He smiled, worked, read the paper, played tennis. She couldn't fake it. School was torture. The rest of her time was spent in her room. She quit cheerleading, gave up her weekend job at a horse farm and refused to see anyone.

George pushed her to go out with friends. He didn't know what else to do. She was so social before. She got her energy from other people. She was never a loner. His boss's son had a formal dance and he asked Victoria to join him. George wanted his sharp-witted, happy girl back. She would remember how to be the belle of the ball. Before her mother died, she was full of laughter and every day was a celebration. He wanted her to remember how to be that girl so he pushed her to go to the formal.

She came home four hours after her midnight curfew. She stumbled in the door, covered in filth with blood running down her legs.

"Daddy," she said before she fell to the floor.

When the tears and panic subside, she drinks the bourbon down, pointing at her glass for Callum to pour another. She drinks that one down too but keeps her seat on his lap and leans into his chest.

111

"How did she know Callum?"

He tells her about the night they cooked the lobster penne. He shares everything he remembers about his conversation with Marina and the rape crisis center talk at school.

"Should I have told you then?" he asks. "It didn't seem right either way."

She turns her eyes to his and he can feel the heat from her bourbon warmed breath, they are that close. He feels a shift inside himself and it is not physical. He feels himself sliding to a different place.

"No," she says. "Marina trusted you and you were right to keep it between the two of you. You did right telling me now though. It is clearly eating at her the nearer we get to Asheville."

He holds her close. He likes having her close. Under any other circumstance on the planet, he would kiss her, undress her, lay her on the floor and devour her. Instead, he plays with the curls at the back of her hair. *This is probably how people fall in love*, he thinks. *Fuck. This is what happens when you don't fuck. The wanting to fuck leads to talking and caring and makes you fall in love. FUCK.*

He must go tense because she sits up straighter. "Callum?" she asks.

There is too much going on here, too much emotion, and he doesn't know what to do. This feeling of wanting to be here for her, not just in her, is growing. How do you comfort a woman when you can do literally nothing to help her? Nothing. *Sex?* He could make her feel so good. Sex is the best he has to offer her.

"Callum, thank you for caring for Marina enough to be honest with me. You have been such a good friend to us both."

He smiles at her sentiment. Maybe he can give her more than a fantastic orgasm. "Do you want to talk or get some sleep?"

She looks genuinely torn. "Sleep, I think?" she asks, more than she says.

They both know talking means talking about the rape. That seems the next logical step. Callum finds it hard to believe that rehashing it and reliving it would be cathartic for her, but he isn't ready to give her up yet. "Just sit another minute or two." *Under any other circumstances*, he reminds himself.

And then she does it. Despite the fact she is reliving horrors, maybe because of it, her lips find his for the second time. Her lips are warm and soft and when her tongue touches his, he can taste the bourbon. My god he loves bourbon. He's never going back to scotch. His hands reach into her hair to pull her closer and her hands find his chest, finally. She unbuttons three buttons, without moving her mouth from his, then a fourth, to get her hands on his skin. When she gets the angle she wants, she exhales with a sigh of satisfaction. Her hands are like a fire on his skin.

He takes his hands from her hair and holds the small of her waist, using his thumbs to lift her shirt an inch at a time. When he finds her skin, he loses the air from his lungs and pulls her closer with a hand on each hip. The smallest sound of acquiescence escapes her lips. *But.* He wants her, but he doesn't want her while she is thinking about a man who hurt her. Suddenly sex as a distraction doesn't seem enough.

"Victoria," he whispers into her mouth.

She appears to take his whisper as a confirmation of his passion and bites his lower lip, just a little. That same delicious sigh escapes his mouth. There is no stopping it. He pulls her hips closer and imagines what it would be like to be inside of her. His hands raise along her back, feeling the heat from her skin. *But.* Damn it.

"Victoria," he says again, more dispassionately, lying his forehead onto hers, breathing deeply.

His tone stops her cold. She slides her hands from his shirt, buttoning four buttons back up again before she rises from his lap slowly and regretfully. His dispassionate voice is not reflected by the fit of his jeans.

"I know," she says. "I know."

"Do you know how much I want you?" He doesn't so much speak the words, as exhale them.

"Of course I do," she gestures to the obvious. "Now is not the time though."

"Sometimes I think you are going to react very differently than how you do. You often surprise me," he says in admiration. This was likely to end with hurt feelings and slammed doors.

"Callum, I hate to tell you this, but you are about as transparent as that glass door."

"Meaning?" he asks, not sure he wants to know.

"You are still working some things through from England. I have to get back into mine in Asheville. When all that is sorted out, we'll see what is between us." With that very accurate assessment, she kisses his lips and goes in to join her daughter, closing the door quietly behind her.

He refills his bourbon once again, drowning his sorrows and his passions. He wonders what Victoria will do about Marina. A girl can't go through life knowing her father was a rapist. Then again, she'll want the truth. They'll arrive in Asheville in less than twenty-four hours. He imagines a little old house on a big hill with peeling paint and an old tire or two in the front yard.

The next morning Callum sleeps later than usual. The bourbon is better than a sleeping pill. They have left him a note about bringing back some breakfast. He showers and dresses and then hears them come in. Marina walks straight to Callum and hugs him tight around his waist.

"Thanks Callum," she says "You were right about telling her."

The smiles surprise Callum. Victoria sends her off to pack and hands Callum a large coffee and a bag from a nearby bakery. "Balcony? Bacon, egg and cheddar croissant," she says. Just the way he likes it. They sit at the table outside despite the cold. "Callum, I had a long talk with Marina."

He leaves the food untouched, waiting for her words.

"I was up most of the night figuring out what to tell her. I can't have my girl growing up thinking her Daddy is a rapist." He realizes she lied and starts to feel judgey.

"I don't want her thinking of me as a victim, Callum. Or that she was unwanted. Or that genetically she is a monster. I can't have any of that. You understand, don't you?" she asks and there is only one answer to give. He nods because he doesn't know what her alternative is. Judgment is easy, solutions are nearly impossible.

"I lied to her Callum. I told her that I got pregnant after high school and that her Daddy joined the military and died. I told her I loved him and he loved me and we were going to get married. I told her my father and I argued and I told her that I left Asheville because there were too many memories. I told her he was an only child and her grandparents have been dead for years. I lied and lied Callum. God forgive me." She holds back her hair in a fist to keep it from the cold wind.

"Does anyone in Asheville know what happened? Is there any way she could learn the truth?" He examines all the angles since he has a fair bit of experience with lying.

"No, my father made sure of that. No one knows anything. Except the boy who did it and maybe his father." She shivers against the cold air, remembering.

"Where is he now?" Callum asks.

"Dead I hope. But I don't know. He never knew about Marina. I didn't want him making a claim on her. My father wanted me to have an abortion. It was his boss's son. My Dad wanted it quiet and forgotten. I wanted to press charges, but he didn't want the embarrassment. At the time I thought he was embarrassed." She pauses and releases her hair. It blows across her face as she looks out over the city. "Now that I have a daughter of my own, I know he was trying to protect me."

"Victoria, is there a chance he is still in Asheville?" He doesn't know how she could handle that.

She nods, showing more confidence than he thinks she feels. "It's a big enough city for both of us," she says, but she isn't convincing. "Callum, I have to go back. Its time. I'm sticking with this story. She never needs to know anything more. If he's there, he'll never know she is his. My Dad would never have said a word about a baby."

They pack up and drive the last leg of their trip through the mountains, into Asheville. By the time they arrive, the sun is low in the sky headed toward evening. They pull into a neighborhood that is not at all what Callum expected. The little old house on a hill is more of a huge beautiful old house on a corner. A low stone wall frames the huge corner setting for this majestic home. Brick chimneys top the turreted roof. A freshly painted white, wraparound porch looks bright against the gray of the house.

"This is where you grew up?" he asks, looking stunned. "It looks out of some southern architectural magazine."

"Mom, this is really beautiful." Marina seems just as surprised as Callum.

"What did you two expect?" Victoria asks, putting the car into park.

"I thought you were poor," Callum says, not bothering to pretend.

"Why?" she laughs.

"The accent," Marina answers before he has a chance to. "It sounds like bad teeth and a long beard."

"And a refrigerator on the front porch," Callum finishes for her. They high five before getting out of the car.

"My teeth are perfectly fine," Victoria says absentmindedly as she watches her father walk the wide front steps to greet them.

Victoria's first thought is that he is too old to be her father. His gray hair has gone white and he doesn't stand as tall. Thirteen years have been hard on him. Her second thought is that his heart is failing. Congestive heart failure ages you fast. *Why the hell did I stay away for so long?* He opens his arms giving her the choice for how to greet him and she throws herself into his embrace.

"Daddy," she says and she cries for the second time in two days. He holds her for a long time before she pulls back to look at him. "You are so old," she cries. It's funny how regret and anguish can sit side by side with hope and joy.

"Same little shit as always," he says and hugs her like he'll never let go, but he does and he holds her at arm's length to take her in. "You are so beautiful. Just look at you."

Marina stands next to the car, hiding behind Callum. Victoria holds out her hand for her daughter to come and meet her grandfather. Marina steps forward tentatively and examines him with critical blue eyes. This is the first relative she has ever met and there is a lot to take in.

"Hello," he says, without forcing a perfunctory hug on her. She doesn't know him from Adam and there is no need to pretend.

"Hello," she says back and Callum steps forward to rescue her from the awkward.

He holds his crutches aside, offers his hand. "Callum Townsend. Very pleased to meet you."

"George Bradley. Pleased to meet you too. Looks like you took a hit there." He points to the leg.

"Apparently I'm not quite the skier I thought I was. Took a little tumble. These two have been a great help to me, Mr. Bradley." Callum ruffles Marina's hair.

"Call me George, please," he says amicably. "Come on in and let's get you settled."

"Can I call you George?" Marina asks.

He studies the face of this granddaughter he has never met before like he would bottle up the moon and give it to her if he could.

"Of course darling. You can call me whatever you want. Your Momma used to call me George when she was being sassy. You can call me George or whatever you like." George pulls a bag from the car, heavier than he should, given his heart condition.

"Daddy, let's get those later. We'll just bring in what we need for tonight. We've got this down to a science." Victoria pulls out three overnight bags that they can manage on their own and George leads them into the house.

The house is large with a two story foyer and wrought iron railing, leading up dark wooden steps to the bedrooms upstairs. "I'm not walking the stairs like I used to, so I've moved down here." He points to an office off the kitchen that has been converted into his living quarters. "All the bedrooms are made up. Rosalie still comes in every day. You all can take your pick and I'll do anything I can to make you comfortable here. If you don't like the beds…"

"I'm sure they are fine, Daddy," Victoria says walking the stairs.

"Victoria, wait, there is one more thing. Your old room. Aside from dusting and changing the linens, it hasn't been touched since the day you left. Now that you're here, it feels odd. All the other rooms have been done over."

This stops Victoria in her tracks. "Oh," is all she says. Marina rushes past her up the stairs and closes the door to Victoria's childhood bedroom. Even the thirteen year old knows that is too much for her mother to deal with today. Callum would have done it, but speed isn't on his side these days. Marina impresses him.

They choose rooms more by color than anything. The master is painted in the palest yellow with a small patterned floral quilt. There is a white chair with a leather ottoman and a mosaic stone covered reading lamp by the bay window with a wide view of the mountains. The light wooden furniture is new and has a western flair. Victoria naturally settles there.

Another room is all dark reds and browns with a king size bed and luxurious large, square white pillows. A leather chair and ottoman fill the corner next to a heavy oak desk. A gray stone fireplace covers one wall with large windows on either side. There is also a private bath with a shower lined with jets and Callum is happy not to share it.

Marina runs back and forth between the last two and chooses the blue over the lavender. Both rooms are decorated with a teenager in mind. Victoria thinks a very smart decorator has recently been in this house.

Marina's double bed is lofted high with a desk and chair tucked underneath. The quilt is covered in blues and greens reminiscent of an ocean. Empty white frames in all sizes line the walls so she can make this room her own. There are Bluetooth speakers and empty bookshelves for her to line with the books she brought.

"Knock knock ya'all!" Victoria knows who that is from just three words. She runs down the steps and wraps her arms around her childhood friend and next door neighbor, Mindy Raines. Mindy sets the baking dish she is holding on a nearby table to return the embrace properly.

"Mindy, why didn't you age? You still look like the homecoming queen." Victoria holds back Mindy's arms and takes in her perfectly shiny, stylishly cut shoulder length blonde hair. She is trim and pretty with smiling green eyes and wearing a green dress to match. "You are gorgeous."

Mindy takes the compliment in stride. This is not a new sentiment for her. She introduces her four sons ranging in age from two to ten and her husband, Will. Despite Victoria's protests, within five minutes the car is emptied, all of the boxes and bags are in the appropriate rooms, the casserole is warming in the oven and then they are gone with promises of a future dinner together at Mindy's house.

"Tonight's just a quick hello not a visiting night. You all get your feet under you and then we'll see you," Mindy makes quick eyes up the steps towards Callum. These are the kind of expressions only old friends understand, but Victoria knows Mindy likes him plenty.

"Damn that girl is a cyclone," George says when he closes the door behind her.

"She sure is. Dad, can we talk on the porch for a while before dinner, just you and me?"

"Sure, sure." He leads the way out to a large glassed in porch making a quick stop in the kitchen for two beers from the fridge. She frowns at the fact that he is on medication and still stocking beer in the fridge. The porch is filled with ceramic potted plants and a seven foot tall lemon tree. They sit in white wicker rocking chairs.

"A beer never hurt nobody," he says popping both caps and handing one to her.

They drink and she looks at her mountain. It looks more like Utah here during the winter. Utah is much drier during the summer and the mountains take on earthier tones. Everything here goes greener and greener.

"Dad, I need you to know something," she starts. "I told Marina that her father died in Afghanistan. I told her we were going to get married after I found out I was pregnant, but he died first. I told her you and I argued and I left." She tells him so he can keep her secrets, but he does her one better.

"Bobby Lindley," he says.

"Oh I remember him. He was such a sweetie. How is he?" she asked.

George shakes his head almost imperceptibly. "He died in Afghanistan not too long after you left. His parents died shortly after. They are buried just outside of the city. He had no other family. I attended his funeral. Marina might need a name."

She sips her beer and considers what he is suggesting. "A name and pictures. I went to a dance with him sophomore year. Poor Bobby. And a place to visit. Dad, this is the right thing to do, isn't it?" She wants confirmation that more lying isn't wrong.

"I don't think I'm the one to be giving advice on the right thing or the wrong thing. I made terrible mistakes with you back then Victoria." He looks older and unwell, carrying the weight of his regret.

"I'm not so sure of anything anymore, Dad. I was so sure about it all back then. The right and the wrong. The crime and the punishment. The

121

abortion or the baby." She whispers the last part just in case Marina is within earshot, but says it in such a matter of fact manner that her father flinches at her words.

"When I look at that girl now, it makes me sick that I was pushing you to…" he stalls as if searching for the words… "to terminate." He keeps his eyes on their mountain. He can't look at her and she understands.

"Dad, I am a completely pro-choice woman. One hundred percent. I just felt like it was all being swept under the rug. I wasn't going to let a baby get swept away too. It happened and I could never pretend it didn't."

"I am sorry for that pretending," George says.

"But Dad, that is my point exactly. Now that she is old enough to understand, all I want to do is pretend it never happened. I think it's called being a parent. I think I can protect her from this."

He looks at her like her understanding might finally give him some peace.

"Last night Callum told me that Marina had her suspicions about things. I didn't really get it until then. Can we be okay again Dad?" She asks because she isn't apologizing for anything.

He lays his hand over hers and nods, "We are Vic. We are okay."

She laughs, "No one has called me Vic in a long time." She feels a hope that this just might work. Maybe you can go home again.

"So Callum?" he asks.

"So Callum," is her only reply.

They settle into George's house over the next few days. Callum and Marina take on planning Christmas dinner. Victoria inquires about a nursing position at the hospital. She isn't rushing to get back to work, but she needs to work for her state of mind, not to mention her checkbook.

The rent on her house will cover the mortgage, but she isn't one to sit back and wait for the worse to happen.

Victoria and Marina go to Asheville Middle School to register for the eighth grade. Since Christmas break is just a few days away, they agree she'll start after the holidays. They spend their time decorating, bringing in a huge tree, shopping downtown and cooking. They all use the time to get acquainted. A few days before Christmas, Victoria decides to be a busybody and steals a number out of Callum's phone.

When Victoria and Marina take a day alone to do some Christmas shopping, George takes Callum on a red trolley ride of Asheville. They ride the hills of the city's downtown business district by the river and the train tracks through the art district, and the elegant old neighborhoods surrounding the stately old Grove Park Inn.

When they exit the trolley, George asks Callum. "Do you eat chocolate?"

"Yes sir, I do. As often as possible."

They slowly walk a few block to French Broad Street Chocolate Lounge. The chocolate specialty shop showcases extraordinary flavors in a way that would bring the greatest Swiss chocolatiers to their knees. George orders chocolate mousse and Callum chooses chocolate crème brulee. They sit at a café table in the window to sip their coffee, awaiting their desserts.

"I'm resisting the urge to interrogate you about your intentions with my daughter, Callum," George blows the steam off his espresso.

Callum likes George already. He can see Victoria's stubbornness in him but also great warmth and kindness. He has been very understanding with Marina, spending time to get to know her, not just waiting for her to know him. Callum respects the difference.

"Interrogate away, George. You have the right as a father and as my host. Ask me anything." Callum offers.

"I'm not asking about any hanky-panky. I don't want to know anything."

"Good. That would be awkward at best." Callum smiles, mildly relieved and very amused.

"I'll keep it simple. Where are you coming from and where are you going to?" A waitress sets chocolate laden plates in front of them. First bites go down in ecstatic silence.

"This is unbelievable. I like Asheville very much." Callum declares and wipes a napkin across his mouth. "I have come from London. I was a chef in my own restaurant. I was a co-owner. That went bad due to my own poor choices and my even worse handling of those poor choices."

"A woman?" George asks.

"Of course." Callum admits, leaning back in his chair. George is a savvy old dog.

"Are you over that? My girl has eyes for you and if you are going to break her heart, you should move on sooner than later."

Callum hasn't really thought about Elizabeth since they left Utah. Elizabeth seems more of a distant memory.

"I am over that George. I have eyes for your girl too."

George works on his mousse for a few minutes and lets a comfortable silence rest between them. "And?" He asks eventually.

"Oh yes, where am I heading to?"

George nods. "That is the question."

"I don't have an answer for that one. I am currently homeless. A man without a country." Uttering these words feels strangely liberating.

"If you had to choose a life for yourself today, what would it be? Don't over think it. Just answer."

"I'd own a little shop just like this one. Right here in the city, but I'd figure out how to use it to help people. Maybe teach kids with dyslexia like mine or help people learn how to work in kitchens." Callum is surprised by his own admission. Altruism has never been his biggest priority.

"Well, that isn't the answer I was expecting from you Callum. Let's finish up, then I want to show you something up the block."

"Sounds intriguing. I'd like to do more to contribute to the house George. I don't expect a free ride."

"I sure as shit don't want your money." George says pretending to look offended.

"I didn't mean to imply…"

"You didn't. I'm just taking that off the table. You are my guest, Callum. Wait, let me see your hands."

Callum shows big hands, dotted with cuts and scars from years of kitchen work.

"You've got good strong hands. Will you chop some wood for me? I lost two trees this fall and I'd like to have done it myself but things slowed down pretty quick. I can hire help but…"

"But nothing. I'd love to cut wood. How does one cut wood?"

George smiles. Callum needs to feel like he's contributing. When they get back home, George goes to his room and emails to cancel the haulers coming to drag off those trees. George has enough firewood for the next two winters stacked along the back fence. He'll find room to store some more.

Callum wakes to his mobile vibrating on the morning of Christmas Eve.

"Hello darling brother. Forgive my calling at this ungodly hour, but I didn't want to miss you." Just hearing her voice, he misses her. "How's that damn leg?"

"On the mend. I can hobble with the best of them now. How are your sweet girls faring in Texas with all those cowboys?" he asks.

"Clara is picking up a bit of a twang already," Anna jokes. "Are you alright there in Asheville? Should I pull the plug on Austin and come to you instead? I would, you know. I don't feel right about you being without family. Without your mother, especially," she says.

"I'm fine, Anna. This has been a good break for me. I am very happy here with Victoria and Marina. Even George." Callum tells Anna about Victoria's father.

"He wants me to look into opening a shop that shut down here a few months back. The owners left the area and George is considering buying the property and equipment. He is suggesting we buy it, open it, turn it into something and sell at a nice profit. I am half game to do it."

"Are you actually considering staying there Callum? Are you and Victoria getting serious?"

He doesn't have the heart to tell her nothing more than a kiss, albeit a very good kiss, has passed between them.

"A conversation for another time? Can I get a Christmas reprieve from making life plans?"

"Of course you can." At his request she tells him John's family gossip. Those Texans are interesting. They vow to spend Easter together at Osprey Island and Callum will meet everyone then.

Callum gets up and dressed and mentally reviews his to-do list for the day. They are cooking for Mindy's family and Rosalie. Rosalie has been working with George for the better part of thirty years. She has no family of her own and they appear more like family than employer and employee. Tomorrow's Christmas dinner will be out at the mansion with just the four of them.

As Callum is laying out the rib roast to trim and tie, he hears a knock at the door. It is only nine o'clock in the morning. George, reading the paper at the kitchen table, doesn't budge. Callum is covered in raw meat so he says, "George can you get that?"

"I'd rather you did," George says without explanation, keeping his focus on the paper.

Callum washes his hands quickly and when he passes through the foyer, both Victoria and Marina are at the top of the stairs. "Why is no one interested in answering this door but me? What is wrong with you people today?"

He opens the door and there is his mother. His mother, who last threw him out of her house with words that he had destroyed his own life and humiliated her by exercising very low morals with her best friend's son's wife. They have not spoken since.

He opens the door wide and she stands looking at him for a long time. When he left her, he was full of arrogance and anger. His hair was short and his face clean shaven. He wore only the latest fashions and he was full of himself and his success. He acted untouchable, going so far as to do what he did with Elizabeth.

A different man stands before her now. The first thing she notices is his smile. She hasn't seen a genuine smile on his face in years. Not ironic. Not sarcastic. He is genuinely happy. His beard is short but has filled in, and his hair is longer. He looks relaxed in jeans and a flannel, resting on crutches.

She does what any mother would do under the circumstances. She forgets all the reasons she is furious at him and pulls him into her arms, hugs him and fake cries. She does a little sniffle sniffle.

She catches him off guard in every way imaginable. The crutches fall to the ground and he hugs her while teetering on one leg. He manages a sniff of his own, but his has actual moisture.

"What on earth are you doing here? How did you find me?" His shock is apparent.

"I am supposed to give you this." She hands him a folded note with a red ribbon.

Surprise! Merry Christmas. XOX Marina, Victoria & George. (Marina's idea)

He looks over his shoulder and they are lined up in the hallway, all looking very proud.

"I am so sorry," he tells his mother, choosing to leave the reasons for his sorrow vague. Details seem unnecessary.

"Not another word about it. For God's sake we are English, even if we are in Asheville, North Carolina, United States of America." She feels his beard because it is so foreign.

By now they have progressed to the doorway and introduce themselves to Caroline Townsend. Callum is stunned and silent. As Marina and George take Caroline inside to sit her down with a cup of tea, Callum sits on the front step. His crutches got away from him and he can't stand another moment. Victoria sits beside him.

"How?" he asks.

"I stole your phone for her number and called her. You should really change your password. I guessed *Mise* on the first try. I told her about the accident and how you have been with us, helping us and it just worked. She was done being angry and ready for this. Is it okay with you? Or are you mad that I butted in? It was a little risky." She smooths a single, out of place, strand of his hair as an excuse to touch him.

He takes her face in his hands and in the simplest way possible, grazes his lips over hers. He is not seducing her, he is letting her know he cares for her. She gets his meaning.

"I will never be able to thank you for this Victoria. Never."

"You already have," she says and rests her forehead on his for a moment before gathering his crutches and leading him inside so they can spend Christmas with their families.

The day is spent getting to know one another. England and western North Carolina have very little in common culturally, but George and Caroline both come from a long line of people who appreciate good manners and they make it work. Caroline is on her best behavior, but Callum knows she is used to getting what she wants.

Around the table on Christmas Eve, Callum marvels at the candlelit smiles he sees. These people have so much history, so much shared pain and an overwhelming amount of love. Callum hasn't spent a Christmas like this since he was a boy and his father sat at the head of the table where George sits tonight. When his father died, all of this died with him. Callum remembers that last Christmas with his father and Jeremy's family. In his memory, it looks like a British Norman Rockwell painting. The goose and ham, twinkling candles, the smell of pine, his father's easy laughter and his mother's smile. She had a real smile back then.

Six mothers later, his father was dead and Callum was getting tied up and left alone for hours, all for the pleasure of a fuck. Life can turn on a dime.

On Christmas morning Callum builds a big fire in the fireplace and sets a Christmas music Pandora station. Barbara Streisand's voice fills the room. It is a little cheesy, but he loves it and sings along to Jingle Bells. He mulled cider overnight and warms it over a low heat before a gift is touched. Smells of cinnamon and orange fill the house.

"Callum, come on!" Marina pleads.

When everyone is seated with cider, Marina distributes gifts. Earrings purchased at the last minute go to his mother. Callum gives George a tablet and George pretends not to know what it is to cover his surprise at Callum's generosity. Marina gets a smartphone.

"Callum you didn't," Victoria cries, watching Marina dance across the living room.

"I did. It is prepaid for two years. After that you have to get a job." Marina throws her arms around Callum and Victoria wonders if they are getting too attached. She can't imagine being here is anything more than a long layover for Callum.

When Callum hands Victoria a box, she can't help the quick thought *I wish it was smaller and a ring*. It is completely unconscious and not even how she really feels. She's just seen too many romantic holiday movies about getting engaged under beautiful trees like this one.

She opens a box to find two tickets to see Andrew Bird performing at *The Orange Peel*. She saw him play there years before. It is one of her best teenage memories. He is coming back next week. Under the tickets is a soft sweater wrapped in white tissue. She lifts it out of the box and it pours all the way to the floor. It is a luxurious, camel colored cashmere sweater. It is stunning and probably cost as much as that diamond ring.

"No Callum, this is too much," she says, feeling it against her cheek.

"It is just enough Victoria."

She shakes her head in protest.

"Be quiet and put it on." He takes it from her hands and holds it up behind her. Her long hair spills across the back. It is the perfect color for her and she pulls it close.

"Callum, I absolutely love it." She kisses his cheek. This kiss does not go unnoticed by the eyes surrounding them.

Marina gives Callum a collection of books on tape so he can avoid reading to himself. George gives Callum an axe, gloves and a how-to video about chopping wood. They share a big laugh and Victoria has no idea why. When Callum opens Victoria's gift, she holds her breath in, hoping he'll love it. The package holds a set of professionally graded knives. He left his behind at *Mise*.

"Victoria, I can't accept this," he says, even as he runs his finger lovingly along the black leather case. "It is far too much."

"You are a chef and you need real knives. Do you like this kind of a knife?" she asks.

"Not like, love. But they are too much," he protests. They are very costly knives.

"They are just enough Callum, just enough," she says.

He is stunned by her thoughtful and generous gesture, and won't argue it with her further. "Thank you," he says because there is nothing else to say.

Caroline hands Callum an envelope. "Something for you," she says. He opens it to find a return airline ticket to England. He tucks the ticket back inside and closes the envelope.

"Thank you Mother." The tone of his voice is anything but grateful and keeps anyone from asking what is in the envelope.

"Give us about fifteen minutes to get breakfast on the table. Marina?"

Marina hops off the couch, thanking her grandfather for the horseback riding lessons. Victoria stays behind to keep an eye on the parents.

In the kitchen, he pulls a *strata* from the oven. Eggs have cooked over the breads and sausages and the cheeses are bubbling. Marina slices a platter of fruit and Callum pulls maple coated bacon from a baking sheet.

"That smells so good." Marina comments before whispering, "Callum, what did your mother give you?"

He shakes his head in disgust. "A bloody plane ticket back to England. She's forgiven me and now I'm supposed to drop my life and follow her like a good doggie." His whisper is equally quiet but harsh and angry.

"I don't want you to go Callum," Marina gives him a pitiful, sweet little girl pout.

"I know Marina. We have a good time together, don't we?" He is in no hurry to leave and gives her hair a good rumple. She is getting attached to him and the feeling is mutual. Still, he doesn't want to complicate her life. What type of influence could he have on her? Making pancakes together is one thing, being a responsible adult is another thing entirely.

"That looks good," he says pointing to the neatly arranged berries and melon on the tray.

"Callum. You and my mom…" she doesn't ask the question, just lets the words hang there.

He just sighs and doesn't tell any lies or make promises he can't keep.

"I care for her Marina. You know I do." Victoria walks into the kitchen and cuts the conversation short.

"Looks wonderful," she says, popping a berry into her mouth, hugging Marina.

Callum can see how happy she is. She is happier here than she was in Utah. He turns back to plating the bacon and wonders if there could be something more between them than the impending casual sex and an ongoing friendship.

After dinner at The Mansion, George takes Caroline's arm and they walk the gardens to admire the Christmas lights. Marina points out her favorites. Victoria takes Callum's arm and hangs back by the gates. She shivers, wrapping her arms around herself.

"Are you cold?" he asks and actually takes the dinner jacket he is wearing and wraps it over her shoulders.

"Wow. Old fashioned chivalry. That is a first for me," she smiles. His small act of kindness gives her a tiny bit of distance from her memories of the last time she walked these grounds.

"You don't look well Victoria."

She doesn't answer, but she makes a face indicating she really isn't well, adding a small smile and a shrug. They have spent enough time together at this point that they can read each other's faces pretty well.

"Did you enjoy dinner?" he asks.

A tear slides from the corner of her eye. She is not a crier so the single tear gives him pause. She places a finger over her lips, telling him to keep it between the two of them.

"Is it this place?" he asks and another tear falls. "Oh my god it happened here, didn't it?

She wipes her eyes with the edge of her finger careful not to smudge carefully placed eyeliner. She doesn't wear eyeliner every day, but it is Christmas.

"What the fuck are we doing here Victoria?" he asks, appalled that they are spending Christmas at the site of her rape.

"He doesn't know it was here," she says pointing to her father. "He loves it here." After a moment, she adds, "When I decided to come back here,

I decided I wouldn't hide from anything. All in or all out, right? I'm all in."

She smiles before handing him back the jacket, takes a deep breath and joins her daughter to admire the beautiful holiday decorations. He is left standing dumbfounded. If he had handled his problems in England the way she was handling hers now, he would be in a very different situation.

Later, Callum sits up reading *Hunger Games*. The house is quiet. By page five, the story became less about sexual fantasy for him and actually quite fascinating. He is a slow reader, but he is steadily managing his way through Katniss' struggle as a Tribute and he can't put it down. About one o'clock, he hears tiptoes outside his bedroom door. Victoria taps with a single fingernail.

"You up?" she whispers.

"I am. Come in," he whispers back and straightens his pillow so he looks less slouchy.

She is wearing a black tank top and red checked flannel bottoms. Her hair is piled on her head and tied into, what he now knows is called, a messy bun. Her face is clean of any make-up and she smells like soap. She is as sexy as any Playboy centerfold.

"Callum, can we talk?" she asks, leaning against the door. He pats the mattress beside him and she sits, bracing her feet on the wooden bedframe.

"What a wonderful Christmas," she stalls. "Having you here with us, meant a lot to me."

"It was indeed. Being here meant a lot to me as well," he says truthfully.

"Callum, my god this sounds so cliché," she stalls again. "About us."

She sits on the edge of his bed, but he wishes she would lay beside him. He is going all wrong in the head with the young and single thing. It was a good plan and it worked for him for a long time, but he's having trouble remembering why. At the same time, he doesn't want to play around with her. There is Marina to consider and he knows how badly these things always end.

"Are you going to tell me you are full of shame and regret for kissing a shallow bastard like me, and you just want to forget it? I understand, Victoria. I do," he says it because it is the right thing to say, but he doesn't mean it. He isn't sure what he means though.

She chooses her words carefully. "Actually no. I don't want to forget it. Just the opposite in fact."

"What do you mean the opposite?" He sits up and turns her chin to face him. Crystal blue eyes speak so much more than what is coming out of her mouth. *Damn her eyes. Damn her mouth.*

"I know you are still getting over Elizabeth."

"No I'm not," he protests.

"Whatever," she says and continues. "I have to deal with everything here. Neither of us is in a position to start something. I don't even know if we'd like each other if your wings weren't clipped." She points to the leg brace. *No strings. She's angling for no strings. I can do no strings.*

"I'd like you even if my wings weren't clipped," he protests again. "Sorry, I'm interrupting. What were you going to say?" He asks, even though he knows, as sure as the day is long, exactly what she was going to say.

"I want you Callum. It's been a while for me, and I don't want to feel guilty about it or ashamed of it. I don't want it to be weird or overly emotional. I don't want to wonder if you want me. I'm not looking for a proposal here. I just want you." She waits for a response. "No commitment Callum. I'm not asking you for anything other than this."

She gestures to the bed. "I like having you here, but I know this is temporary."

He studies her face for a moment and then two, silently asking questions he isn't ready to ask out loud. *Could you love a sexually impulsive, dyslexic with limited prospects? Are you better off with or without me? What can I possibly offer you?* The answers to these questions elude him.

"Callum?" she asks waiting for some type of reaction.

Without another thought, he sets Katniss aside for the living, breathing woman in front of him. He tosses the book and misses the nightstand. Katniss falls to the floor.

Callum slides his hand under Victoria's tank, up her back, just to test the feel of her skin. It is warm and soft and he thinks he is too late. He is already falling for her, like Elizabeth, not like the others. With the others, it was all about taking. With Elizabeth, maybe now with Victoria, he wants to give something. He just isn't very good at knowing what to give.

She closes her eyes and tilts her head to meet his hand rising along her back. When he reaches the nape of her neck he wraps his fingers around it gently easing the tension from her muscles. Her head falls forward to let him, already responding to the skill of his touch. In bed, he knows exactly what to give. It is out there in the world where he gets a little lost.

"Is there anything I need to know about you?" With her history, she might have concerns with sex that need discussion.

"I can't have your weight on top of me at all and I can't be restrained in any way." She meets his eyes with her own. "Thanks for asking that, Callum."

She gets up and turns off the bedside light but opens the curtains to let the moonlight in. She releases her hair from the tie and carefully, to avoid his incision, climbs on top of him, wrapping her legs around his waist. He lifts her tank over her head and she does the same with his gray tee

136

shirt. His hands rest on her waist and hers lay over his chest while they both pause and feel the power in this moment.

He thinks she is more than he expected in every way. Strength and generosity flow from her despite her pain. He takes her in with his eyes. The moonlight shines over her shoulder and glows around her hair. It looks darker, redder in this light. Her fair skin is like cream and feels like silk under his hands. He hesitates kissing her or touching her. For a moment, looking at her is enough. He can feel his defenses falling away and even though it scares the shit out of him, it is probably inevitable. *This can't just be sex.* And just like that, he loses his hold.

"You are so beauti…" he starts to say, but she stops him with her mouth on his. Her tongue finds his and she tastes like honey, intoxicating him more than a kiss should. *Damn it.*

Although he has been with nearly a dozen women since Elizabeth, he has not kissed one. Just Victoria. He is motionless as Victoria explores his mouth with her own. She would hate him if she knew the choices he has made these last months. He almost wants to protect her from himself. She'll regret this, he is sure of it. All women do. But he is no saint and he doesn't stop it.

He comes unfrozen and pulls her closer to him. Finally he can touch every inch of her skin, every curve and angle he has been dreaming of since the day they met. Her breathing deepens in his ear. This is where he knows best. No doubts follow him into bed.

When she unties the string on his pants, Callum pulls back and lays her down. He finds his way over her with his mouth, his tongue. He quickly learns what she likes and slides from the bed taking her pants with him. His tongue leads on the decent of her body and finally he pushes her legs over his shoulders, lifting her hips to bring her closer to his mouth. The tension in her calves dissipates quickly and her sharp intake of breath encourages him on. She hasn't been in this position many times in her life and he has. He is a man who is all about taste and this is what he has been waiting for. He knows what he is doing and, before long, she comes with a pillow stuffed in her mouth to muffle her sounds.

He gives her a moment to catch her breath while he finishes undressing, then he picks her up and brings her to the leather chair where she can sit above him, and she won't have to bear his weight. She hands him a condom because she is a smart, prepared woman. She guides him inside of her and as they move together, he immediately thinks of Elizabeth. He thinks Elizabeth was nothing and Victoria is everything.

They move together like they have done this a thousand times before, together. Elizabeth leaves his thoughts after just a moment. He holds Victoria's face because he wants to watch her when she comes this second time. Her eyes close as she finds her way and when she does, she whispers his name, "Callum." It fills his heart in a way it has never been filled before. He feels like he could climb mountains. This is what falling really feels like. He closes his eyes tight when he comes and lays his forehead against hers. He has just one thought. *Fuck, I love her.* He clenches his eyes for a long time after, regretting nothing but feeling like a school boy after his first lay. *This isn't love, this is orgasm, just really good orgasm.* He lies to himself. *I don't love. Fucking and cooking, that's all I do.*

"Callum?" she asks searching his eyes. "Is it your leg?"

He wants to say, *It is my fucking heart, damn it,* but he doesn't. "No. That was just amaz.." She stops him with her lips on his again. She won't let him talk.

They dress just in case Marina wakes up, and lie together on Callum's bed. They face each other and stare into each other's eyes in a way that does not feel casual. Victoria smooths his new beard and he plays with the curls resting on her shoulder.

"I'm glad Marina took the room down the hall," Callum says, tucking Victoria into his shoulder. *Maybe I can be good to her.* Callum catches himself wondering what she is thinking and suddenly wants to jump out the window.

"Jesus Christ," he says before he can stop himself. He's on a rollercoaster and the bottom just dropped out.

"What?" She gets up, alarmed.

"Please ignore me. I'm already getting weird. And I never get weird."

"Are you regretting it?" she asks sounding hurt.

"No. Not for a single second. But I don't do this. I don't gaze into a woman's eyes. I don't snuggle. I don't wonder. I don't do any of this."

She giggles out loud.

"You are fucking laughing at me?" He is disgusted. "Shush, you'll wake Marina."

"Callum, are you feeling actual human feelings?" She mocks him.

He wants to protest but can't.

"Callum, for a thirty year old man, you are a hopeless romantic. Sweetie that was great sex. And we are becoming really great friends. But that's it, okay?"

Damn her.

"First of all, I don't know what you are talking about. Secondly, what is love, if not great sex between great friends?" He really does not know the answer. And then he realizes he said *love* aloud. He is completely out of control.

The question stops her giggling. She doesn't have an answer either and the use of that word is not lost on her. "Well that wasn't weird for about four minutes," she says moving toward the door. "Best affair ever, Callum."

He hops to the door to stop her exit. "What do you mean? That's it?"

"You're blocking me, Callum. Do not block me," she warns. He moves away from the door.

"Don't go Victoria," he says as she walks past, into her own room and closes the door.

Callum is left standing alone.

Victoria wakes up later than intended. It was a late night. She can smell the pancakes and bacon. There is always bacon. When she passes Callum's room, the bed is made and his suitcase is no longer in the closet but against the wall by the window. She tiptoes in to see if he has packed and he has not. She wonders if he is taking his mother's ticket and flying back to England. She sits on the edge of the bed and tries to be honest with herself. She tries to let go of her fear and desire and just be honest. *What do I want?* Honesty is too difficult with bacon in the air so she goes down to the kitchen.

They are all seated at the kitchen table. Caroline is dressed in a red suit even at this early hour, formal as usual. Victoria says her good mornings and takes a seat. She gets a cool hello from Callum and bites into a pancake. They are delicious as always. My god he cooks. He makes her daughter happy. He is unbelievable looking. He is fantastic in bed. He is shockingly considerate. He's absolutely perfect. Except for all the ways he isn't. He's shallow, unemployed, in love with another woman and hiding out here from a very different life in England.

"Callum, we will leave in thirty minutes," Caroline states. She rarely asks questions.

"George," Callum says pointedly. "Is it okay with you if we leave in thirty minutes since you are driving?"

"Of course it is. Anything you need, Caroline" he says to keep the peace.

"Are you leaving us already Caroline?" Victoria asks.

Caroline grimaces slightly at Callum. *You tell her*, that face says.

"Mother has decided to go on to Austin to see my sister, a woman she has no biological connection to whatsoever." He is angry.

"Oh, well isn't that nice? She is your sister and if things were different, she would have been a part of your life. She could have been like a daughter to Caroline, right?" Victoria says, not really understanding why Callum is so annoyed.

"Exactly Vicky. Thank you. She is my stepdaughter and I would like to get to know her better." All goodwill was lost with the *Vicky*.

"Her name is Victoria, Mother. She prefers Victoria."

"I apologize Victoria," she overly annunciates the name of course. "I don't understand why you are so bothered by my going to Austin, Callum."

"Girls, maybe we can finish our breakfast in front of the TV," George says lifting his plate and rising to give them privacy."

"Please George stay," Callum takes George's plate from his hand, centering it firmly on the placemat.

Marina watches Callum and his mother's back and forth with the excitement of a spectator at a Wimbledon match. Victoria tries to focus on her pancakes, but she is fascinated too. Aside from the first days in the hospital, they have seen very little in the way of irritation from Callum. He looks like he is very quietly seething. Victoria wonders if this is the British way. Hold in ninety-five percent and let the last five percent show.

"You are going to Austin because you are angry that I won't come back to England with you. You are again punishing me. Your means of punishment are certainly getting more creative, I have to hand it to you,

Mother. You were marvelous with the strap but this, surprisingly, hurts more."

Victoria sits up straighter in her chair. "You are staying?" she asks and a smile, brighter and more telling than she would like, sneaks out.

"George has asked me to stay for the immediate future and I have accepted. Do you have any reservations?"

Callum's statement lies heavily over the table. Victoria thinks George wants Callum to be there when he dies so Victoria and Marina are not alone.

Callum seems to realize the unintended weight of his words and backpedals to soften their meaning. "George has purchased a building with a wonderful storefront downtown. We are considering going into business together." Callum says a little defensively.

The jaws of two grown women and a teenage girl drop in unison.

"Are you both comfortable with this arrangement?" Callum asks Marina and Victoria. They both nod despite their shock.

Caroline is the first to find her voice. "Do you mean to tell me you are staying here in Asheville, North Carolina? The United damn States of America to be a shopkeeper." While it is worded as a question, it is not a question.

Callum smiles at her rage and leans back in his chair as he pops a piece of bacon in his mouth.

"Now who is punishing whom?" she does ask.

"I'm not punishing you. I'm just choosing a different path. I want to be closer to Anna and her family. I want to be an uncle to my nieces."

"From Asheville?" She is finding her way back to asking questions.

"Sure." Now he is being cavalier. "It is a hop, skip and a jump as compared to traveling the Atlantic."

"And Victoria? And this sweet child?" She lays her hand on Marina's head but falls short of a loving touch. She doesn't do the loving touch well. "Do you mean to play with their lives as you did with Elizabeth and Jeremy's?"

Callum rises to his feet. "This conversation is over." He clears plates from the table and tosses them carelessly to the counter by the sink. It is almost funny how intent he is to do it with one leg, but it is more tragic. Victoria takes a plates from his hand.

"I'll get it." She wraps her fingers around his wrist, stroking his anger warmed skin with her thumb. She takes the dishes from him. She looks to his eyes, desperate not to be another conflict on his mind. She can't believe he and her father have been plotting. She is completely touched by his promise to George. At the same time she realizes George is not expecting to make it very long.

"Go on, take your mother to the airport. We can talk later?" she whispers, wishing they were alone.

She can see his struggle to focus on her face and release his anger. She lays a hand on his shoulder and remembers their time together last night. She remembers holding him and having him inside of her. Her knees feel weak and if they were alone, she would kiss him. He's watching her face and she knows he feels it too.

"I would like very much to talk later," he says quietly and she thinks he is using talk as a euphemism for very different words.

After the run to the airport, George takes Marina to a movie. Having no friends over winter break can be lonely for a teenage girl. George tries to fill the void as best he can. Victoria finds Callum sitting in her bedroom, on the white chair, waiting.

"After last night, I thought about taking a flight to Austin. I wasn't sure if it was time for me to go." he says. "I think you want to fuck the nanny Victoria," he says.

"Manny," she corrects absentmindedly, thinking she'd very much like to fuck the manny.

He doesn't laugh this time. "Am I a punch line to you? I thought I was supposed to be the shallow one. I'm starting to feel like a joke here."

"I thought you would be comfortable keeping things casual. You don't really seem a serious kind of guy, Callum?"

"I don't feel casually about you. Do you feel casually about me? Be fucking honest with me, Victoria. Just for a moment here."

She doesn't have a response for him. She can't protect his feelings without risking her own. It isn't a tough choice, especially now that she is back here and remembering things she doesn't want to remember.

"Are you feeling something for me and you don't want to? I know you have a lot of demons to confront here, but I'm not sure I want to be one of them."

She sits on the bed and lays back with her feet on the floor. She doesn't know what kind of arrangement he made with George. She can't even consider that. She has to protect herself and Marina, but honestly, she really doesn't want him to go.

"Yes, I am feeling something for you."

That is all he needs. He locks the door and stands over her at the bed. He frees her from her pants and pulls himself from his own. He is frantic to get closer to her. She reaches for a condom and when he is ready, she wraps her legs around him. He uses his arms to prop himself high off her and buries himself inside of her. This is not the gentle sharing of passions as the night before. This is faster, rougher and a little angry. She comes quickly and by the time he comes, she joins him a second time. It is frantic and intense. After, he falls to her side, both of them facing the ceiling with their feet on the floor.

"Huh," she says simply.

"Huh?" he asks.

"You are something Callum," she sighs. "I can't image what you are like without that." She half-heartedly points her chin to his brace.

"I'm a fucking dynamo," he jokes. "Victoria, I want to let myself feel for you. Will you just bloody let me?" He asks because if she says no, he can stop it. He can mindlessly fuck her and be polite and turn it all off. He can be here until George dies and see them through his death and burial. He promised and he'll keep his word.

"Callum, I think you want to feel something for me because you feel good here. You feel good about you. Not necessarily you feel good about me. You like how we are getting along. You like spending time with Marina. You feel better here than you did in England after Elizabeth. But Callum we can't be a hideout for you. You'll get bored so fast. I don't want to be your plaything until you want to go back to your life," she says. "No matter what you and George agreed on."

"No."

"No?"

"No, damn it. I have been living my entire life proving I'm not a moron. Dyslexia tends to equate stupidity to most people, my mother included. I played into it. I made bad decisions because they were expected of me and I didn't have the respect for myself to be better."

145

She scoots closer to him and pulls his arm under her head, holding his hand in hers, imagining a little boy Callum being beaten with a strap. It so fits into what she knows about him.

"You do what you need to do, Victoria. But what I need to do is right here." He says giving her a squeeze.

"Did you just say you need to do me?" she asks.

"It's the dyslexia. I get confused by words sometimes," he lies before turning to face her and kiss her again.

"Are you staying?" she asks pulling her lips from his.

"I am." This time he undresses her properly.

On New Year's Eve, they go into town to see Andrew Bird.

"I don't want you two driving around on New Year's Eve. I got you adjoining rooms at a hotel right on the same block as The Orange Peel. My treat."

Victoria protests. She doesn't want to leave her Dad alone with Marina. "What if there is a problem?" she worries.

"Rosalie is staying over in the guest room. She'll keep an eye on us both. Marina is cooking dinner and we got all the Twilight movies, lord help me. We'll have a great time. Go have fun,"

George has his doubts that they'll use both rooms, but the cost of an additional room was well worth avoiding a sex talk with his daughter. Grown woman or not, she's still his little girl.

When they pull up to the hotel, Callum realizes it is the same one where he spent his first evening in Asheville. Not the night, just the evening. It was the first night on his cross-country "blow me and I'll give you the fuck of your life" tear. Walking into the hotel turns his stomach. He glances nervously into the bar to make sure she isn't sitting on a stool looking for her next lay.

They only check into one room. Victoria declines the second. They have never spent a night together for fear of Marina finding them in the morning. The room is modern with a European flair.

Callum sits on the bed. "I've something to show you." He hands her an envelope.

Victoria reviews Callum's lab work. Callum was tested for STDs and HIV before the surgery in Utah and he was clean, but he needed another round of tests to ensure his good health.

"Did I ever tell you that I'm on the pill?"

He shakes his head and smiles wide.

"No more condoms!" she cheers and thanks him for his diligence in this matter by lowering to her knees in front of him.

"No, no. I want you up here with me." He pulls her to his lap. He faces a chair identical to the one where he sat with another woman between his knees not too long ago.

"Are you sure?" she asks with surprise. This is unusual.

He undresses her fast and takes off his leg brace, tossing it across the room. "This thing is horseshit," he says and pulls her into his arms. They rush into it, knowing they are truly alone, no one in the next room or downstairs or coming home soon. Just the two of them for twenty four hours.

He presses up on his arms to give her the space she needs between them, careful to keep his weight from her and for the first times feels himself inside of her without the protective barrier that has kept them apart.

"Come closer to me Callum." She pulls his shoulders toward her. When his skin grazes hers, he freezes, knowing this is something she has not done before. He moves inside of her slowly and she pulls him even closer. They meet chest to chest and she wraps herself around him. She moves without hesitation, syncing to his rhythm.

"Is this okay?" he asks to be sure. He would never want to cause her fear or regret or any discomfort. He holds her face and moves with her slowly at first to be sure.

"I trust you Callum," she says. "It is perfect."

For a split second he realizes the enormous responsibility of having her trust. He must never hurt her, but he hurts everyone. He leans his lips to hers and breathes in from her. He breathes in her goodness, hoping it can take seed within him. She pulls him closer still with her calves pulling his hips. The connection is overwhelming, out of body, religious. It is magic, yet real. He is weightless. He feels himself falling. He desperately doesn't want to fail her.

They choose a little restaurant with a big bourbon menu for dinner before the show. Callum introduces Victoria to John's brand of Kentucky bourbon. They celebrate John with steaks and more than a little bourbon before walking down the block into The Orange Peel. This quintessential Asheville music venue is a big room with a big stage. Because of Callum's leg, they are invited to seats at a table against the side wall.

"Asheville is a great city," Callum says as they study the crowd before show time. "It reminds me of Camden in London."

"Do you miss London?" Victoria asks.

After a moment's thought he answers, "I don't."

"Not at all? Not even the bright lights, big city? The restaurant? Your home?"

"I really don't," he maintains.

She frowns. "I'm not sure I believe you."

"You told me you trusted me three hours ago and now you are accusing me of lying?" he laughs. "I liked the trusting much better." He takes her hand to his mouth and glides her index finger along the inside of his lower lip to remind her. The gesture makes Victoria forget her thoughts.

"Keep that up and I'll believe anything you tell me," she says and the lights dim.

"Then I'll be sure to tell you only truths." He takes her hand and pulls her to stand between his legs. She leans her back against him, listening to the music. He breathes in deeply, smelling her hair. There is a hint of vanilla. "I promise I'll never lie to you, Victoria."

"I don't like promises, Callum," she says.

"I promise to promise you nothing, then." He moves her hair and licks the back of her neck to end this nonsensical conversation. "Please believe me," he whispers in her ear. "I want nothing in London. All I want is between my knees."

She leans back into him hard, feeling his intentions against her back. She smiles at his sharp intake of breath against her neck.

"I love this sweater," Callum says, enjoying the music. Victoria is wearing her Christmas sweater for the first time with blue jeans and brown Frye boots.

"It is absolutely beautiful Callum. Thank you."

The music is loud and the lights are low. The room is packed with new fans and old fans of this great musician. Callum slides his hand into the pocket of the new sweater which he himself cut out. The hole in the pocket is large enough for his hand to fit through.

"What is that?" Victoria startles at her torn sweater.

"Watch the show. Forget I'm even here." He tastes her neck again and slides his hand along the waist of her jeans, touching her smooth belly with his thumb. He feels her grow heavier against him. Her neck falls farther to the side to give him greater access with his mouth. He breathes into her ear.

"I'm going to make you come." He unbuttons her jeans under the safe cover of her gorgeous cashmere sweater.

"Callum," she says, neither encouraging nor stopping him. The bourbon helps the inhibitions float away. Among these thousand people they seem to have a perfect privacy. His hand finds its way into her jeans and he dances his finger along her wet skin, slowly exploring and easing her to that other place, in the middle of this concert that she loves.

When she comes, breathless and quiet, he decides he will love her. There is no deciding, really. It is done. After, she turns to him and wraps her arms around his neck.

"The sweater?" she asks not understanding.

"Would you believe special order?"

"No," she says and then there is a smash and shower of glass behind Callum's head.

Callum instinctively pushes Victoria away from the glass. His hair is full of shards. He can't see what is going on behind him. But he hears it.

"You fucking piece of shit," a woman screams at him. "You motherfucker."

The crowd backs away from her. Callum brushes glass off Victoria. When he is sure she is not hurt, he pushes her behind him away from the screaming woman.

"You put your fucking hands on my throat. You made me do things. My husband saw those marks on me. He left me, you piece of shit."

Callum knows who she is now. She looks very different after just over a month. She has lost the glamour she had in the bar up the block and looks more like an aging drunk.

"Callum, what the hell is going on? Who is this woman? Are you bleeding? You can't have another concussion." She tries to examine his head, but he is almost a foot taller and he isn't cooperating. "Are you crazy?" Victoria asks the screamer like she might get a sensible answer.

"You are the crazy one, cunt," she slurs and turns again on Callum. "You're fucking a rapist."

Victoria looks wide-eyed from Callum to the crazy woman and back again. "You are out of your mind."

"Bullshit," she screams. "He is a pig. You are fucking a fucking rapist pig."

Victoria tries to get around Callum, but he is having no part of it. He manages to keep Victoria back for the five seconds needed until two bouncers intervene, grabbing her, kicking and screaming, and they pull her away.

Callum freezes, trying to process what happened. He looks to Victoria and she is walking out the door, fast. *This is the end.* He got to love her for five minutes. Suddenly she stops. He can see her stopping and he can't really believe it. She stops, turns and holds her hand out to him. *No. This is over.* He crutches past her, out and onto the street. The crutches make a dramatic departure difficult. He pushes hard to try to get away from her.

He is ashamed and disgusted that his choices have brought him to this. He has finally completely ruined his own life.

"Callum stop," Victoria nearly begs. "Talk to me. She was just some crazy woman, why are you so upset? Did that glass hit you? Please let me look."

"No Victoria. I need to get out of here."

"Callum stop. Please talk to me." She pulls him into a nearby bar and slides into a booth in the corner. She orders two more bourbons because they need them.

"Talk Callum. Please."

"No Victoria."

"Callum what the hell is going on?" she pleads.

Against his better judgement, he takes a deep breath and begins. "She is not just some crazy woman. I knew her." He could have lied, but he's not doing that anymore. He's doing things differently this time around. "She wasn't like that before."

"Did you sleep with her Callum?"

He nods.

"She says you're a rapist Callum?"

"I did not rape her."

"Why does she think you did, Callum?" Her voice sounds like the voice she uses when she wants Marina to focus.

He shakes his head. "I don't want to discuss this with you."

"Yet, here we are with glass in our hair covered in beer." She manages to keep calm. He doesn't know how. He's not calm. "So fucking talk Callum."

"I think we are through," he says. "You and me. I think this is the end of us."

"Are you telling me you raped her, Callum?"

He can tell she is trying to keep control of her voice and he doesn't answer.

"Callum, you have been nothing but gentle and kind and understanding and giving with me every second we have spent together in bed and out. You are damn near polite in bed, Callum. It just doesn't seem possible."

He speaks to the bourbon, gazing at the deep caramel color. "I picked her up in a bar on my way west. We had sex. Everything I say now makes me sound like I did something wrong, but it didn't feel wrong at the time. I don't want us to be done Victoria."

"Tell me, Callum. I trust you. Now trust me."

"We had sex. It was anonymous, the way she wanted it. It was rough. I liked it. She liked it. After, I asked her if she was satisfied and she said she was. It was one hundred percent consensual."

"What were the marks? How rough were you?"

He closes his eyes. He can't look at her, but he does tell the truth. "I held her throat. Auto asphyxiation. She liked it. She came twice. It was consensual."

She stares at him blank faced.

"I'm not a rapist, but she was right. I am a piece of shit."

He throws some cash on the table and walks from the bar. She follows him silently. He knows it is over between them. He crutches up the hill. He feels her hand on his back. She can't hold his hand with the crutches. He really thinks it is over between them. Then her hand rubs his back, soothing his worries away.

"Stop Callum," she says and pulls him into an alley. They are surrounded by red brick and endless colors of graffiti. Her arms encircle his neck. "Just stop. I'm not the same person I was when we met. Knowing you and being with you has changed me. I was afraid of opening up and needing anyone. I was hiding out in Park City alone with my very unhappy kid. Look how you helped me change my life. I don't think you are the same either. Remember that day we met in the hospital and you were screaming and swearing at me? You are different Callum."

She's right, he is different. He had thought this would be the end of them, but he thinks he was wrong. It might actually be the beginning of them.

"Let's be who we are now and forget the rest," she says.

"I wasn't nice to her. There were others too. I treated them poorly. I was so pissed off at Elizabeth."

"I believe you Callum. I believe every word you say."

Their kiss in the alley is the start of something honest. Something that is more than great sex or a great friendship.

Eight

By the end of winter break, Victoria has a job at Asheville General Medical Center. Her start date is the day after Victoria begins school. George and Callum are working on a few projects together. One involves chopping what seems like an awful lot of wood. Victoria has done some hiding behind the curtain whiles Callum swings the axe over his head. George sits nearby in a rocker on the porch providing pointers and making jokes about England's loss of the colonies. There is also an effort to convert old slides to videos. Victoria is glad they found something to do where they can both sit. Callum does too much walking considering he is still healing. George should be taking it easy too. Callum has also taken on the challenge of duplicating George's mother's chicken and dumplings. There is no written recipe, just much talk about flavors and textures and every week there is a new version of chicken and dumplings for dinner. They are all good but never quite right.

The first day of school, Victoria and Marina go into the kitchen to sort out a lunch. Callum stands at the counter despite the hour.

"You're up early," Victoria says. She feels like she wants to kiss him, but it isn't right. Not in front of Marina.

"Perk of having a chef in the house. The lunches are top notch." he says. "I packed you a grilled chicken and roasted vegetable wrap, crisps and a banana. Don't you dare toss the banana either. Eat it."

"You made my lunch?" Marina says, like maybe he just cured cancer.

"Of course. What were you going to pack? A pb and j?" He says the letters with disdain.

"What are crisps?" Marina asks with her nose in the bag.

"Potato chips of course."

Marina hugs him and reluctantly follows her mother to the door. Callum follows them. "Marina, something I learned years ago. A question and a compliment get people talking."

"Callum," Victoria says with surprise. "That is really good advice."

"I was the new kid many, many times. You develop strategies. Marina your number one directive this morning is to find someone to sit with at lunch. You have two choices. You might turn off your ears for this Victoria.

Marina is fascinated. "Tell me."

"Go with the question and compliment and get yourself in with anyone you genuinely like. That friendship will build. This is a small city and new kids are exciting here. If all else fails sit with the, sorry Victoria, sit with the kids with disabilities."

"What?" Victoria says with shock.

"It's all about aligning yourself. She'll come off as kind. If she sits at the strays' table, kids with no friends, she'll be in danger of becoming a stray.

Victoria opens the door and pushes Marina through. "Thanks bunches Callum," she says sarcastically.

Marina runs in for one more hug. "You are a genius," she says.

"Just be kind to everyone, you'll be fine," he lies, but it makes Victoria smile.

Victoria signs Marina into school for her first day and her heart breaks a little as she watches Marina trudge off to class. When Marina is out of her sights, Victoria turns to leave and there he is. Christopher Augustine holds the door open for his daughter. She is a year or two younger than Marina. She has Marina's exact same chin, there is the slightest point to it. He has aged well, dark hair is clipped short. An easy smile rests on his face as he walks with his hand on his daughter's shoulder, laughing. Victoria steps out of his way and he walks by without noticing the woman he raped.

She drives home, vision blurred by tears and rage, parks poorly, and runs into the house wiping her eyes. George sits at the kitchen table, reading a paper, drinking coffee. Callum sits close by, reading the second book of Hunger Games, *Catching Fire*.

Victoria storms into the kitchen, seething. "Why didn't you tell me he is here? You had to know?"

"Now wait a minute Vic. What's going on?" he asks, looking confused.

"Christopher. He was at the school, Dad. He has a damn daughter. Marina has a sister." At the word sister, Victoria storms from the kitchen and runs the stairs to her room. She slams the door with everything she's got.

George folds his paper neatly and lays it at his side. Callum sets his book aside.

"That was faster than expected," George says. "I wanted to give her some time here, first."

"You knew all along?"

"I did," he says.

Callum wants to ask why he didn't mention it, but he doesn't. Callum isn't interested in berating George.

"She's probably packing Callum. Can you stop her?" George pleads.

"Truthfully George, I'm not sure I should. What does this mean for Marina? She is the bastard rape child of this fucking asshole? Sorry. Were they better off in Utah thousands of miles from him?"

"I'm not sure Callum. This is not an easy situation. Marina has family," George says.

"George, he has no rights. He's a rapist."

"But Marina has rights."

"Her father is a rapist," Callum repeats.

George doesn't reply. Callum reaches for his crutches to go to Victoria. He finds her in the foyer.

"I'm going for a ride," she says.

"I'll join you." He pulls his coat off the rack and follows her to the car. They drive the mountains. The last weeks have been warm and the trees are barren but free of snow. Evergreens hold their color in these aptly named Blue Ridge Mountains. They drive without conversation, without music for an hour before she parks in an overlook with a view of the valley below. All these miles later, Callum still has no idea what to say to her. What are the guidelines for this type of situation? Running does seem to be her best option.

She sits back and her eyes scan the view in front of them.

"Should you take Marina back to Utah?" he asks. "I'll stay here with George. He won't be alone. I'll stay with him until the end."

Fresh tears flow. "It is really hard to act like I can handle anything when you are so damn nice." She smiles because, even now, he can bring a smile to her face. "Please say something mean so I don't have to sit here and cry. Something really terrible. Right now. Go." She tries to joke.

"You have snot running from your face," he says.

She immediately reaches to wipe her nose.

"Just kidding," he says and she manages a laugh.

"Damn him," she lays her forehead on the steering wheel. "It's not entirely his fault. Truthfully I didn't come here really thinking that Christopher was gone, but I didn't imagine our damn kids would be in the same damn school. Does he have a claim to her Callum? Can he try to take her from me?" The fear shows on her face.

"I can't imagine he does, but let's go talk to a lawyer. Or let's get you and Marina the hell out of here." He is ready to pack their bags. As much as he doesn't want to be without them, he doesn't want Marina finding all of this out now. She has been lied to a lot.

"Should I have told Marina the truth, Callum? Did I make this worse?" she asks.

He doesn't know the answer. All he knows is that he is going to protect them. He will protect them both, no matter what. There is a lot he cannot do. He can't fix things with Elizabeth or Jeremy. He can't change his mother's view of him as anything other than a stupid little boy. He can never be the golden angel surgeon like his brother. He can never do those things, but he can do this.

"Tell Marina she's mine. Tell everyone she's mine. I'll be her father."

"What the hell are you talking about Callum?" She asks in disbelief and confusion.

"He can't have any legal claims to her if he never knows he is her father. Tell her we met years ago when you came to England and we had an affair. Tell her I found you. Tell her."

"Callum. Stop it," she says in frustration. "Just stop. You are talking fantasy."

"Victoria, we can do this." He is insistent.

"Callum, Marina found you. She ran into you on a mountain. You are not being rational." She lays her hand on the back of his neck. "It's okay, Callum. We'll be okay."

He takes her hand from his neck and holds it in his own hand. "I don't want you soothing me. I'm fucking soothing you."

Victoria's mobile vibrates. She answers and Callum can hear a panicked voice on the other end but not the words.

"I'm coming," Victoria says and throws the phone onto the seat. She starts the car, immediately throwing it into reverse.

"Rosalie found my Dad. He was unconscious on the kitchen floor. Oh my god Callum he can't die before I get to him. Not like this. Not after we fought."

They pull up to the emergency entrance at the hospital. Callum sends Victoria in. He can drive with his left leg to park the car. Inside Callum finds that George has already been admitted into the Cardiac Critical Care Unit. When Callum arrives, he is conscious and smiling. Victoria is sitting at the edge of his bed and her relief is obvious.

"It's okay. They just need to adjust his new medication. The fall wasn't too bad."

"I didn't fall. I laid down abruptly," George argues. After a while, George sleeps and Callum and Victoria move to the lounge to talk.

"Callum, my head is telling me to get Marina the hell out of here."

He wants to pull her to his lap. He likes when they talk close and she lays her head against him. He likes how it feels when she leans on him, literally and figuratively. This isn't the place though, so he doesn't.

"Callum, thank you. For everything you said earlier, everything you offered."

"I meant it all. I still mean it."

"You are the most wonderful man." She holds his face in her hands and touches her lips to his. "Honestly, will you tell me what you think?"

His jaw and fists tighten and he hesitates sharing the truth, but truth is the only option. "Victoria, sometimes when I think of Anna, I get so angry. I will never forgive her adoptive fucks, who called themselves her parents, for keeping Anna from me. Never. Victoria, she was just across town. We could have had a life together. I could rip their heads from their bodies and kill them both."

"I get the picture." She takes his hand to smooth out the clench. "Marina needs to know something, but I don't know what. I made it worse in Nashville. I told her such lies, Callum." Her eyes fill with guilt and Callum decides *fuck it* and does pulls her into his lap.

"You don't have to decide anything right now. Your Dad gets out of here tomorrow?"

She nods.

"I'll pick Marina up from school."

Paige Randall

"You can't drive Callum."

"It's been six weeks. I can probably drive."

"You need six to ten with the brace and the crutches," she says.

"What time is Marina out? Three-thirty? Its ten now. You stay here. I'm going to the ER. It seems I have fallen and need an orthopedist to look at my leg. I'm so sick of this fucking brace Victoria. It's coming off today. Let me take care of this. We'll talk in a few hours."

Because she has someone who genuinely has her back for the first time in a very long time and she trusts him, she takes his face in her hands again and tells him clearly and openly, without reservation, "I like you so much Callum."

"Well good, because I am completely in love with you," He kisses her before she can say a word, gets up and crutches away with a smile.

Callum makes his way into the ER and tells them he had surgery six weeks ago but took a bit of spill today and wants to verify that his leg is still healing well. Within three hours he has been thoroughly examined and is cleared for driving and the brace is off. Some sweet talking is involved. There are instructions for physical therapy which he promptly tosses into the trash.

He returns to George's room without the brace or crutches.

"I've always been a fast healer," he explains. My brain is a mess, but my bones are fantastic."

Callum takes the keys and programs the address of Marina's school into his mobile so he can navigate there. "We'll talk later and figure this out. Okay?"

Victoria watches him walk down the hall. She has never seen him walk before. He walks like a man who owns the world, like he has all of the answers.

As Callum drives to Marina's school he decides that, one way or another, he will get his eyes on Christopher. He wants to know what they are dealing with. Callum easily finds his way to Asheville Middle School. He doesn't know the protocol for picking up a student so he parks and waits by the doors. Then he realizes he doesn't want to be too close and risk embarrassing Marina.

With the brace off, he is thrilled to be able to walk and start rebuilding muscle in his leg. He has nearly twenty minutes until dismissal so he loops the circumference of the parking lot, the sidewalk and then the playground where a collection of parents play with their younger children. Callum takes a seat on a bench by a group of men. Callum has always suffered the sadness that accompanies growing up with poorly managed dyslexia, but he has also enjoyed the benefits of being a very tall, very good looking, very confident presence. People, men and women alike, are drawn to him and he knows it.

There is a mutual exchange of nodding and some *heys* and a *what's up*. Within ten minutes, Callum has the rundown on their group. They are stay at-home Dads — a writer, two techies, a bartender (nights only), and a sculptor. Asheville is loaded with artists. One of the techies is named Christopher. Callum studies him hard. He has sandy hair, not unlike Marina's. Inconclusive. His eyes are dark, unlike Marina's. Inconclusive. It is the chin that gets him. It is his fucking chin. There is a tilt, an angle and a slight point. He is Marina's rapist father. Callum wants to punch him in the face. Impulse control is not a strong trait of Callum's. His muscles tense, he can nearly feel the blood moving through his veins, his breathing quickens. Their voices becomes distant. He knows he is in trouble.

"What do you do, Callum?" Ryan the writer asks, shaking Callum from violent thoughts.

Callum forces himself to rejoin the seemingly innocuous conversation. He scrambles for something but wants to be vague. But punching

Christopher in the face would feel oh so good. Suddenly a small child, a boy, runs up and grabs Christopher's leg.

"Juice, Daddy?" he says. He looks like Marina miniaturized. There is a sister and a brother. Oh my God. Callum isn't sure why, but this makes him want to cry. Callum doesn't cry so he takes a deep breath and answers Ryan's question.

"I am considering opening a shop in town. I've been running a kitchen in London for the last eight years and I'm looking for a different pace of life. That is 24/7. I'd like to cut it back a bit."

"How old is your kid?" Christopher asks.

"Eighth grade," Callum says and doesn't know how long he can control the impulse. Thankfully, he hears the bell.

"Good to meet you," Callum says before making his way to find Marina.

Ryan calls after him. "We all work out at Asheville Fitness after drop off in the morning, if you are interested."

"I'll think on it," Callum calls back without turning around.

Marina finds him quickly. She looks happy and that is good news after a first day in a new school. He hopes there is no corporal punishment here in school. They loved that when he was a young. He remembers getting a ruler to the knuckles often.

"Hey kid," he says and when she notices he is without crutches, "surprise."

She has a brother and a sister he thinks and bites back his regret that he is now part of the lie. She gives him a hug in full view of her classmates. They go for an ice cream before he tells her the news of her grandfather and who knows what else. Let the kid enjoy thirty happy minutes before dumping on her again.

Marina tells him every detail of her day. She found a nice group of girls to eat lunch with using his technique. They encouraged her to join *Best Buddies*, a group that supports students with intellectual disabilities. Victoria will be happy.

"Callum I have to tell you something."

He wipes Ben & Jerry's New York Super Fudge Chunk from her chin with a napkin. *That damn chin.* "Tell," he says forcing a smile. He was trying to lie less, but now he is lying more.

"What happened on the mountain with you was the best and worst thing I have ever done in my life."

He knows what she means, but he wants to hear it from her anyway. He stuffs a large spoonful of Chubby Hubby into his mouth and speaks through it. "Explain."

"I am so sorry I hurt you Callum," she say and her eyes fill with tears.

"You are forgiven and you should never be saddened by it again. Ever." He holds her chin and speaks right into her eyes. He hates her guilt. She is a kid. Guilt and regret and self-loathing are for grownups. "You probably saved me Marina. I wasn't on a good path, but I am now and I have you to thank for that. You are forgiven. Understood?

She nods and wipes her eyes with the back of her hand.

"Why the best?" He fishes for the compliment because an emotional boost would be lovely.

"The best because you belong with us. I remember what it was like before you were with us, but I can't remember. Do you know what I mean?"

"I know exactly what you mean." He wonders if Marina would be best served by his just killing Christopher. He would be dead, the brother and sister would be hers. Very tempting. The thought of prison is not appealing though.

When they are done with their ice cream, Callum tells Marina about George and they go to the hospital. Marina sits on the edge of George's bed and tells him all about school. At five, Rosalie comes in.

"You all go home. I'll stay the night with him," Rosalie insists. Callum wonders why George and Rosalie insist on pretending their relationship is platonic.

After homework and a late dinner, Victoria sits Marina down for a serious talk. Marina waits in a chair across from Callum and Victoria looking from his face to hers with a worried frown on her own face.

"I want to be completely honest with you Marina. Callum and I are becoming more than friends." Victoria confesses.

"Duh Mom. Is that it?" They nod. "Goodnight." Marina says and kisses them both before going to bed.

"That was easy," Victoria says.

"She's a smart kid," Callum says. "Very intuitive."

An awkward silence falls between them. Callum's declaration of love earlier sits heavily in the air. Victoria scoots onto his lap and lays her head against his chest again, in the exact way he loves. She can act words of love without saying the words and that is enough for now. They sit for a long time before Callum tells her. He doesn't want to break the moment, but she needs to know.

"I met Christopher today." He holds her tight against him.

"Go on." To her credit, that is all she says.

"There is sort of a dads' group. Is there such thing?" She doesn't reply. "Anyway, he and a few other at-home dads, is that a thing? Whatever.

They meet up at the gym every morning. They invited me to join them. I need to rehab this leg anyway and I'm not going to PT."

She silently takes in all he has said.

"I need to know what kind of man he is. He is married and has two kids, a daughter a year younger than Marina and a little boy. He looks a bit older than Clara."

"A brother and a sister." she says in a whisper. "How can I keep her from them?" This time he doesn't answer.

He knows she can't keep Marina from them. He knows without any doubt that Marina will never forgive her if she does. Regardless of the circumstances, Marina will want to know she has family. But that has to come from Victoria, on her own. Callum can't force her into it.

"You are going to the gym with them?" she asks and he nods. "I don't know what I would do without you, Callum. I never meant to rely on you like this, but I do, and it's hard for me. I'm so used to being alone."

"You'll get used to me." He knows she is trying to explain herself for not returning his words of love. He can wait.

"Today, when I was with my Dad and you were with Marina, I was thinking. You need to go back to England," she says.

He has no intention of going anywhere. "Stop Victoria," he nearly whines.

"No Callum, I'm serious. You need to resolve things with Elizabeth and Jeremy. You can't hide here. It will all catch up with you eventually. You'll have regrets if you don't tie up your loose ends."

"I'm not going back to fucking England. That is over for me," he insists.

"For now, maybe it is over for you but not forever," she insists back.

"Will you stop fucking pushing me away," he pleads. "I just told you I loved you."

"Callum," she says getting angry. "How can we love each other if you have all of this unfinished business? We can't."

He shoves her from his lap and she lands on the sofa next to him with a bounce. "Off you go," he says and crosses his arms over his chest. He gives his brain a moment to consider her words. What if Elizabeth showed up this minute on his doorstep, done with Jeremy, ready to spend her life with Callum? Is that what Victoria is asking? Is he over Elizabeth?

"I love you. Will you fucking let me?" He begs. "I'm going nowhere."

"I can't say it yet Callum. I'm not sure you are really ready for those words."

He'd like the words, but he doesn't need the words. For now her mouth on his will be enough. He kisses her to stop her from talking. They make out a while, old school. Eventually she slides from the sofa and lowers herself to the floor between his legs, reaching for his zipper.

"No," he says, as a reaction to a feeling he doesn't understand. He doesn't want her there, like that, with him. Not now, not ever.

"Why Callum? We've never done that. You aren't interested? I find that hard to believe," she emphasizes the word *hard*.

He thinks about all of those women. All of the women he treated in a way that he would never want Victoria treated. He wasn't kind to them. Christopher wasn't kind. Does Christopher think he wasn't kind or does Christopher know he is a rapist? What the hell is rape? Where are the lines? Victoria sits on the floor while he is running these thoughts through his head. He has been judging Christopher very harshly and he should, but he isn't sure where the line is and it is making him uncomfortable.

"Callum?" she asks.

He doesn't bother answering. He takes her into his arms, switches off the lamp and carries her upstairs to his bed.

Weeks pass before Callum goes to Asheville Fitness in the morning. The leg needed easy strengthening before he hit the weights and he doesn't want to look like a pussy. Callum works out alone the first two weeks, in the afternoons.

As February approaches, Callum finally hits the gym after he drops Marina off at school in the morning. Christopher and Randy are spotting each other over heavy iron on the bench press. Callum doesn't want to get into a pissing match over weights until he is in better shape so he says hello and hits the treadmill to work the leg through an easy run. An hour later, Callum finds himself sitting in a coffee bar with Christopher the Rapist and Writer Randy. They talk about their families and careers. Callum listens and talks as little as possible.

"What about you Callum? Any progress on that shop you were thinking about?" Christopher asks. "My father-in-law is a developer if you need some help."

Callum tosses his empty coffee cup six feet into the trash can. "No, nothing yet. The leg has slowed me down. I'm just bullshitting around."

"Must be nice," Randy says.

"It is very nice. I like Asheville. I want to spend some time exploring the area." Callum opens the metaphorical door and Christopher walks right through it.

"Maybe we could hike tomorrow instead of the gym. Randy, let's take him to Craggy Rock. Not much climbing, but it's a good hike."

"Shall I pack a picnic lunch?" Callum asks.

Christopher and Randy just stare at him.

"I'm a fucking chef. It's the least I can do."

"Yeah. Let's picnic." Randy says, a little dumbfounded.

"Men can picnic," Christopher says.

Callum decides not to tell Victoria about the hike with Christopher and Randy. She leaves for work early and then Callum packs the cooler. Rosalie spends the days with George. Callum meets Randy and Christopher in the school parking lot after dropping off Marina. He wills himself to keep an open mind as he climbs into the back seat of Christopher's truck. No, an open mind is too much. He'll just get through this day without committing murder.

Once they are clear of the city, they drive the mountains for about an hour. Led Zepplin fills the car so small talk isn't required. Robert Plant singing *Ramble On* calms the savage beast inside Callum. They drive though mountainside neighborhoods with sprawling homes, manicured lawns and golf courses. This isn't the trailer trash area Callum expected. The day is unseasonably warm and the sky is blue. Callum relaxes enough to study Christopher. He can only see the back of his head and his eyes in the rear view mirror. It is enough for now.

Finally, Christopher parks the truck and Callum moves the contents of the cooler to his backpack. They walk into the woods. The trail runs alongside a creek for two miles up a slight incline until it finally crosses the creek and makes a sharp incline up into the hills. They climb a fairly steep hill for about half mile and then climb almost straight up for another thirty feet. Reaching the top, they sit on the summit of large flat rocks, catching their breath. The view into the valley is breathtaking.

"I've lived here most of my life and this still gets me," Christopher says. Hunting hawks circle the tall evergreens in the distance.

Randy takes a camera with a long lens from his backpack. For a large man, he moves gracefully with a camera. His long hair and straggly beard are a stark contrast to the impression of a graceful artist. Callum thinks he looks more like a moonshiner or one of those duck men. He shoots photos silently and writes notes onto a small white pad with a short pencil.

"Capturing this with words is really hard for me. I feel too close to it sometimes. Blue sky, white clouds, barren trees, bluish green evergreens, but what else?" he asks himself more than the others.

While they unpack lunch, Callum asks Randy what he is working on. Randy describes his novel's setting and characters but doesn't say a word about plot until Christopher interrupts.

"Tell him Randy."

"He's too new. I'm not sure if I like him yet." Randy looks Callum over with serious brown eyes.

"Well no fucking sandwich for you then, buddy." Callum jokes.

Christopher prods Randy. "Dude, you have to learn to trust a little."

Callum watches Randy expectantly and silently. Randy watches him back and Callum can see the struggle within. It takes a few moments, but Randy finally finds his voice.

"I'm gay. I write romance. I faked hetero for years until my wife caught me fucking my barber and she left me. She left the kid too which shows what a shitty hetero I was. I married a woman who left her kid."

"I am fucking stunned," Callum admits.

"That I'm gay?" Randy asks defensively.

"No, I'm stunned that you have a barber." Callum rubs Randy's mess of hair and gives him a hug. "Like me Randy. I am fucking delightful," he begs.

Randy hugs him back and Callum watches Christopher out of the corner of his eye. Callum can tell he is pleased with Randy's share and Callum's response.

"How about some food," Christopher says.

Callum unwraps a brick flattened round of crusty bread filled with roast chicken, prosciutto, pesto, arugula, peppers and asiago. He unwraps a cutting board and a sharp knife and slices the sandwich into wedges, pulling them into a wide circle. He fills the center space with thick cut, hand sliced homemade potato chips and hands out napkins. Christopher and Randy look on with shock.

"The fuck," Randy comments.

"Did you bring a cutting board on a hike?" Christopher says. "I thought we'd be eating Subway."

"Wait, I'm not done." Callum produces a flask and three short plastic glasses. "Midday bourbon?" He offers.

"Yes!" Randy says.

Christopher shakes his head. "Not for me. I'm in AA."

This news stops Callum in his tracks. "Yeah?" he asks, wanting to know more. Maybe this means something. Maybe there is a reason for how he treated Victoria. Maybe something is different now.

"Sorry man, I forgot," Randy says.

"You two enjoy. I've been dry for twelve years," he explains. "I'm good. Have a drink." The flask sits untouched.

Callum can't let it lie. He needs to know more. "How did you get into AA?" he asks.

"Years of being a drunk piece of shit tends to get you there one way or another." Christopher bites into his sandwich, nodding and gives a thumbs-up. "This is great."

"This is truly excellent Callum," Randy agrees.

"Did you get a DWI or kill someone or something?" Callum doesn't mind if he comes across like an asshole. This is important.

Christopher considers his answer and stuffs a few chips in his mouth. "I was going to lose my wife and daughter. She put up with a lot of shit and she was coming to the end of her rope. I was drinking a lot and getting rough at home. The choice was clean up or get out."

"And you cleaned up?" Callum asks.

"I did. It was no choice really." Christopher smiles ironically and chews a few more chips.

The news takes the angry wind from Callum's sails. He immediately relaxes and decides to get to know Christopher better. He may be a completely different man now. Maybe he was a lunatic drinker, had a terrible night with Victoria and that was it. He got help and now he is a good dad and a productive member of society. Maybe he blacked out and doesn't even know he raped her. *Maybe.*

Somehow February eases into March and Easter is on the horizon. Callum has continued to spend time with Christopher and Randy. He even bought Randy's latest novel, *The Ashes of Asheville*. It is a historical romance set after the great flood of 1916 in Asheville. Randy is quite a writer. Callum gets to know Christopher better and better. They work out most mornings, hike the mountains every week or so and, most importantly, they talk. Callum is surprised by Christopher's willingness to talk. He is open about his alcoholism and the early struggles in his marriage. Callum thinks he understands what happened between Christopher and Victoria. He was completely out of control back then and he had no idea what he was doing. *No idea.*

George is slowing down but hanging in. He wants Callum to visit his family on Osprey Island over Easter and he wants Victoria and Marina to go to. George can see the connection growing between them. Best if Victoria gets to know Callum's family. Rosalie will stay with him and he promises not to die while they are gone.

Victoria refuses. As much as she wants to meet Anna, she won't leave her father. Marina, Victoria, George and Rosalie will enjoy a quiet Easter at home, but she insists that Callum go see Anna. Reluctantly, Callum agrees to go to Osprey Island alone. He is inclined to stay in Asheville, but he needs to see his sister. It has been too long. The last time he visited he was a whining mess and he is anxious to make a better impression with John.

Victoria sits at Callum's desk while he packs. "Callum, you fold clothes neater than anyone I've ever seen."

He zips the bag closed and sits down on the bed with a hand on her knee looking serious.

"What?" she asks. "You look angry."

Callum doesn't know where to begin. He has things to say, but he doesn't want to say them. He just wants her to know them.

"Did I do something?" she asks.

"I am not angry, but there is something on my mind." She looks at him, willing him to speak. He takes a few breathes and with a hand on each of her knees, he looks her straight into her eyes. "I want more."

"I don't understand," she says, but of course she does.

"We have been at this for a few months now. I am head over heels in love with you. You like me very much." He leaves the words there. No more is really needed.

"Callum, Marina, my Dad, Christopher. It all feels so unsettled. And you, too."

"Me too what?" he asks, but he knows what comes next.

"You need to go back to London."

"Oh bullshit. This isn't some set something free and, if it is yours, it'll come back shit." He isn't sure if he is angrier than he should be, but he is trying to be honest.

"To me it is Callum. I need you to leave so you can come back and stay." She begs him to understand, but he doesn't.

"Can you fucking hear yourself? It is absurd. It is childish. You want *The Officer and the Gentleman* factory scene. But this is real life."

She moves from the chair and curls into his lap. "I feel like Deborah Winger now. You'd look great in whites."

"You're mocking. I'm serious here."

"You have to leave me Callum. You have to go back to England and face everything. I won't love you until you leave me."

"You sound insane. I'll not leave you. I'll…"

The conversation ends when she puts her mouth over his. The kiss makes him forget his words. It always does. He finally smacks her bottom to get her to hop off. "I have a long drive. Up up."

He kisses her once more and taps her nose with his index finger. "I know you are afraid, but I love you and I want more. I don't need to go to England to know this is where I want to be. One day you'll understand what you mean to me?" He touches her check and leaves.

Six hours later, Callum drives over the bridge onto Osprey Island. The weather is warm for this time of year so he pulls off his jacket and opens the windows. Any tension he felt on the drive about Victoria or his future dissipates immediately. Osprey Island has a magical effect on its visitors.

Anna is waiting on the porch swing with baby Lynn sleeping in her arms. He parks the car, climbs the steps and sits by her side, kissing her cheek. Anna lays her head against Callum's shoulder and they watch Lynn sleep together for a moment.

"She's grown so. She's a dream, Anna." Callum whispers and glides his thumb over Lynn's tiny hand.

"I couldn't get her down. Clara is so excited to see you. They have been preparing for Uncle Callie all day."

He just smiles because his words get trapped with her sometimes.

"How are you? The leg? You look wonderful." Of course she reaches to feel his beard. Anna can't keep her hands out of a good beard. "You look happy. You've put on a few pounds. You were looking a little too Billy Idol last visit. Not you look more like Eric Northman." Anna says referencing the vampire from *True Blood*.

"I am well. I feel good. Where are John and Clara?" he asks.

"On the beach, will you run down and say hello? I promised Clara you would."

Callum walks around the house and down the wooden walkway to the beach. He kicks off his shoes and walks through the sand calling to Clara. She hands her fishing rod to John and runs right into Callum's arms.

"Uncle Callie's here Daddy," she yells to John.

Callum hugs her hard, smelling her little girl hair. The minute she wraps her arms around his neck, he knows. He knows that he wants a Clara of his own, maybe two or three. He wants to be a Daddy and fish the surf with his own little children. He wants babies to sleep in his lap and he wants Victoria to be his wife. He doesn't just want the love, Callum wants the whole life.

Easter is a crowded weekend at Osprey Island. John's parents, Conrad and Jane, Aunt Susannah and her partner, Meredith, come and stay in the house next door. Anna's mother, Ellen, and her husband, Rodrigo, stay in the house with John and Anna. Easter dinner includes neighbors and friends. Everyone brings a covered dish or desert and John cooks a ham and two turkeys. Barbara and Joe from next door organize an Easter egg hunt for the kids. It is like a weekend out of a magazine.

As much as Callum loves his time with his sister and he enjoys this perfect place and these wonderful people, he misses his life in Asheville. He has found a family there.

On Callum's last night, after the kids have gone to bed and grandparents and aunts and uncles have returned to their respective cities, Callum, John and Anna sit up late with a bottle of wine and a roaring fire. John and Anna sit on the leather couch, legs entwined, looking relaxed and content, even after the chaotic holiday.

"It's been great having you here Callum. My family was happy to get to know you." John says.

"They are marvelous John. You are so blessed. The kids, this place, this life. Both of you are so lucky."

Anna frowns. "That is a load of crap."

Callum laughs. He likes having a sister very much. "Whatever do you mean sweet sister?"

"Sure. It is all sunshine and rainbows. We have certainly lived happily ever after. But getting here was hard work. We aren't fucking blessed. We aren't lucky. We did the work."

John nods, agreeing with Anna. "Things started out rough for us Callum. What's the story with you and Victoria? We haven't really had a chance to talk with the crowds here."

Callum debates what to tell them. He sips his wine and watches the flames dance over the logs and he considers what to share. He is done lying. What is the damn point? If he wants a relationships with Anna, he can't only show her the best possible version of himself. He wants to be a real person.

"I love her, but she won't love me." He lays his head back into the leather of his chair. Saying the words out loud feels good, even though it hurts like hell.

"Doesn't love you or won't love you," Anna asks.

"Won't. I think she does. But she won't engage with me on a deeper level. We are sort of dating and sleeping together but living like housemates. I want more."

"What do you want Callum?" John asks.

"I want what you two have," Callum says and drains his glass. "I want love and kids and all of this."

Anna frowns again. She looks to John and even Callum can tell she wants John to do the talking this time.

"I know it's fast," Callum says defensively.

John holds Anna's leg and takes his turn. "Callum, I am sure Victoria is an incredible woman and sometimes these things happen fast. Anna and I were married inside of three months. But Callum, a few months ago you were here and damn depressed over another woman."

"I know that," Callum admits.

Anna sits up, leaning towards her brother. "Does Victoria know that?"

Callum nods.

"Callum, she doesn't trust you. You are coming off a bit fickle." Anna says as gently as she can. "What do you want in the longer term?"

"I want to marry her. I want to make a life in Asheville. I want to be a father to her daughter and I want children with her." Freeing these words is both liberating and terrifying.

"And what does she want?" Anna asks.

"She wants me to go back to England to face Elizabeth and Jeremy. She doesn't believe I'm done with England and serious about Asheville."

"Are you working Callum?" John asks.

Callum shakes his head. "First the leg and then, well, it just didn't make sense to commit to something if Victoria isn't interested in being together longer term."

Anna gets up and sits on the coffee table in front of her brother. "Darling, Victoria is never going to take you seriously unless you commit to something besides her. You seem to be biding time to go back. I can't blame her a bit."

"I'm completely devoted to her and to Marina. And George for that matter. I don't understand how I am coming across as cavalier."

John empties the bottle among their glasses. "Here it is Callum. She thinks she's your layover and you are biding your time until you get on the next flight. You can be as devoted as you want, but it isn't a commitment unless you commit to something. Or else it's just words."

"More doing, less talking about doing, Callum. She'll see you're serious when you show her you are."

179

"Fuck," Callum says. He wonders if he should tell them the rest. The rape is her business, hers and Marina's. His friendship with Christopher is becoming complicated. He has been spending more and more time with Christopher and Randy over the last month. There has been talk of a cookout and getting families together. Callum doesn't think he can keep this deception going much longer. He decides to say nothing more about it.

"I need to shut everything down in England. I need some closure with Jeremy and even Elizabeth, don't I? And I need a fucking job. Fuck." He runs both hands through his hair in frustration.

"You'll get there Callum. It's a process," John says, quoting his therapist, Dr. Lane.

Nine

As the weather starts to warm and spring takes hold, Victoria knows she can't go on living in limbo. George is holding on, but the indecision over what to do about Marina is keeping her up at night. She knows Callum is uncomfortable with the secrets. After his Easter visit, it is especially obvious that Anna means the world to him and keeping Marina from her siblings just seems cruel. Victoria considers seeing a therapist to talk through the possibilities, but she can't bear the thought of telling it all to another person. Callum knows and that is enough.

After Easter, Callum seemed very determined to move forward with opening a business. Victoria doesn't think he is serious, but he has spent the last few weeks in near seclusion with George, out at some site he has kept a big secret from her. His easy smile has been replaced with a serious, determined, somewhat absent-minded scowl.

On her way home from work, Callum texts. *Marina and George are set for dinner. Will you meet me? I have a bit of a surprise.* He includes an address downtown and she parks in front of a storefront her father owned years before. It was a café for many years and, before that, a bakery. The large glass window is covered with brown paper so she can't see inside. Very ornate black and gold lettering on the window reads, *Townsend Cooking*

Academy. Victoria drops her handbag to the sidewalk and stands and stares until Callum opens the door.

"Surprise!" He smiles a very proud smile with his arms open wide, gesturing to his school.

"Are you serious?" she says.

"As a heart attack. Oh, that isn't as funny given George's condition. You get my meaning though." He waits for her to jump into his arms. He waits for smiles and gushing and declarations of love. He waits, but all he gets is her staring dumbfounded at the lettering.

"What do you think?" he asks, growing impatient.

And she starts to cry. Not heart wrenching sobs. Not tears of joy. But tears of genuine sadness.

"I don't understand," he says. "I thought you might be happy."

She touches his check and then kisses his lips. "I am Callum. I am so happy you are making a life for yourself."

"That isn't my meaning at all," he protests. "I want to make a life with you."

She kisses his lips again, gets back in her car and drives off. It is all Callum can do not to put a hammer through that window. He goes back inside and decides to finish the paint. He can sleep when he's dead. The paint is dark brown, a stark contrast to the stainless steels counters, ovens and sinks, but it complements the exposed pipes in the ceiling and the ancient woodwork and wrought iron trimmings. He loads paint into a roller and takes out all of his frustrations on the walls. Hours later, he is exhausted starving and still devastated when he hears a light tap on the glass.

Callum opens the door and Victoria steps in, not bothering to survey the space at all. She takes his face into her hands and kisses him. She can apologize without words. He locks the door and leans her into it, hard. His mouth, lips, devour her neck. His hand holds her hair while he pulls at her clothes. Within moments, her skirt is around her waist, panties are on the floor and his pants are around his knees. He grips one of her knees to his waist and is about to bury himself inside of her. He is frantic and angry, and it is exactly what he needs, but it feels wrong... too rough. He won't let her be an object, something he uses to blow off steam. He drops her knee and walks away from her, abruptly.

"Callum, come back here, what are you doing?" she asks in genuine frustration.

He shakes his head. "No, it's too much. It's too fast. It isn't who I want to be with you."

"Callum get back here right now and finish what you started," she insists.

He hesitates, but complies after adjusting the level of his own sexual intensity dramatically. He slows his pace and tends to her with the care she deserves. She comes, but not loudly, before he comes too. He catches himself on the door and slows his breathing, before kicking off his pants, pulling off his tee shirt and walking naked to the cooler to get two bottles of water.

He hands one to Victoria, sits on the dark wood steps that lead to the second floor and drinks his water down. Victoria reassembles her skirt and sits cross-legged on the floor, leaning against the door, finally surveying Callum's cooking school.

"Nice place you've got here," she comments too lightly.

"What the hell Victoria," he says. You can't fuck away this level of anger. "Am I doing the wrong thing? I really did think you'd be genuinely pleased."

She shakes her head and frowns. "I don't know Callum. I don't know anything anymore."

"What do you mean? Did you prefer the thought of me as a temporary fixture? Fucking the nanny and all?" he asks with growing frustration.

"No. Of course not, but I feel like I'm just hanging on sometimes Callum. Seeing you do all this reminds me that I have done nothing about Marina. This is a huge step for you. For us."

"You don't want this, do you?" He is finally starting to understand.

"Callum, I can't do anything. I can't move forward in any way until I figure things out with Marina."

He leans his arms onto his knees. "You need to tell her Victoria. She needs to know. He needs to know too. He seems very different now. Maybe it can work out."

"I don't want him in my life Callum. I don't want him anywhere near my daughter."

Callum debates for the one hundredth time if he should tell her what he knows about Christopher. Would it help her to know he is in recovery? Would she let Marina be a part of his life then? His best friend is a gay, divorced romance writer. Would knowing that help? As much as he wants to tell her, he knows he will come across as standing shoulder to shoulder with her rapist. She'll never hear any of it.

"She needs to know," he says again.

Victoria is done talking so she gets up and walks the shop. She studies the appliances, word work, counter tops.

"This is something Callum." She is truly impressed.

"There is classroom space upstairs," he says. "The third floor is an apartment."

"Are you moving out?" she asks with the perfect amount of fear in her voice. Finally, he is pleased at her reaction.

"Not now, with George sick I'm not. But I can't live off you forever. Look at the shop across the street," he says changing the subject. "That is where you should start."

Christopher's wife owns *Augustine Arts*, the gallery that is Callum's new neighbor.

Callum dresses silently and covers the paint can. He sets the brushes and rollers to soak. Finally he switches off the lights and they step out onto the curb. Callum takes Victoria's hand and lays the keys to his building in her hand.

"My life literally rests in the palm of your hand," he says, always good at theatrics. He closes her palm around the keys, brushes his lip across her fingertips and walks off to his car.

The next day Mindy calls to coerce Victoria to join the middle school Spring Auction Committee. Reluctantly, Victoria agrees to visit a few local shops and pick up donations for the fundraiser. Of the shops that need to be visited, Victoria selects *Augustine Arts* because Callum is right. Christopher's wife is the place to start. Enough avoidance. She has to do something.

When Victoria walks into the gallery, a gentle bell announces her arrival, and the smell of vanilla tickles her nose. Local landscapes are well spaced for effect on stark white walls. Exquisite pottery and sculptures cast from recycled metals are displayed on tables around the small room. She is dressed in stylish, probably expensive, cream-colored slacks that flow around heeled black boots, and she greets Victoria with an easy smile. Her simple black tee shirt and blonde ponytail give an entirely different impression. Casual, down to earth, simplicity. Her face is clean of make-up except for a slight tint on her lips. A few freckles dance across her nose under warm green eyes.

"Good afternoon, thanks for coming in today?" She offers Victoria a hand and the easy gesture makes Victoria wonder if Grace already knows who she is, what happened, and that their daughters are sisters.

Victoria doesn't know why, but she has an urge to embrace this woman she has never met, like family. The urge is strong and a little bewildering. Instead she introduces herself, taking the offered hand.

"Hi there," Victoria clears her throat because the words are sticking. "I'm Victoria. I…"

"Of course, Victoria," Grace's smile never falters, "My, you are gorgeous and you have your Daddy's eyes."

Victoria smiles at the compliment, but the smile is a little forced.

"I heard you were coming back to town. I am so happy to meet you. Welcome back to Asheville," Grace speaks in a voice that is as inviting and welcoming as only a born and bred southern woman could manage, under challenging circumstances.

And then the unthinkable happens. Grace pulls Victoria into her arms. They are about the same height and Grace squeezes her top to bottom, hard. This isn't one of those polite hugs where shoulder meets shoulder. This is the hug of friends or family who have been reunited after many years apart. Victoria's eyes threaten to fill.

"I'm sorry, I guess I should tell you who I am." Grace smooths Victoria's jacket back around her waist and turns the sign on the door to *Closed*.

"Do you drink tea?" She asks, already moving toward the back room, holding a red curtain aside for Victoria. Grace fills a kettle at the sink. A small, mosaic-topped bistro table with two blue cushioned chairs rests against the back wall. Brown boxes are stacked against the side walls. Victoria follows her to the table and she doesn't even want to dart out the back door. She is mesmerized by this woman's simple, understated elegance and her manner that perfectly suits her name.

"My Daddy and your Daddy used to work together. Asheville is such a small world. Your Daddy works with my husband's Daddy. I think you might have gone to school together. Christopher Augustine?"

Victoria nods silently.

"Not long after you moved... west I think?"

Again Victoria nods.

"Not long after that, our Daddies were working for the same firm. They partnered on a few big projects. You know that new shopping center down by the mansion?"

Victoria nods her head robotically.

"They worked that one together." Grace sets out cups with spoons and sugar, and then a small blue plate with Madelines. Victoria can't resist Madelines.

"Oh," is Victoria's only contribution to the conversation.

"A million years ago, there was a conference in Disneyworld of all places. I met my husband at Cinderella's damn Castle. Have you ever heard anything more cliché? Anyway, all of our families went, there was an award for development in Asheville and all of our families were invited. The end. Too much me talking. Tell me about you."

Grace sets a steaming cup of tea in front of Victoria. Victoria bites the soft, orange scented cookie.

"How long have your been married?" Victoria asks.

"Going on twelve years. But that's not about you, that's me. Tell me about the great west. Where'd you live?"

"Utah."

"Oh lovely. More mountains." Grace says and then sips her tea expectantly, but Victoria has nothing else to say and she shifts in her seat wondering how she let herself get into this.

"Do you want to donate an item for the middle school spring auction?" Victoria asks.

"Of course. I have something picked out already. It's all boxed up behind the register. Are you here to pick it up?"

Victoria nods.

Grace sets her cup down. "I am so embarrassed. You were just popping in and I railroaded you into all this." She waves her hand at the tea and cookies. "I'm so sorry Victoria."

Victoria shakes her head. "No, no. This is nice. What's your husband like?" She asks a little abruptly because she'll never have another opportunity like this.

"Do you remember him at all?" Grace asks.

"Some."

"Then you know he is driven. Fiercely driven. I love him dearly, but he is driven to a fault. And he is sweet and kind and an amazing father. He loves his kids like no one else."

Victoria works hard to keep a neutral facial expression and not frown.

"Are you with anyone special?" Grace asks.

Victoria wonders if this is a polite way of redirecting the conversation away from her marriage. Or is she just asking if Victoria is married, gay, boyfriended, divorced, single, etc. Victoria has no idea how to explain Callum so she shrugs and then realizes the looks like a spoiled teenager.

"Sort of, in a way. It is a long, strange story. Can I get away with it's complicated?" she asks.

Grace smiles and shakes her head slowly. "Nope."

Victoria can't help but like her. "Okay then. I am sort of living with someone. Well really he is sort of living with me. But we aren't really dating, but we kind of are seeing each other. Of course we see each other. We live together. But you know, we are maybe seeing each other." Victoria sighs in frustration. "See? It's complicated."

Grace sips her tea and smiles at Victoria over her cup. "Not complicated at all. You are sleeping together, but you aren't fully committed. I get it. The living together is interesting though."

Victoria blushes and offers no more of an explanation.

"Is he cute?"

"He is fucking gorgeous. And British," slips out of her mouth before she can stop the words from flowing.

Grace smacks her hand on the table with a loud laugh. Tea cups sway for a quick second.

"I like you already Victoria."

In spite of every reservation, Victoria says, "I like you too Grace. " She can't believe she is talking to the wife of the man who raped her. "How old is your daughter?" Victoria asks.

"How'd you know I have a daughter?"

Victoria panics. Because I have been stalking you at school, on the internet and I might hire a lawyer and an investigator before this is through. Then Victoria remembers she is on the auction committee. "Just chatter at the meeting. I was assigned to visit your store."

"Of course. More power to you, braving those PTA mommas. Did you meet Mindy?" Grace rolls her eyes.

"Oh I've known Mindy since I was three years old. She'd been bossing me around most of my life. But I love her."

"Well, you go on ahead darling. I'm sure she has a big heart. But she is a little scary on the PTA. There are too many rules and not enough booze. Do you know she has a little gavel and a Lucite name plate she sets in front of herself at meetings? It is terrifying."

Victoria laughs because Grace has Mindy pegged. She has a big heart, but she is a little terrifying.

"Will ya'all come to dinner Saturday night?" Grace asks out of nowhere. "I'd love to get my eyes on the gorgeous Brit. And your daughter? What's her name? George, too of course."

As Grace goes on, Victoria rises sharply, pushing her chair back into the wall with a thud. "I'm sorry. My Dad's not well and we aren't able to get out much." She moves toward the red curtain. "Thanks for the tea." Without waiting for a response, Victoria darts out the door. She doesn't see Grace chasing after her, waving the package for the auction.

Victoria pulls into the driveway at the same time as Callum and Marina. Callum insisted on taking over the lease on George's Lexus when George stopped driving. Marina runs over and kisses Victoria's cheek and takes the stairs two at a time into the house. Victoria lingers with Callum in the driveway to tell him about meeting Grace.

"She is wonderful. I could be friends with her Callum. How is she married to that piece of garbage?" she asks.

Callum understands how she could be married to that piece of garbage, perfectly. He really isn't a piece of garbage, but Victoria isn't ready to hear it. "I don't understand it at all Victoria."

"She asked us to dinner. I really stuck my foot in it this time. Dinner!" Victoria punctuates her frustration by grabbing Callum's arm.

190

He doesn't know why, but he has an overwhelming urge to shut her up. To pull her close and explore her mouth with his tongue. He'd like to undress her here in the yard. He'd rather rip her clothes from her body and bury himself inside her than continue this conversation.

Two things are clear to Callum. Number one, he can't help keep Marina away from her sister and brother anymore. Number two, pretending he can behave like a normal, supportive, decent human being is getting harder and harder.

"No dinners, certainly," he says, keeping a smile. "Marina seems very happy here, doesn't she?"

"She stopped giving me that peck on the cheek after school years ago. She does seem happy here. I think a lot of it is you."

He tenses almost imperceptibly but not quite.

"Callum?" she asks, because she noticed. "Are you starting to feel pressured here?"

"Of course not Victoria. I am exactly where I want to be. I thought you could see that?" He speaks to the wind rushing through the treetops. It isn't pressure he feels, it is obligation. He feels obligated to help Marina find her way to her family. He takes a moment to decide. What if he can't have both? What if he can get Marina to her sister and brother, but he loses Victoria in the process? He decides he needs to think that through and make a choice. He's not sure he can have both.

"You have an exit strategy too. You have an apartment." He won't meet her eyes. "Callum, look at me."

And he does. He looks into her blue eyes, so full of hope and promise that he can be a different man. "I just want us all to be happy Victoria." But there is that leopard and spots things. And the scorpion and the frog thing. There is only one you. In this case there is only one Callum. He smooths his thumb along her lips. She has wonderful lips, full and red without tint. *Why won't you love me?* He wonders.

"I am just starting to realize that if you break up with me, you are breaking up with Marina, too. You poor man. You'd have to break up with two women who are coming to care for you and rely on you." Her tone has an edge to it. She is mocking him.

That isn't what he wants. "And I care for and rely on you both. More than you can imagine. Stop talking about break-ups you lunatic. Are we breaking up? No we are not. One of these days you'll ask me about my school and you will see how serious I am." When he brings his mouth close to hers, she parts her lips and invites his tongue. It affects him more than a kiss should. Sometimes he feels like an adolescent with her. His pants tighten at just a kiss.

"I will Callum. I promise. Soon," she says and kisses him again. "Are you angry with me?"

"No," he lies. Lying comes back too easily. "I understand things are complicated. I do. I'm just a bit mopey. I need to go downtown for a bit. I'll be back in an hour." He kisses her nose and gets into the car. He watches as she walks up the stairs and into the house, letting his pants settle back into place. He loves her, but he is growing impatient with her. He is growing impatient for Marina to have her siblings. If he isn't careful, he is going to make Victoria hate him.

Callum knows that Christopher takes Jessie to dance class on Tuesday afternoons and he knows where. He also knows they often stop in for dinner at *Early Girl Eatery*. Callum drives the city streets and parks nearby. He times it well and within two minutes Christopher and Jessie are walking down the street in his direction.

"Callum, hey man. What's up?" Christopher slaps his back.

"Well fancy meeting you here young miss. Hello Jessie." Callum rumples the hair. Her smile is all too reminiscent of Marina's. It eats a hole right through Callum. He can't let this go on. *Victoria will never see reason.* Keeping these children apart is criminal.

"How was dance class?" Callum asks.

"Good." These girls are all about one word answers.

"Jessie have you met Marina? She is a year ahead of you," Callum asks even though he hates himself for it.

"I think so. We don't have any classes together though," she answers. "Is she your daughter?"

"She is the daughter of my lady friend." Callum heard the expression on TV and he liked it.

"Lady friend? I didn't even know you had a lady friend." Christopher over accentuates lady friend. "What's with the secrets?"

"Sorry, I thought we were men. I'll share more if it pleases you." Callum over accentuates share.

"Where are you headed?" Christopher asks.

"I'm picking up a little something for my Mum. Some birthday trinket to send back to England," Callum lies well.

"You want to grab a bite with us? It's just the two of us tonight. Grace has Jack at a soccer party. Divide and conquer."

"No no, you go ahead. I have something in the oven at home. Thanks though." Callum backs up a few steps with no intention of leaving. Christopher holds the door open.

"At least sit and have a beer," Christopher demands with an easy smile and Callum agrees, walking through the open door.

Christopher and Jessie order breakfast for dinners, apparently a favorite of Jessie's. Pancakes of course. They chat about school, working out and a contract Christopher is trying to win. Jessie mostly texts and plays games on her phone. *Typical.* After a few minutes, Callum downs his dark lager and pulls his wallet from his pocket.

"No, I got it," Christopher protests.

Callum leaves the wallet behind his draft glass and stands to go. "Thank you. I'll see you later in the week. I won't make the gym for a few days. Lots going on, as they say."

Driving home, Callum is sure what he did is unforgivable. He makes calls to furnish the apartment. Staying close by for George is essential, but if Victoria cuts him out, he has a place to go.

Callum ladles chicken and dumplings into a large white tureen edged in ivy. He arranges a platter of roast broccoli. Marina love roasted vegetables. Callum's pulse becomes erratic with nerves. He waits, but not for long, and then there is a knock at the door. Marina jumps to answer the door with Victoria close at her heels. Callum keeps his place at the kitchen counter facing out the window at the beautiful mountains surrounding the city.

He has come to love Asheville. He could have made this his home. He tries to remember if his suitcase is in the closet or if he stored it in the basement. He will miss them, but Marina needs this more than she needs him. He knows it in his heart. You can't change the course of someone's life without sacrifice.

With that thought, he decides he'll head to Osprey Island and spend more time with Anna and John. He likes spending time there. Maybe he could lease the space here and set something up there. The beach is as good a place as any to recover from a broken heart. Callum sees George sitting alone at the table. He almost feels the worst about George. He feels bad about Marina and Victoria, but he made them no promises. He gave his word to George. *Why won't she love me?*

"Look out the window first, don't just open the door to anyone," Victoria instructs. Every moment is a teaching moment when you are a mother.

"It's a man and a girl. She goes to my school." Marina opens the door wide. The night air is warm.

And there he is. He stands with hands in his pockets leaning against the railing. He appears easy, relaxed. His daughter stands at his side. Victoria's memories hit her like the falling snow of an avalanche.

She danced to be polite, but her heart wasn't in it. Her lilac dress was itchy and her shoes hurt. Her mother would have helped her to choose better. Christopher and his buddies were drinking from a flask and drinking a lot. She'd probably have to call her Dad to pick her up before the night was done. Damn him for making her come. But Christopher's Daddy was her Daddy's boss and his date fell through at the last minute. There wasn't a real choice in the matter. An orchestra played loudly and she was getting a headache. She excused herself to visit the ladies' room.

"What's wrong? You don't look like you are having much fun?" His words were starting to slur and he grabbed her arm roughly. "What's wrong?" He repeated for no reason.

"Nothing Christopher. I'm just a little under the weather. I need some air." She pulled loose from his grip and moved toward the gardens outside. She lifted a link fence intended to keep her from the gardens and went through anyway. When her feet hit the grass, she took off her shoes and enjoyed the freedom of wiggling toes in the lush grass. She walked by the rose bushes and touched a new, pink bud. She thought how lovely it was and wondered at the short life span of roses. As soon as they open, they are dying.

She didn't even hear him come up behind her. In one move, he swept her legs out from under her and pinned her to the ground with the full weight of his body. He was a wrestler and he knew how to restrain her with minimal effort. She was completely over powered but she fought for traction with her feet, her hands. Everything. Her brain struggled to accept her circumstance. His hand was over her mouth so she couldn't scream.

"I'll make you feel better. You just need a little loving. You miss your Momma. Let me help you." As he spoke, he pulled her dress around her waist and pushed her underwear down with his foot. She screamed and screamed into his hand as he kissed her neck.

"That's better, right?" he insisted.

When he forced himself into her, she stopped screaming. She stared at the roses and suddenly understood.

She stays standing, but the nausea hits her hard. She won't stay standing for long. She takes her eyes off the face of her rapist and studies his daughter.

"Oh," he says. "Sorry. Come on Jessie, we have the wrong house."

"No Dad, this is Marina." Jessie points to her sister. "Callum lives here."

"Victoria?" Christopher asks.

She nods. She is nowhere near accessing words.

"Does Callum live here? With you?" he asks, looking confused by this information.

Again she nods. Marina steps outside to chat with Jessie. Victoria wants to stop her, but she can't.

"I don't understand. I thought you moved west years ago. Callum lives here?" He asks again since he is getting no answers.

He hands her Callum's wallet. "Callum left this at Early Girl. I found his gym card inside with this address. I thought maybe your Dad had sold the place or something."

Victoria ignores him and watches Marina and Jessie sitting in the porch swing both looking at Jessie's phone, watching a video and laughing. The sound of a little boy comes from the phone, "I like turtles," he says over and over again. Victoria studies their faces. Their coloring is different, but the shape of their eyes is similar. Their chins are identical.

She finally finds her voice. "Come on Marina. Say goodbye to your friend." *Sister.*

"Callum and you are together?" He asks, still understanding nothing.

Marina reluctantly slides from the swing and waves goodbye with one hand held low.

"Victoria, I..." He starts to talk, but the door closes in his face.

Marina runs into the kitchen to reclaim her seat at the table, but Victoria freezes at the door, bracing herself with a hand on the heavy wood. *What did he do?*

"What did you do?" She says to the door in a low voice. "What did you do?" She says, louder the second time. "Callum, what did you do?" The third is loud enough to hear next door. She turns just as her father falls from his seat onto the floor.

Dammit George, you are such a drama queen, Callum thinks when he catches George's eye on his way down.

"Oh my God, Daddy," Victoria cries, runs to his side and grabs his wrist to take a pulse. "Callum call 911. No, we can get him to the hospital quicker. Pull the car up to the steps."

Callum pauses before following Victoria's instructions and glances at George just as his eyelids flutter.

"I'm okay, I was just a little lightheaded. Everything is okay," he lies.

Marina holds George's ankle looking afraid but bewildered.

"George?" she asks.

"Marina, I am perfectly fine. I might even be a little hungry. Just help me back up into my chair." He struggles to get his hands under him.

"No Daddy. Hold still. We have to get you to the hospital." Victoria protests, all words of Christopher forgotten. *Damn, George is unbelievable.*

"They can't help me a lick, Victoria. This is called dying. But I'd like to go with a full belly and that chicken smells good so please just help me up." George demands.

They get him into the chair and serve him a bowl piled high with chicken and dumplings.

George smiles at his frightened daughter and takes a big bite of chicken. He makes a face of very great satisfaction and then tastes a dumpling. "Callum. You did it," he says chewing thoughtfully.

"I did what?" Callum thinks, wondering if George is going to out him right here and now for bringing Christopher to their front porch.

"Chicken and dumplings, just like my momma made." George leans over and kisses Callum's cheek.

"Really?" Callum asks.

"Absolutely," George answers smacking his lips.

Callum decides to play along. "I got it? It's the thyme. It was so simple all along. Just a bit of thyme." Callum has been adding thyme all along. George is so full of shit.

"That's it Callum! It is the thyme," George agrees.

Marina cheers. "How many was that Callum?"

"I've lost count. Fifteen? Twenty?"

Victoria remains silent, looking conflicted over George's quick turnaround. They finish dinner with an apple pie Marina baked. George eats every bite, making easy conversation, and goes back for a second piece. When he is done, Marina joins him in front of the TV for one of their Discovery channel fishing shows or mining shows or something with little people. Callum isn't sure. Callum swirls a knife into the dirty pie plate, creating van Gogh's Starry Night sky out of pie remnants, in his imagination at least.

Victoria sips her wine and watches him. She says nothing and her mouth forms a thin line of anger. Those beautiful lips are absent from this conversation.

Finally, he tries to explain. "I know what he did to you Victoria. I do. I started going to the gym with the men from school because I wanted to see what kind of man Christopher was. I wanted to kill Christopher every day. I would imagine the feeling of his throat in my hand, squeezing the life out of him." He regrets the strangling analogy immediately given their experience at The Orange Peel with the woman in Asheville. He continues anyway. "But I didn't. I owed it to you and Marina to try to learn more about him. We spent time together. He and Randy and I. Randy is a writer. He's gay and his wife left him with his kid and Christopher is a good friend to him and he's a good father, too. He was not what I expected at all. Christopher was an alcoholic. Is an alcoholic? Whatever. He's in recovery now. He's been sober for thirteen years. I know this is hard to hear Victoria, but he is a good guy. Maybe he got some therapy. Maybe he is medicated, I have no fucking idea, but he has changed." Callum speaks to his apple pie Starry Night because he can't face Victoria.

After a moment and then two, Victoria speaks slowly in a low voice that barely contains her rage. "Are you that stupid Callum? Are you truly that fucking stupid?"

She repeats herself and he knows she is just trying to hurt him.

He doesn't bother answering, just swirls his knife, creating a beautiful night sky, only he can see.

"You need to go Callum. Now. We are through." She says it low and quiet, but clear and sure. He can see she is trying hard to restrain her volume.

"No." He says simply.

"No?" she asks like she is talking to a poorly behaved three year old. "Did you just say no to me?"

"I'm not leaving. I made a promise to George and I won't break it." Callum almost smiles at the thought of George's theatrics, but now is not a time for smiling.

"You have Daddy issues Callum. That is on you, don't put it on us. I can take care of my own father. I'm sorry your father died, but I don't really give a flying fuck right now. Get the hell out."

She might be right, Daddy issues are a possibility, but he loves her. He knows he is impulsive and immature and vain, but he fucking loves her. He isn't going to Osprey Island. He isn't moving downtown. He is staying right here and fighting for her.

He takes her hand and looks into her eyes. Amazingly, she lets him, probably more out of shock than conciliation. "I did say no. What I did may have been wrong, but I did it for all the right reasons and I think you will come to see that one day. Look Victoria, I may have Daddy issues, but you have pretty severe commitment issues. I'll fight for you Victoria. I'm not going to England to face my ex. I'm not going to have a reunion with Jeremy. That part of my life is over. My life is here now with you and Marina and your father. You all are my life now. Love me or don't. I'm here to stay."

He gets up to join the others by the TV. She can work through her anger on the dishes.

After the house is quiet, Victoria tiptoes across the hall to her childhood bedroom for the first time since her arrival back in Asheville. She ignores the sliver of light under Callum's door. With her hand on the door knob she decides to make this quick. Just get in, get what she needs and get out. No drama. No laying across the bed soaking her pillow with tears. She doesn't have time for that nonsense.

The checkered lilac quilt immediately takes her back to lying on the bed with her Momma reading her goodnight stories, even years after she could read on her own. She closes her eyes to remember the smell of her mother's red hair and the feel of her smooth check lying close to Victoria's own. Her eyes grow wet despite her intentions. She almost changes her mind about this and takes a few steps, backing up to close the door. But she doesn't. She walks across the room and slides the closet open, reaching up high on the top shelf in the back for a metal lockbox. Without a look back, she closes the door behind her silently.

The floor is cold under her feet when she taps on Callum's door quietly. He doesn't answer with words, just opens the door enough to see what she wants. The fire cracks behind him. His beard has filled in and he keeps it trimmed neat. He has been working out and looks beautiful and strong. For a moment, she ignores his commitment to her father and daughter. This is just about the two of them. His eyes hold her gaze waiting silently for her to speak. All he wants is her love. Of course he has it, but she can't rely on it. This is a man she could spend her life with, but how long will that commitment last for Callum?

"Talk?" she asks.

"Are you throwing me out again?" he asks back.

"We'll see."

"Fair enough," He opens the door wide and she sits on the bed with legs crossed under her. She holds the box in her lap with her hands flat on top. A burning log shifts in the fire spreading orange sparks.

"Why did Christopher come here, to my damn house? What did you do Callum?"

"I left my wallet on the table at Early Girl. I knew he'd come," he starts.

"You said you were going to work out with them, not be drinking beers and hanging out. Why didn't you tell me any of this?"

"You weren't ready to change your opinion of him. You weren't ready to hear any of it."

"Are you friends with him?" she asks.

He holds her gaze while considering her question until finally, he speaks reluctantly, but honestly. "I didn't mean to be, but I am."

"But why would you do that Callum? It is such a betrayal." Her eyes beg him to understand the simplicity of this equation.

"You can't keep Marina from those children. You can't. It is just that simple." His eyes beg her to understand the simplicity of this equation. "Those children are her brother and sister. What Christopher did to you was monstrous, unforgivable, but Marina mustn't be kept from them. Finding a sister at thirty…"

"Callum, Marina isn't you and that child…" Victoria struggles for her name.

"Jessie. Jessie is Marina's sister," Callum whispers.

"I don't care what her name is, but she isn't Anna. Marina is my daughter and, as her parent, I can do whatever the hell I want to."

He shakes his head at her words. "No Victoria. This is wrong."

"You are a moron, Callum."

His incredulity at her word choice is obvious and satisfying.

"Really?" he asks. "I let the *stupid* go downstairs, but did you really just call me a moron?"

She shrugs, maybe a little ashamed, but standing by her words.

"Out with you. Time for bed." He opens the door for her to go, but she leaves the box.

"Take your little sex toy box with you. I'm not in the mood to play with you tonight." He whispers as she passes.

"You are an absolute fucking moron," she says. "The combination is 1-2-3-4. I know, brilliant."

When she gets back to her room, she climbs into bed and cries the tears she saves for times when she is alone and sure no one is looking. She cries for her mother. She cries for her daughter and the sister and brother she will never know. She cries for her father who is dying. Lastly, she cries for Callum because she thought there was something there, but she was wrong.

Callum opens the cabinet and pours himself a bourbon, a tall one. He drinks it down quickly before taking the box to the desk and using the given combination. Inside is a lot of fabric. Callum holds it up and shakes it out. The dress smells musty and old. It has been balled up in the tiny box for a long time. The wrinkles seem permanent. Smooth, delicate lilac is wrapped around some type of netting. *Tulle perhaps?* The netting is covered in brown stains. It takes Callum a moment to realize it is blood. The back of the dress is streaked in green. *Grass stains?* This is the dress Victoria wore the night she was raped. The night Marina was conceived.

He has a quick thought about dresses and past presidential events and realizes the power in the tangible. Words are one thing, holding it in your hands is another thing entirely. Callum's first instinct is to toss it into the fire, but he doesn't.

Callum folds the dress in half at the waist and then in half again. He folds in the sides and rolls it with the expertise he would roll a roast or a strudel. He tucks the dress back into the lock box and sets it in his bottom desk drawer. Callum considers crossing the hall to Victoria, but he has no idea what to say to her. Maybe he is a moron after all.

The next morning, Callum finds George at the dining room table. Marina and Victoria are nowhere in sight.

"Morning Callum. How'd you sleep?" George asks, chipper for a dying man who was lying on the floor last night.

"Shitty, thanks to you. After your antics I was up half the night."

"Antics? What antics?"

"George you are a lot of things, but you are no actor." Callum pours himself a coffee, refills George's cup and joins George at the table.

"I take offense at that statement. I had the lead in my school play in third grade. I was a hell of an Oliver. *Please sir, can I have some more.* Did Victoria know?"

Callum lays the back of his hand over his forehead and uses a terrible, female, southern accent. "That you were faking a spell? No, she had no idea."

They sip their coffee in silence. George shakes the paper to catch the fold and begins reading an article. Sparrows fight for their place on the feeder, outside the window.

"What the fuck, George?" Callum asks after a minute.

George lays the paper down with a pat. "I thought it was obvious."

"Nothing is obvious to me."

"I know you have been spending time with Christopher. I know you are trying to decide if he is fit to be a part of Marina's life. I know you aren't happy with Marina being kept from her brother and sister."

"And how in the fuck do you know all of this?" Callum asks feeling a little stunned.

"You are a lot of things Callum, but good at hiding how you feel, isn't one of them." George smirks over his steaming coffee cup.

"Really? I thought deception was one of my better talents." Callum is genuinely surprised.

"If it was, you lost it. Maybe you were a better liar in England. The United States is bringing out the shred of integrity you had hiding in there." George taps an index finger at Callum's heart. Callum suddenly misses his father. *I do have Daddy issues* he thinks a little disgusted at himself.

"Callum, I will be gone inside a few months. Are you going to be here when I go?"

"Bullshit George. You look good. I don't think that timeline is accurate."

George looks out at the sparrows on the feeder. "I'm not staying around for the bad parts Callum. No one is feeding me or changing my diapers. I don't want tubes or respirators or hospital food. I'll go when I am good and ready. I have what I need, when the time is right."

Callum sets down his mug hard. He hasn't thought about pulling the plug on his Dad in a long time, but he does remember that day.

"My Dad had an aneurysm. His brain basically exploded when I was at boarding school. He was in a coma for a month, before my mother had to make the horrid decision to let him die. Tubes and respirators and all of that shit. I was thirteen."

Callum doesn't tell George how agonizing that decision was. In the end, his mother, mother of the year, decided the boys might blame her for killing their father. She forced them to turn off the machines together. A young hospital nurse tried to talk her out of it, but she was adamant and she never lost an argument.

"So you understand what I'm going to do?"

Callum nods "I do."

"Callum you owe me nothing. If you need to go, go now. But if you are staying, you need to make things right with Victoria. She needs to decide one way or the other what to do about all of this. Marina is too smart to live in this town and not figure things out."

"Where is Victoria, by the way?"

"She picked up a shift at the hospital. They were short-handed. Be warned, I think Marina has plans for you today."

"Okay," Callum says. "But wait. George, why didn't you say anything? Did I do the wrong thing? She is furious at me."

George sips his coffee, thoughtfully. "I have been doing the same thing for years."

Callum is shocked. "Tell me George."

"I almost killed him for what he did to my daughter. He put his hands on my baby, Callum. That next day, I went over there with a handgun. I sat in the car for three hours with a bottle and a gun, trying to talk myself out of it. In the end, I decided I had to protect Victoria. Revenge would have been right. I don't doubt for a single second that killing him would have been within my rights as a father. With her mother dead though it wouldn't have made things better for Victoria. She'd have no one. I didn't know how to help her, Callum, so I sent her away... to Europe. She thought I was hiding her, ashamed, but I was trying to protect her. When she came back, she told me she was pregnant. I thought we could still get her back to a normal life if she got rid of the..."

George shakes his head and stares off at visions of memories Callum can't see. "I'm so ashamed of how I handled it. I was wrong in every way a father can be wrong. And I knew this day would come eventually. I tried to be ready for it. For Victoria and Marina. I'm still not sure..."

Callum nods to the stairway to let George know Marina is headed their way. She bounds into the kitchen.

"What's up buttercup," George asks rumpling her bedhead.

Marina smiles at her grandfather. "Did you tell him?"

Callum can see the love between them.

"Nope," George says. "I left that to you."

"What's on your mind kid?" Callum asks.

"Since Mom is working and it is Saturday and the weather is good, I had a plan for the day. But, it is a surprise. And it is about an hour away. And then we have to hike about a mile or so."

"I'm in," Callum says, happy for a day on the mountain. "Breakfast at *Tupelo Honey?*"

Marina claps her hands. *Tupelo Honey Café* has the best bacon in town.

"George, are you up for some breakfast?" Callum asks.

"No thanks, just you two today. I have some papers to get organized. There is a lot to do around here for an old man."

"Okay then. Hop to it Marina. Out the door in thirty. I'm hungry."

Marina runs the stairs to dress for their adventure.

"I'm staying George," Callum says watching after Marina. "I'll be here for them until the end."

Two hours later, bellies full of biscuits, gravy, bacon and eggs, Marina navigates and guides Callum through the mountains, neighborhoods and finally into Dupont State Forest. The mountains hold uncountable shades of green as they approach the summer months. They park in a long lot and Callum reads the sign.

"Triple Falls?" he asks.

She nods, sure he won't know why it is special.

"Is this where they filmed Katniss finding Peeta in the mud in the first *Hunger Games* movie?"

Marina smiles wide and nods her head.

"This is awesome!"

"How did you know?" she asks.

"I can read on occasion," he says. "When I learned they filmed outside of Asheville, I was intrigued," he says.

Marina pulls her backpack from the car. She has a few water bottles, a camera, the book, and something else she wants to talk to Callum about.

"You ready? Want me to carry that?" he asks.

She shakes her head, slides the straps onto her shoulders and their shoes crunch through the graveled lot into the woods. There are few hikers for a Saturday. The trail is well marked and easy to follow. Birdsong fills the air and the sun filters through tall trees. After twenty minutes, they descend downward to the falls, walking the dozen flights of stairs that guide them onto the rocks.

Falling water drapes the enormous stones surrounding them. They are able to walk out into the middle of the falls onto massive dry, flat stones. Water falls on three sides. They speak in loud voices to be heard above the pounding water. They take a few pictures including a selfie to send to Anna. Marina points out where Katniss found Peeta and they watch the video clip on her phone. Finally, they sit on a dry ledge and watch the beauty around them.

Marina tries to decide how to start the conversation she wants to have with Callum. She wants to have it here, just the two of them, with her mother and grandfather far away. After dinner last night, she asked her mom if she could have Jessie over and she said no.

"Callum can we talk?" Marina asks, facing the man who somehow has become an important part of her life.

"Oh no. Sounds serious. Am I in trouble?" he jokes.

"No, but it is serious. I think it is anyway." She rolls her phone end over end in her hand, delaying the next sentence.

"Come on. Out with it." He says with a slight shake to his voice.

She knows he knows everything she wants to know. She also knows he doesn't want her to know anything her mother doesn't want her to know. But she needs to know. And she won't get an answer from her mother. She just knows she won't.

"George was faking last night. I can't believe Mom didn't know."

Callum laughs out loud, sounding relieved. "Your grandfather is quite something," Callum admits.

Well at least Callum isn't lying about that too. "He didn't want Mom mad at you," she says and Callum stops laughing.

"Oh Marina, just us men sticking together. We have done a lot of male bonding, George and I. He's just looking out for the other guy in the house, is all." He stands up like it is time to go. Marina keeps her seat on the hard stone.

"Callum. It's all about me, isn't it?" She pulls his sleeve to guide him back to the seat next to her. "Isn't it?" she repeats.

"Marina this is a conversation you should be having with your mother. I'd like to help, but I'm a nobody in this. You mom will talk to you," he says with a surety that she knows he does not feel.

"She lied to me already, Callum. Everything she told me in Memphis was a lie. I know it was. I believed her until we got here Callum, but it just isn't true. When Jessie came over last night, I knew for sure. I really like her and I asked Mom if she can some over. You know what she said Callum?"

Callum's face remains impassive. He even manages a small smile. "What did she say?"

"She said, no."

Callum keeps the smile plastered to his face. "Marina she has a new job, her Dad is sick, she has a lot going on." He almost pleads for Marina to believe him.

"Bullshit Callum. She said Jessie is younger than me and I shouldn't hang out with seventh graders. That is bullshit, right?"

Marina holds onto his arm like he is her only means to safety after falling into the center of the ocean, begging him to be honest with her. She unzips the backpack and takes out a white piece of paper. She unfolds it slowly and hands the paper to Callum. It is a photo, just a headshot, of two smiling girls, side by side on the front porch. He stares silently, holding the paper in one hand.

"She wouldn't even talk to Jessie's Dad last night. She was really weird." Her voice falters under the weight of her words. Callum just shakes his head, but he doesn't deny it. "And then George faking all that?"

Callum watches the water fall and avoids her stare.

"Callum, please."

He shakes his head slowly. "I can't. It has to be your mom," he says.

"She'll lie." Marina knows she will.

"Maybe you should let her," Callum says, finally meeting her eyes. "If your mother is so sure she needs to lie to you, maybe you should trust her that the lie is best for you."

"Lying is never a solution. That is what she says all the time. Lying is never a solution. Stand up and deal with your life. Lying is never a solution." She repeats for the third time.

Callum does nothing more than watch the water mercilessly beating the falls.

"You know everything don't you, Callum?" she asks.

"I don't know which way is up sometimes, darling," he says.

"Will you tell me just one thing? Answer yes or no and then I'll leave it alone. I promise I'll leave it alone. Just one question Callum?"

He takes a deep breath before answering. He smiles a charming smile at her. She nearly killed him just a few months ago, and somehow he has become one of the most important people in her life, in her heart. She wishes he was her father. She knows he feels the same way.

"One question, Callum?" she repeats and waits for his answer.

"No," he says finally, then grabs her backpack and walks back to the stairs to climb out of this place.

She stares at his back as he takes the steps two at a time. She waits a minute and considers not following. She can run into the woods and lose herself for as long as she wants. Let him chase her and call her name, worrying all damn day. Let him tell her mom that he lost her only daughter in the wilderness. She knows she'll never learn what she needs if she runs away, not yet anyway. Finally she gets off the stone and meets him at the top of the stairs.

He is sitting on a bench waiting for her. His elbows are on his knees and he rests his forehead in his hands.

"Ask it Marina," he says finally, not moving.

"Is Jessie my sister?" She holds her breath and waits for the answer even though she knows it already.

He nods the slightest nod and her whole world changes.

They ride back in near silence. The conversation is over. Marina, true to her word, asks no more questions. *My god she is unbelievable.* Callum would be asking a thousand and one questions if he was in her shoes. When he stops in the driveway, they sit a moment staring at the house. Victoria isn't home yet.

"Thanks," Marina says, before heading inside.

Callum opens the window and calls out to her. "Marina, I'm going to run an errand or two. I'll pick something up and we can cook a special dinner tonight. I'll be back in a bit. Alright?" She looks at him like she knows he is lying. She nods anyway, waves and goes into the house.

The drive to Christopher's house is short. Within ten minutes, Callum is walking Christopher's front steps. Before he can knock, a lovely woman, the same woman Victoria described, opens the door with a surprised, "Oh. Hi. Can I help you?" She has an easy smile and she reminds Callum a little of Victoria.

"I'm Callum. Is Christopher at home?"

She gives him the once over. "He is. Can I ask, are you from England?"

"I am. London."

"You may know a friend of mine. Victoria? She mentioned she had a friend from England and she described you to a tee." Suddenly the door opens wider and Jessie and her little brother face Callum. Jessie greets Callum by name.

"You two know each other?" Grace asks Jessie.

"Yeah, he and Daddy are friends. His daughter goes to my school."

Callum doesn't clarify his relationship with Marina and he clears his throat to speed things along since he doesn't want to talk to Grace anymore. He pulls his eyebrows together to give his face a little more seriousness and it only makes him more intriguing to look at.

"Christopher?" he asks when she doesn't move.

"Sure, sorry. We are just heading out. He's around back. You want me to call him to the door or you can just go on around?"

He opts to go around. Christopher rides on the mower, driving in straight lines across the lawn. The lawn is well manicured and heavily landscaped. At least ten different flowering plants Callum can't name are in bloom without a weed in sight. Christopher wears a tee shirt and shorts, headphones atop his head. He looks like the perfect suburban dad on a Saturday afternoon. His secrets are safe. Callum doesn't call for him even when Grace's car is clear of the house.

Now that Callum is here, he isn't even sure why he came. He just knows he needs to do something. He needs to do something for Marina and Victoria. *Something. Anything.* Callum walks quickly across the yard with long strides and great purpose. When Christopher sees him, he waves, happy to see his friend. He turns off the mower and takes off his headphones. Callum walks up behind Christopher, wraps his arms around Christopher's neck and pulls him over the back of the seat, slamming him onto the ground, hard.

"What the fuck?" Christopher tries to yell with the wind knocked out of his lungs.

Callum outweighs Christopher by at least fifty pounds and he has maybe four inches on him. He also has the element of shock working for him and years of wrestling experience. Christopher wrestled too so Callum goes for his dick, pinning Christopher down, forcing his legs apart. Callum presses the full force of his weight between Christopher's legs by pushing his hip into Christopher's dick as hard as he can. The potential and imminent pain freezes Christopher and Callum holds his hands together above his head. Christopher doesn't resist. He is Callum's bitch.

"Feels good, doesn't it?" Callum whispers into Christopher's ear. "You know you want it."

Callum knows he has Christopher's full attention so he puts his hand up Christopher's shirt, groping him like he would a woman, pinching his nipples hard for good measure.

"Oh baby you feel so good," Callum whispers into Christopher's neck. Callum takes his hand out of Christopher's shirt and uses it to slide down Christopher's shorts, cupping his ass, baring his pubes. Christopher is panting, red in the face. His eyes are wet. Callum keeps his hip in place tight.

"What the fuck?" Christopher asks again.

"You want to scream. Go ahead. Call the neighbors right over. I just might ass fuck you before I'm done. I'm liking this a lot." Callum forces his hip deeper into Christopher's dick. He gasps in pain and Callum starts thrusting and moving his hips in circles, dry humping Christopher's groin.

"Mmm, nice. I actually think I could come like this. Fascinating and good to know in case I ever go to prison. I'll probably end up in prison eventually."

"Callum?" Christopher asks. "Why?"

"Victoria, that's why." Callum says and then notices her watching everything from the gate. "I'll tell you what Christopher. I won't come on you, if we can have five minutes of honest conversation. If you bullshit me I will consider raping you. I've never considered myself gay, but these lines can blur, can't they. And rape isn't about sex, it is really just about power. I'm not above it."

"Anything Callum, just get the fuck off me," Christopher begs.

Callum stands up and Christopher pulls his shorts up. Christopher looks weak and scared and Callum thinks that it must be horrible to be a woman. The ease with which Callum can overpower another individual is a little frightening. Being vulnerable to that all the time must be terrifying. Callum offers his hand. Christopher hesitates, takes it and Callum pulls him to his feet on unsteady legs. As soon as they are both upright, Christopher sees Victoria standing at the gate watching their every move.

"Callum?" she asks, looking Christopher over. His face is splotched with red and covered in shame.

"Be quiet Victoria," he says, taking her hand and standing between the two of them. "I didn't mean for you to see that. Don't even talk to him."

"What are you doing here Callum?" she asks bewildered.

"I'm not sure what I'm doing here. I'm trying not to kill him," Callum admits.

Victoria says nothing and seems to be processing an awful lot of information.

"Do you have anything to drink Christopher?" Callum talks like he wasn't just grinding his buddy. "I'm suddenly quite thirsty."

Christopher is silent and stares at Victoria then at Callum. The light of understanding slowly comes into his eyes.

"You two are together?" he asks.

"We are together," Callum says, even though he isn't entirely sure Victoria would agree. She doesn't disagree which is a good sign. "I think you owe Victoria some honesty. If you lie, I'll rape you right here for Victoria to watch. I think she'd be alright with it, wouldn't you Vic?" He has never called her Vic before, but it feels right.

Victoria shrugs, wordless and noncommittal.

"Can we at least be civilized? I'll help myself to three beers from your fridge. Let's sit at the table." Callum walks into the house, takes three beers and shuffles through the kitchen drawers to find an opener. He finds it on the first try. Callum understands kitchens. When he goes back outside, Victoria and Christopher are sitting at a black wrought iron table. Obviously no words have passed between them. Callum hands each a beer and draws long on his own. Being an asshole is hard work. He is exhausted and outrageously horny.

"Speak," Callum says.

"What do you want me to say?" Christopher asks.

"Hold on. Victoria, what are you doing here?" Callum asks. He was so wrapped up in the heat of the moment, he almost forgot that she didn't come with him.

She shakes her head and doesn't answer.

"Are you not sure why you are here?" Callum asks.

"I needed to do something," she says finally. "Anything. It is time. You were right, at least about that."

"Does this mean you have had a change of heart?" Callum asks with his eyes on Victoria.

Victoria shrugs again with her eyes on Christopher.

"Christopher. I think you should just talk. Maybe start with the last time you saw Victoria."

Christopher leans back in his chair and closes his eyes. He takes a few moments, but eventually he speaks slowly and quietly.

"That night. I was too rough with you Victoria. I have regretted that for a long time."

"Too rough." she repeats. "You were too rough? I don't understand exactly what you mean by too rough."

Christopher shakes his head silently.

"You're going to need to say it Christopher," Callum demands. "Honesty please."

"Victoria, I have a wife and kids. I am different now. I was drinking then but I haven't had a drink in over twelve years. That night with you seems like a million years ago," he pleads.

"It was fourteen years ago and it seems like yesterday to me," she says.

"This will ruin my kids," he pleads.

"What about your wife? What about Grace. How is she going to react when she finds out what she is married to?" Victoria seethes at him.

Christopher sets down his beer and speaks more to Callum than Victoria. "She and I have had tough times, but we are good now. Let us be good, please."

"Look at me Christopher. Say it or I will beat your head in with that shovel." Victoria nods to the garden where a shovel indeed stands tall and ready, half stuck into the dirt.

Christopher holds a hand over his mouth, keeping the words in. Finally he moves his hand away and sets the truth free. "I raped you Victoria. I wasn't rough with you, I raped you. And I have been sorry for it every day of my life."

Victoria stands up and walks across the yard to the gate. She looks back once and then goes through, carefully latching it behind her. Callum follows Victoria out, but she is already gone when he reaches the driveway.

Callum drives into the city. He knows where Victoria is headed. He parks illegally in front of Grace's shop and is glad to see it is closed. He leans against the bumper waiting and Victoria walks around the corner within minutes. She never parks illegally. She took the time to park in a garage down the street.

Victoria ignores Callum and pulls the handle of Grace's shop, ignoring the closed sign. The locked door shakes under her force. Callum simply walks up behind her and wraps his arms around her. She leans into him, letting herself fall into his embrace.

"I am a moron. You were one hundred percent right. I am an idiot as well. Everything you said was true." He whispers into her hair. "I need to tell you one more thing before I turn you around. You'll have one more chance to hate me today. If you can't love me, I'll have to bear it, but I will be honest with you." He doesn't wait for her to answer. "Marina asked me if Jessie is her sister. I did not deny it. I couldn't lie to her Victoria. I love her too." He can feel her shoulders go and the sobs comes out of her.

"It's over, isn't it Callum?" She cries, turning around and leaning into his chest. "It is all over."

He lets her cry and holds her hard. "No Victoria. It is all just beginning." And he is sure it is true.

They leave Victoria's car in the garage and drive back to the house in Callum's.

"I should call Marina," she says reaching into her handbag. "I have to figure out what to tell her, Callum. Where is my phone?" Victoria asks.

"Did you leave it in your car? You need it? Mine's here." Callum reaches into his pocket, but it isn't there. "I must have dropped it."

"When you were attacking Christopher?" She smiles but just at the corners of her mouth. "And thanks for that by the way." She unbuckles and slides closer to him on the seat. "I needed that."

"What will I tell her Callum," she asks. "If this was Anna? What would you do?"

He has given this a lot of thought. He has had months to figure out a way to incorporate Christopher and his family into their lives.

"Victoria, I know you don't want to believe this. But he is a changed man. In my heart I think you can have him in your life. In time you may come to trust him as I have. This is not me being an idiot or a moron."

"I'm sorry about all that, Callum."

He smirks but forgives her. "At the same time, I don't think Marina can know about the rape. It could destroy her. And if Marina can't know it, you inadvertently have to protect Christopher and his wife and his kids and lie. You have to leave it in the past, Victoria, and forge a new future."

And there it is. Callum has laid out the path forward and the path forward begins with sweeping her rape under the rug. Denying the rape. Letting the rape go. Why is she letting her rapist get away with it? Why does she let him get a big house and happy marriage, kids and soccer games and dance recitals and lawnmowers? *Why?* The answer is simple. *For Marina.*

"What on earth?" Callum pulls into the driveway and puts the car into park.

George and Christopher are standing on the porch speaking heatedly.

Callum runs to the stairs, "Christopher, what the hell are you doing here? George are you okay?" Callum demands, stepping between them.

"I'm fine, I'm fine. I have been trying to reach you both. Why aren't you answering?"

Christopher throws Callum his phone. "I think you left this at my house. When we were having that beer."

"Thanks so much. Sorry about that. I didn't mean to put you out." Callum says, noticing fourteen missed calls from George.

"Marina ran off," George says in a panic. "First, she tore apart Victoria's room."

"What?" Callum says looking up the stairs to see papers and photos strewn across the hallway.

"Jessie's gone too." Christopher adds. "Grace was supposed to pick her up after dance class, but they said she never showed up. Grace dropped her off and she never went in. I saw George calling over and over and I answered."

Victoria doesn't say a word. She just gets back into the car.

Callum follows her. "George, Victoria left her phone in her car downtown. We'll go back for it and see if Marina called."

When they get to Victoria's car, there are no calls from Marina. Victoria wipes her eyes with the back of her hand. "Where the hell is she, Callum?"

Callum answers quickly. He thinks he knows. "Did you ever see *The Parent Trap?*" he asks out of nowhere. "The two sisters who find each other at a camp and go stay in a cabin together, just the two of them.

She nods and says, "Call Christopher."

They arrive at the local camp within twenty minutes. It is closed and the gates are locked so they park outside and go in on foot. Fresh bike tracks line the mud.

"All of the local kids come here in the summer. First graders go for an overnighter. Scouts come here and older kids do longer stays. Victoria will do a week at the end of ninth grade. It is a rite of passage. Kids get

221

survival training, learn to hunt and most of us smoked our first cigarettes here." Victoria easily opens the chain link fence blocking their way onto a boarded footpath surrounding the cabins.

The bike tracks lead directly to a cabin and inside they find two backpacks, two sleeping bags, some canned food and water bottles against the wall. The girls are nowhere in sight.

Grace runs up the path looking frantic and breathless. "Are they here?"

"Looks like they aren't far off." Callum points to their supplies.

"Thank god." Grace sits down hard on the wooden floor. She crosses her legs and Victoria sits beside her.

Grace smiles, despite her stress. "We have a lot to talk about Victoria. We'll be alright though. Our girls will be fine. You know that, don't you?"

Grace looks hard into Victoria's eyes asking for assurances that she doesn't begin to understand. "I think so," is the best Victoria can offer. "Where's Christopher?" she asks.

"He's with Jack. I wanted to come alone. I think this is a mom thing, don't you? Let's get our girls and then talk, just you and me." Grace offers. "We have to talk so we can figure out how to work this through."

"Callum, too," Victoria counters. "He is part of this."

"What do you know, Grace, about the girls?" Callum asks.

Grace hands him an envelope. Inside are photos, stacked one after another. Baby pictures, school pictures, in front of a Christmas tree, a tiny Marina on skis, baby Marina dressed as a fat orange pumpkin then an M&M. Older Marina dressed as Harry Potter and finally the Marina he knows with a long braid in her hair and a quiver. Marina was Katniss Everdeen for Halloween just this past fall.

"I found these on Jessie's desk. They were kept in a lockbox in Christopher's office. She picked the lock. Christopher and I have always known about Marina."

Before further questions can be asked and answered, they hear the girls coming up the path singing a song about monsters by Eminem and Rhianna. Callum picks up the girls' meager possessions while Grace and Victoria walk the path to meet the girls. Callum feels a little guilty that he started all of this. He pulls out his phone and looks at a picture of Anna that he uses as her contact id. She is smiling with wild hair on the beach after Easter dinner. Looking at Anna, he is sure he did the right thing, no matter how this turns out.

Victoria tries to take her daughter into her arms, but Marina shrugs her off and walks to Callum. Victoria stands helpless with both arms limp at her sides. Jessie stays close to Marina, avoiding her mother. It is clear the planned conversation is not going to happen. The girls look furious.

Grace takes Jessie's hand and tries to lead her out of the camp. "Let's go," she says. "We can talk at home with your father."

"No," Jessie screams. "He is a liar. So are you. You are both liars."

"Why did you tell Jessie before we could talk it through with your mother," Callum asks Marina.

"I didn't tell her Callum. She told me," Marina says.

"Okay ladies, why don't we sit down and take a breath. Let's talk this through," he says and points to a wooden picnic table under a tree. "Come on, take a seat." Marina reluctantly sits down next to Callum. Jessie takes her big sister's lead and sits down too. Victoria stands. "Let's get a few things out in the open," he starts, but Victoria interrupts.

"Marina. I'm sorry this is the first you are hearing about this from me. I haven't been honest with you and I handled things badly. I let my own hurt and anger be more important than, well, more important than anything. Jessie's Dad and I dated when I was young. We broke up and then I found out I was pregnant. He was very gallant and wanted to take care of us, but it just didn't work out." Victoria falters and Grace steps in.

"Then he and I started dating pretty quickly," Grace adds.

"I wanted you all to myself and I left," Victoria says creating a fiction that she ran away as the jilted lover.

Marina stares at her and takes everything in. She looks like she has a thousand questions, but she doesn't ask one. She lets everything her mother says be true, just like Callum told her to.

"Will you forgive me, Marina?" Victoria nearly begs.

"I owe you an apology, Victoria. Everything happened so fast back then. I wasn't supportive of you at all. Will you forgive me?" Grace fills in details that aren't true. Victoria lets her.

Tears stream down Victoria's face and Grace embraces her. Victoria cries silently into Grace's shoulder. To the girls they are tears of forgiveness. Callum knows they are tears of defeat.

"Daddy, why?" Victoria asks him. Marina is asleep in her own bed. Her day as a runaway is over. Callum is cleaning the mess from Victoria's teenage room, ransacked by Marina as she searched for proof of her parentage.

George tells his daughter about the dark days after she left Asheville. How George thought he would kill Christopher. In three months, George lost his wife, his daughter and his future grandbaby. Christopher was responsible for two-thirds of that loss. George thought about telling Christopher's parents, but he wasn't a child. He was a man. He followed Christopher at night, stalked him during the day. He wanted to understand this man who destroyed his family and who would be the father of his grandchild. He learned that Christopher was a Jekyll and

Hyde. He had a sunny smile until the drinking started. George watched him get thrown out of bar after bar downtown. He was a common drunk. Not too long after Marina was born, Victoria started emailing and sending him photos.

"It was Rosalie who convinced me to help him," George says.

"I don't understand," Victoria asks, because she really does want to.

"He is a drunk, Victoria. Maybe something happened to him, I don't know and I don't really care either. I had two choices, to kill him or to help him be a better man in case you ever came back."

George tells the story of how he scraped Christopher up off the sidewalk one night and brought him home. The next morning, they had a pretty severe dialogue, to say the least. They talked about forced sex, pregnancy, destroyed lives and making changes. Christopher sobered up and got into AA. By then, Christopher was with Grace and things weren't going well.

"He agreed to stay away from you if I would keep tabs on Marina and share photos. He understood that he forfeited any rights he had to be a part of her life, but he still cared. He told Grace about Marina. In the early days, he and Grace had a lot of problems. She would have left him, but he turned things around when he sobered up. He's been dry ever since."

"Daddy, are you really dying?" Victoria asks hopefully. "Or was that another lie to get me here?"

"I wish it was darling. I wish it was." George pats her cheek like he did when she was a little girl.

"I wish I came back sooner. I wish we talked. I wish so many things were different," she says.

"You did everything right Victoria and I did everything wrong. I need you to know that. All the regret is mine. I should have come to Utah and pounded on your door. I should have been a better father to you and a grandfather to Marina. If your mother had been here, I would have known…"

She stops him with a finger to his lips. "I know Dad. Everything would have been different. I love you so much Daddy."

She falls into his arms and they cry together, just a little, for their lost years and mistakes.

"Will you forgive me?" he asks.

"I do. And you forgive me?"

"I won't even answer the question," he says shaking his head. "There is nothing for you to ever apologize for Victoria. Nothing. Understood?" She nods and kisses his cheek.

Victoria decides to help Callum clean up her room. When she is halfway up the stairs, there is a quiet knock at the door. Callum sticks his head around the corner. "Is that the door, this late?"

She turns on the outside light. Christopher is leaning against the railing, hands in pockets. "It's Christopher," she whispers to Callum.

He descends the steps quickly before she opens the door.

"Victoria," Christopher says.

She faces him wordlessly.

"Can we talk?" he asks.

She steps out onto the porch with Callum at her side. He is not letting her face this alone.

"Talk," Callum says.

Christopher stands to face Victoria and looks directly into her eyes. She doesn't flinch or step back. She holds her ground, holds his eyes with her own, and remembers how he forced himself into her, tearing her open.

226

"I raped you," he says. His eyes fill. "I raped you and I am so sorry. I don't mean it to be an excuse, but I was drinking heavily. Your Dad saved my life. I am damn lucky he didn't kill me because he could have. He certainly wanted to, but he wanted me to be better for you and for Marina. I am better, Victoria. I haven't had a drink in twelve years. I am a good husband and a good Dad. I am begging you for a chance."

For the first time she notices his chin. It is Marina's chin. This is Marina's father.

"For the sake of my daughter, Christopher, I forgive you," Victoria says and to show herself she means it, she offers him her hand. He take her hand in both of his own hands. She forces herself not to cringe at his touch. After a moment, she goes back to the door. "Will you all come for Sunday dinner? I think Marina would like to meet..." she stalls.

"Her brother?" Christopher says. "His name is Jack."

"Marina would like to meet Jack," Victoria repeats.

"We'd like that. Thank you Victoria," he says. "I am grateful for this chance."

"One last thing," Callum says. "It is just that. Victoria is giving you a chance, an opportunity to be everything a little girl could dream of. I want your word, as a gentleman. If you fall off the wagon. If you even slip up. You are gone. We are all letting this go forward under the assumption that the drinking turned you into a monster. Assuming that is the case, praying that is the case, you can never falter. Ever. Understood?" Callum offers his hand to shake on that agreement.

Christopher shakes his hand but has one more request. "Can you ask Randy and Jenna to join us? He is sort of family and I can't have secrets from him."

"Of course. And Christopher, the children should never know anything more than we had a bad break up. They don't ever need to know the rest," Victoria says before she goes into the house.

Ten

The Sunday dinner cook out turns into weekly dinners together as a family. Jessie spends the night most weekends at Marina's house. Grace tells Jessie that George is ill and Marina needs all of the time she can with him, so the girls stay only at Victoria's house. Grace understands Victoria's reluctance. When Grace started dating Christopher he was like Prince Charming until he drank. Then he was mean and rough. When Grace learned of the child with Victoria, she guessed that Victoria had some experience with that darker side of him. By then, he was sober and Grace was in love with him.

One morning in late May, as Grace unlocks the door to her gallery, she can see Callum pulling the brown paper from his glass. She crosses the street to visit her gorgeous British neighbor, opening the door with a verbal, "knock, knock."

"Hi Grace," he says, folding the paper into small squares to recycle. He is very tidy whether it is paper, food or clothing.

"This is really something, Callum! Is it ready for students?" she asks.

"The building is. I'm not sure I am though," he admits.

"Are you advertising?" she asks, assuming his hesitance is business related.

"Not really. I do have some students though. I have an arrangement with a local organization that helps individuals with disabilities find employment. We are developing a program to provide job training for work in kitchens. It will be a ten-week course and restaurants are already committing to hire graduates from our program. I'll also offer classes to kids and teenagers who aren't likely to go on to college."

Grace giggles into her hand.

"What? Am I funny?" Callum asks bewildered.

"No, of course not. Callum, I had the wrong idea entirely. I thought you were going to teach bored housewives. You would have a booming business, don't get me wrong, but this isn't what I expected from you at all."

"Yeah, I get that a lot."

"What does Victoria think?"

Now it is Callum's turn to laugh. "She thinks nothing. We actually haven't discussed it at all."

"I don't understand," she says.

"Let me put it this way. I am head over heels in love with Victoria and she is very busy keeping me at arm's length. She doesn't think I'm serious about all this." He waves his arms around his cooking school.

"You look very serious to me," Grace says. "She's afraid Callum. She's been on her own for so long. With everything that has been happening and George slowing down, she has a lot on her plate."

That night George calls Callum into his room. He shows Callum where his papers are. Everything is in order. "I named you the executor of my estate."

"Are you joking George? I'm dyslexic. I can hardly even read these papers," he says in a panic.

"There are lawyers for all that. You just have to oversee it. It takes the burden off Victoria. I made my own funeral arrangements. I left a substantial amount to Rosalie. I don't want there to be any surprises about that. She should never have to work again. The rest is Victoria's. Except one thing. The property downtown, Callum. I left my half to you."

"That's incredibly generous George, but not necessary." Callum is awestruck.

"Callum, I have no illusions about what you have done for my family. My debt to you is far more than that building."

Callum starts to deny it, but he doesn't. They both know what these last months have meant to both of them and it doesn't need to be said aloud. "Understood George." Callum looks at the stack of papers in his hand. "Is this happening now George?" Callum asks with a lump in his throat.

"Not yet. Let's throw Marina a hell of a birthday party this weekend."

"We are all set for that. Everyone is coming." Callum confirms.

"After that, we'll see."

Marina's birthday is officially the best day of her life so far. There has never been a June 3rd like this before. She spends the day with Christopher, Grace, Jessie and Jack. They take her on a hot air balloon ride while Callum and Victoria prepare for the party. Callum takes the day off from cooking and hires a caterer. He was picky and sampled many caterers in town before selecting *Luella's Bar-B-Que*. He wants to give his full attention to this day.

Victoria decorates the yard and covers tables with white clothes and blue flowers. There are balloons everywhere. When the time comes they are joined by new friends and old friends and even a few PTA moms. Victoria got Jessie's help inviting all of Marina's friends from school. Randy and his barber partner bring Jenna. Rosalie sits beside George as he oversees the festivities. Everyone comes and Marina is obviously overjoyed.

"Callum. Somehow I think all of this is because of you," Victoria whispers in his ear, circling her arms around his waist.

"Not possible Victoria. You did this. You did all of it," he pulls her into his arms. They watch Marina, smiling ear to ear, pulled to the karaoke microphone by her friends.

"Speech, speech," they chant.

Reluctantly, but not very reluctantly, Marina takes the offered microphone. "Really? I have to make a speech? Okay." She hesitates for just a moment. "I'd like to thank everyone for coming. I'd like to thank Luella's for the great food." The caterer walks over and hands Marina a ten dollar bill, everyone laughs.

"Thanks to Christopher and Grace for the balloon ride today. That was amazing. Thanks Dad, she smiles and salutes Christopher." She is trying out the *Dad*. Again everyone laughs. There are few secrets in this crowd.

"I want to thank my Granddad." Victoria and Callum gasp quietly. This is the first time she has called him anything but George. "Grandpa, I love you so much. Thanks for this great party." George blows a kiss to his granddaughter. Victoria thinks she's never him as happy.

"And Callum. And my Mom…" she drops the microphone and runs into their arms. She can't say it out loud. It is too much, but they know. There are lots of *aawwws* from the crowd and finally applause. After she hugs them both, she goes to George and hugs him hard.

Victoria watches her daughter, happy and secure, with all of these loved ones surrounding her. It is everything a mother could want for her daughter and she is sure that Callum is the cause.

"I love you, Callum," Victoria says simply and walks away to go and speak with her father.

"Wait," Callum protests, calling after her. "Wait. I want to say it back. That was too fast. It fucking sucked." She turns back laughing and blows him a kiss. "It sucked!" he says and, even as he says it, she can see the joy and relief on his face. Victoria mouths *I love you*, taunting him. She'll tell him again properly later when they are alone.

George waits a week. It is the tenth of June when he does it. He is on oxygen and getting weaker by the day. Within a few weeks, he will be bed bound and he won't tolerate that. Rosalie finds him in the morning, as he planned. She wakes Victoria and Victoria wakes Callum. He still sleeps in his owns bed. He is a little old-fashioned about this.

They bury George next to his wife, Victoria's mother. It is ironic that the funeral attendees include everyone who was at the party only a week before. Years of business associates, community leaders and friends also come to pay their respects.

After the service, Victoria wonders about the beautiful blonde woman who snuck in late and sat in the back. As the last of the guests trickle out, Anna taps Callum on the back and introduces herself to Victoria.

"Anna! Why the hell didn't you tell me you were coming?" Callum asks, controlling his joy at seeing his sister at this sad event.

"Of course I was coming Callum. You had enough on your plate and you certainly didn't need to worry about making arrangements for me. John was so sorry not to attend, but babies are nothing but a pain in the ass at these things. Right?"

Victoria loves her in three sentences and hugs her hard. "Thank you for being here. I am so glad to finally meet you. Sometimes these things are a blessing in disguise."

"I am sorry about your Dad darling. Callum told us wonderful things about him. Is this Marina? Aren't you lovely?" Anna says taking a hug.

"Will you stay with us, please?" Victoria asks.

"I'm registered at a place in town, but my plane was delayed so I haven't checked in yet. I don't want to impose," she says, fully intending to impose.

Later that night after a quiet dinner remembering George and getting to know each other, Anna and Victoria sip wine on the deck while Callum tucks Marina into bed.

"Are you okay sweetheart. I hope today wasn't too much for you," Callum asks, smoothing Marina's hair from her forehead.

"It was sad but nice. I think," she says. "I'm going to miss him."

"I'll miss him too. George would have liked the service a lot," Callum agrees.

Marina sits up, suddenly very serious. "Callum. I want to tell you something. I don't want us to have any secrets." Her face is so young sometimes.

"Of course," he says. "Neither do I. You can always tell me anything." He can't help but brace himself. Her confessions are never simple. They often tear his heart out.

"That day we went to Triple Falls and we talked about my sister?"

He'll never forget that day. He nods to encourage her on.

"You told me maybe I should let my mother lie to me. Maybe she had her reasons for keeping secrets and it was for my own good."

Oh my god, he thinks. "Go on."

"I'm doing what you said. I got my sister and my brother and Grace and my Dad and that's all that matters. Right? If things were different a long, long time ago, that doesn't matter now. Right?" she looks at him with the eyes of an angel. She looks to him, and he feels that she is a lamb to slaughter and he is the slaughterer.

"I love you Marina. I'll be here for you every day of your life." He hopes that is enough. "I have a secret too." He tiptoes to his room and brings back two black boxes. One has a solitaire round diamond ring and the other has three varying sized silver bands inside.

"This one is for your Mom and these three are for us. I had them specially made. They are family rings. They bind us all together forever. I'm going to propose during the fireworks when we go to Osprey Island for July fourth."

Their embrace holds all the promise of a life he never even imagined. Callum knows that the last years of his life have been like the labors of Hercules. Instead of earning Hera's good will, he was challenged to find his way here. To become a man who could be a father to a little girl and a husband to a woman, like no other woman he has ever known. A woman who bases her life on courage and honesty and finding truth. Most importantly, to become a man worthy of their love. The mobile in his back pocket vibrates a text message.

"Goodnight love," he says kissing her forehead.

"I love you Callum. Good night." She rolls over, pulls the quilt to her chin and closes her eyes. She looks as peaceful as Callum has ever seen her. He closes the door before reaching for the mobile in his pocket. His mother wants Victoria's address to mail a sympathy card. Her lack of depth never ceases to amaze Callum

Eleven

Marina leans her head out of the window and breathes in ocean air for the first time in her life on the bridge to Osprey Island. They cross the sound onto the barrier island and pull into John and Anna's driveway ten minutes later.

Three houses are full of friends and loved ones. John's brother, Brian, and his wife, Stephanie, are in the smaller house, 517, with their two boys, Mikey and Sammie. Anna's mother and her husband have rented house 518 for the month of July. They are hosting John's parents, Conrad and Jane as well as Jordan and his partner Jerome. Rodrigo's daughter and Anna's best friend, Pemberley, died from cancer a little over a year before. Jordan was Pemberley's tireless, loving, nurse. Rodrigo reluctantly opened his heart to this man despite his initial misgiving about Jordan's checkered past. A collection of Pemberley's cousins from Connecticut fill in the remaining rooms of the enormous house.

July 4th marks a year since the memorial service that was held for Pemberley on Osprey Island. Rodrigo decided to honor his daughter every year on this day by gathering family and friends for a celebration. Pemberley would have loved it.

As is always the case, John and Anna are waiting outside with the girls to greet their guests. After greetings and many introductions, Callum and Victoria take Marina around back to see the ocean.

"John and I will bring out a beach happy hour. Relax and stretch your legs before you get settled in," Anna encourages. "Put on your suits if you like."

Marina runs straight though the silken sand into the blue surf, screaming with joy. Callum silently counts in his head how many people will be on the boat during the July 4th fireworks. Twenty-six? No, friends too. More like forty. Plus a captain, plus caterers. Suddenly the idea of a very public proposal seems absurd. In his heart, he isn't sure Victoria will say yes.

Despite the fact that she finally, albeit inauspiciously, declared her love for him at Marina's birthday celebration, this proposal isn't a slam dunk. At his insistence, they still keep separate rooms at the house. Their lives are merged and in perfect sync and they are so happy. *Still.*

"What do you think?" Callum calls to Victoria as she wades into the ocean with Marina.

Victoria hasn't seen the ocean in many years. "It's incredible! Beautiful! I love it!"

I love you, Callum thinks. *Be my wife. Share a life with me.* Here and now. He could just utter the words and that would be that. They could announce at the fireworks and maybe that would be better.

Marina and Victoria come splashing out of the ocean to go inside and change into suits.

"I'll be right there," Callum says and plants himself in the dry sand. Within two minutes, John sits at his side and hands Callum a bourbon.

"My god, I've missed you so, dear John," Callum lays his head in John's lap.

"You'd better get out of there unless you mean business, Callum."

Callum gives him a kiss on the cheek to let him know he could probably be talked into it. John shares a good laugh.

"You look good brother. You're bulking up a little. Feeling good too?" John asks.

"Very good," Callum holds his bourbon up to the sun to look through the amber filled glass.

"Talk," John says. "You've been here five minutes and you look like a very bad cat that ate a pretty tasty canary."

"Are we really not related by blood, John? I feel like you are in my soul," Callum says seriously enough to get another laugh from John.

"Am I right?"

"You are," Callum smiles. "I brought a ring. I intended to propose on the boat on the 4th, but suddenly that is seeming like a recipe for disaster."

"No shit!" John says and smacks Callum's leg. "Are you having second thoughts about proposing or proposing in front of all those people and then being trapped on a tiny vessel over the ocean for hours and hours if it goes bad?"

"Not second thoughts. That," Callum says. Victoria, Marina, Anna, Ellen, Rodrigo, and about ten other people, whose names he can't remember, come down the walkways with coolers, tables and chairs. John and Callum jump up to carry the heavier items into the sand. Within five minutes, everyone has a drink in their hand and platters of food are passed along with stories and endless laughter.

Callum can't remember the last time he experienced this kind of setting. It had to be in the restaurants. He hosted monthly staff meals to keep the staff knowledgeable about the ever changing menu. Those meals often meant hours of wine and laughter, much like this. But he was always the boss, so some of that laughter was polite. This is family. This is wonderful.

"Take Victoria to dinner tomorrow night, just the two of you. Drive her into Charleston. Anna and I fell in love there. It is perfect," John suggests in a whisper.

Callum agrees and decides to blurt it all out to Marina later. That child needs no more surprises in her life.

John gives Callum a few restaurant recommendations but in the end, Callum can't think about food. If they are in a restaurant and getting engaged, he should be the fucking chef. He regrets that he didn't propose back in Asheville. Maybe he should wait until they get home. The box is burning a hole in his pocket and it feels 600 pounds. He can't take the waiting anymore. If it isn't tonight, he'll self-destruct. He considers Angel Oak. This magnificent old tree is a few miles outside of Charleston, but it is where Anna and John were engaged. Callum wants his own place.

"Callum, I think you missed the exit." Victoria says.

Callum drives, gripping the wheel too tight. Tree no. Restaurant no. *Where the fuck does one propose?*

"Callum. What's going on? Aren't we going into the city?" she asks.

Callum follows signs to the Arthur Ravenel Jr. Bridge. This stunning suspension bridge joining Charleston and Mt. Pleasant calls to him. Why not at the top of the beautiful bridge? They can walk the pedestrian lane hand in hand. A breeze blowing her hair, overlooking the harbor.

"There is a walking lane. Can we?" he asks and points to her sandals.

"Sure. If you want. It is beautiful."

"Let's just go to the middle and come back."

The bridge is 2.7 miles across so they take a long time to get to the center. The afternoon sunshine is hot and the wind picks up. Victoria walks with one hand holding her skirt in place and the other holding her hair in a ponytail to stop it whipping her face. Cars honk unnecessarily and often. The walk isn't as romantic as Callum had hoped, but he is committed to it. When they reach the middle, Callum surveys the harbor and the city. Not quite what he imagined, a bit industrial, but this is the place. Without further thought, he drops to one knee.

"Callum? What are you doing?" Victoria asks with a perfectly unconcealed look of horror.

He ignores her harsh tone. She'll get over the shock of it fast enough. He has to keep going.

"Victoria. I love you. These last months with you have been the best months of my life and I want to spend the rest of my life with you and Marina. I want to make babies with you and grow old with you and live my life on your mountain. Will you have me? Will you marry me?" He opens the box and decides if she says no and he can get to the side of the bridge in two steps and throw himself over.

"You want to marry me?" she asks, like she isn't really understanding what he is saying.

"That is the general idea. Yes. I'd like to marry you."

"Callum... I...I..." Car after car passing lays on their horn celebrating a perceived engagement. She tries to talk, but she can't speak above it. She drops to her knees, facing him and closes the box.

"No?" he asks in a panic. "Is that a no?"

She tries to hold his face in her hands, but he avoids her touch. "Callum. Stop. Listen to me. I love you with all my heart."

"Then why am I holding a fucking closed box?"

"Because I'm not sure. Is this what you really want? I love you, but I can't help feeling like we are still a little temporary."

"No Victoria. With you I have everything I could ever want. I love Asheville. I have my school opening in September. I love Marina. I love every moment of our life together." He tries to sound serious and keep the slight whine out of his voice.

"Callum, I feel like you are holding back sometimes. I feel like we have eighty or ninety percent of Callum, but that last ten or twenty percent isn't there. I'm scared to death that when it comes back, it will claim you and take you away from me."

He brings her lips to his and kisses her lightly. "This is all I am. Please believe me. Marry me."

She speaks slowly, almost to herself. "I love you, Callum. You are everything to me. You are giving and caring and kind. You have taken my daughter and my father into your own heart."

"I'm staying Victoria. You are all I am," he says, hoping she is hearing him. "Don't let your fear cloud your thinking. Let me spend my life trying to make you happy."

She stares silently into his eyes while the traffic screams around them. He can see her weighing her love against her fear, questioning her own worth and fighting her self-doubt. Then she smiles and he knows she'll be his forever.

"Yes Callum," she says finally. "I'll marry you."

He hands her the box and she opens it this time. He takes the ring and slips it onto her finger. He kisses her with all of the hope and promise of a life together, a life he never thought he would want. But that life is somehow the answer to his dreams.

"Callum, can we get the hell off this bridge?" she asks as another car blows its horn at them.

He carries her in his arms the 1.35 miles back to the car. With her arms wrapped around his neck, he suddenly realizes he should toss her over the side.

"What the fuck was that closing the box? I nearly jumped the bridge," he says.

She doesn't bother answering him, but she does give him a nice series of licks and kisses along his neck. *Forgiven.*

Twelve

The drive back to Asheville is long and traffic is thick with holiday travelers. By the time they pull up to the house, they are cranky, hungry, exhausted and all racing for a pee. Marina and Victoria run inside to the bathroom, but Callum insists on unloading the car first. By the time he has lined up the bags by the front steps, Victoria is back outside and pulling at a note from the front door.

Callum lifts the top of the recycling bin and tosses in a collection of water bottles littering the car "What's that?"

Victoria hands over the white envelope. *Callum* is the single word written in all large black capital letters across the front.

"What is this?" he asks, taking it from her hand. It feels heavier than it should. It feels like anger or bad news or change. Nothing good is coming from black Sharpied lettering like this. It feels nothing like a simple white envelope with a piece of paper inside.

"What the hell?" he wonders out loud. No one leaves notes. Anyone in his life would text or email or use the damn phone.

"Open it," Victoria demands. "The suspense is killing me."

He opens an envelope with the same fastidiousness that he folds clothes and trusses a roast. He separates the back flap from the envelope without shredding the paper at all. The stationary is from a hotel downtown. He reads it out loud.

Callum, I am in Asheville. I must see you. I think you are out of town and I have no phone number for you. Your mother gave me an address but would not share your phone number. She is such a bitch. I traveled across a fucking ocean because you changed your cell number and you don't look at email. Anyway. I'm here and I need to talk to you now. – Elizabeth

She includes a phone number. He crumbles the paper into a ball and tosses it into the recycling bin.

"Jesus Christ," he mutters. "She's here, in fucking Asheville." His accent suddenly becomes far more pronounced just talking about his people from England.

Victoria suddenly doesn't understand English. "What does that mean?"

"She wanted to talk with me and my manipulative mother refused her any information about how to find me but an address. My mother has sent her here to coerce me back to England. They probably need a fucking chef at *Mise En Place*. Well, she can fuck herself up and down and sideways."

"Oh shit. She's really here? Oh shit. I knew it. I knew it. Your chickens are coming home to roost." If Victoria was less freaked out, there would be a taste of victory in knowing he should have gone back to England to face his life. There is no feeling of victory though.

"Callum, will you go back?" She asks, sounding confused and helpless, a little dazed.

"Of course I'm not fucking going back. What are you talking about? Are we not getting fucking married?" Comforting Victoria while he is tired and cranky with a full bladder and furious at his mother is essentially impossible.

"What does she look like? Is she gorgeous? I am disgusting. I smell like pee from the damn rest stop. Will you meet her somewhere? Will you have her come here? I look like shit. What if she comes back and ..." Victoria is interrupted by a car coming up the driveway.

"Three guesses," she says and her heart sinks.

"I only need one," he says. "Motherfucker."

"That is a weird word," she says absentmindedly. "I'll go inside and leave you alone. Should I put on some tea? Don't you British have a cuppa with everything?"

He doesn't answer and Victoria stays at his side. Curiosity is stronger than vanity in this instance. "I really wish I took a shower this morning," she mumbles.

Elizabeth parks the car and steps out. She is elegant in white pants that sway in the breeze and a lightly colored denim shirt that could use one more button buttoned at the top. Her hair is pulled into a glamorous, not so careless, pile on top of her head. Black horn-rimmed glasses give her the sexy librarian look and generous cleavage seals the deal. While Victoria and Callum watch in silence, she reaches into the back seat and pulls forth a baby boy.

"What a bitch," Callum whispers. "I can't believe she brought her marriage saving baby to stick in my fucking face."

As Elizabeth walks closer, it is obvious to Victoria, but Callum is too angry to see it. "I don't think that is her marriage saving baby," Victoria says. "I think that is your son Callum."

"You are out of your mind," he whispers then stares into the little face. The little blue eyes are Callum's. The bits of blonde hair are Callum's. The button nose and slight cleft on the chin are all Callum.

"Elizabeth," is all that Callum can say. He can't take his eyes off the boy. After a minute of silent staring, he turns and walks into the house.

"Callum?" Victoria calls after him.

"I have to take a fucking piss," He calls without turning around.

After the fucking piss, Callum splashes cold water on his face and then splashes more cold water on his face. He can't get himself to leave the bathroom. He paces sink to wall, sink to wall. If the walk was more than one stride he might never leave that bathroom. He takes four deep breaths, smooths his hair and beard then walks back to find Elizabeth sitting at the kitchen table in George's seat. This makes Callum angry all over again. Victoria is filling a kettle of water for tea.

"Callum, I set out some cups for tea, but I'll go on upstairs and give you two a chance to talk alone." Victoria says and walks from the kitchen.

"No," Callum says simply. "We have nothing to talk about that doesn't include you." He ignores Elizabeth and prepares the tray for tea, even pulling a tin of cookies from the cabinet. He doesn't use mugs but reaches for delicate blue cups and saucers. He is civilized and British, even as he is falling into a great abyss.

"Victoria," Elizabeth says. "Please stay. This certainly concerns you too. Funny we are both named for queens. It must say something about us. Or maybe it says something about Callum."

"I think you should probably talk alone," Victoria repeats.

"Judging from that ring on your finger you should stay." Elizabeth demands. "Please sit down."

The baby starts to cry and Elizabeth reaches into her diaper bag for a bottle. Wordlessly, Callum takes it from her hand and heats it with leftover water from the kettle. He learned a lot watching Anna with Lynn. The gesture gets a big smile from Victoria, even though she is clearly in the middle of a silent heart attack.

247

"Were you going to mention this to me at any point?" Callum finally asks with the quietest fury he can manage. "Him. Were you going to mention him to me at any point?"

She pops the bottle into the baby's mouth and he sucks gratefully. "I could beat around the bush all day long, Callum, but I really need to just be honest with you."

"That would be delightful." He leans back onto the counter and crosses arms over his chest. He absolutely can't control the sarcasm.

"The answer is no. I was never going to tell you about him. You have guessed correctly that he is yours. His name is Marcus by the way."

Callum tosses the tea kettle into the sink. Poor Marcus jumps in his mother's arms. "Are you fucking joking?"

This news is too much for Callum. He walks to the backyard and lets the door slam loudly behind him. At the edge of the yard, there is a spot with four comfortable low chairs and a fire pit. They never sit out here. They should bring wine out in the evenings and roast marshmallows and use this lovely space. Now, it is the furthest spot from the kitchen where he can avoid sitting in the grass.

He sits and stares at the extraordinary layer of colors that make up this mountain view. He can see for miles. It is a clear day.

Victoria approaches quietly, tentatively. She sits by his leg in the green grass. Fury radiates from him in waves. "Callum, I don't understand. What is going on?" she asks.

"She tried to pass off my baby as Jeremy's. Apparently she was pregnant when I left. She was never going to tell me." The hurt is almost inconceivable.

"How do you know?" she asks.

"Marcus is Jeremy's father. She named the baby for Jeremy's father."

Victoria holds his leg and finally lays her head against his knee. He lays a hand in her hair and the contact does begin to calm him.

"I want to have babies with you Victoria. We haven't discussed it and now is not the time to bring it up, but I want to have babies with you. I want little Victoria's filling our house."

She props her chin on his knee. "That does sounds nice Callum. It does. But you have a tiny little Callum in there right now that needs your attention."

"How am I not to kill her?" he asks seriously.

"Be merciful Callum. As much as I want to throw up about it, and I do, she is the mother of your baby." Victoria moves her hand to pull the diamond ring from her own finger.

"What are you doing?" He shouts in horror, grasping her hands.

"It think she's here because she wants you back. You love her and you have a baby together. This is crystal clear to me."

"Do you think so little of me?" he asks.

"Just the opposite. I think so highly of you. Callum, you are the most honorable, loving, gentle, rock solid man I have ever known. You can't live here with your baby across an ocean. It will kill you." Again, she reaches to pull off the ring.

"Stop, just fucking stop. I am going nowhere. Whatever she wants, it doesn't involve getting me back I assure you. And if it did, she can't have me. This is all yours for better or for worse, love me as I am." He pulls her from the ground to his lap and kisses her lightly.

"I think you are mixing metaphors."

"It's the dyslexia. I get confused by words," he jokes. At least he is smiling. They hear the baby cry from inside the house. "Oh shit.

Marina." Callum says and pushes Victoria to her feet so they can rejoin Elizabeth in the kitchen.

When they push through the swinging screen door, Marina is holding the baby at the table.

"Fuck," Callum says. "Marina love, I think we need to talk for a bit here. There is a lot to explain, but I have no idea what it is."

"Is this the whole clan, then?" Elizabeth asks, sipping her tea with hands finally free.

"I have a father and half brother and sister, Jack and Jessie. Oh, and a sort of stepmother too." Marina says proudly. "That is the whole clan."

"That does sound interesting. Well, here it is…" she says turning to Callum.

"Wait. Let's step outside. Marina, will you watch the baby for a few minutes?" Victoria asks.

They walk back to the seats far in the yard. Callum is likely to get colorful in his language.

"Elizabeth. An explanation. Please." He summons all of the restraint he can.

"Alright Callum. Here is the truth. I'm going to come off sounding a bit of a monster here, but I don't have all day." She turns to Victoria, "Apologies Victoria, this may be hard to hear, but you deserve the truth, too. Right?"

Victoria nods, silently pleading for her to continue.

"Callum, I could never have taken you seriously. You just aren't marriage material. Maybe you are now, I have no idea what with the beard and the mountains and whatever. You were a lot of fun though and I had been a good girl all my life. I followed all the rules and I married Mr. Perfect, but it wasn't very fun. Except the restaurant. *Mise* was everything I ever dreamed of. Callum you were an amazing chef. The best, but you were getting a little bored with it."

He shrugs to show her he is listening, but he is doing his best to keep his hands from her throat.

"So we had the affair and it was wonderful and exciting and wrong, but oh so right." Those last words are uttered slightly orgasmically.

"Moving on," Victoria says.

"No, really. I need to explain this. With Jeremy it was all a continuation of before. I was a model daughter, then a straight A student, and the perfect wife. I wore my damn mother's wedding gown for fuck's sake. I was suffocating in it, losing my mind to be something else. You didn't even like me, Callum. You didn't hide it well, but you were bored with *Mise*, and I think that's why you got things going with us. The thrill of the affair made *Mise* fun for you again. With you, I could be someone else completely. I could let go and be wild and daring and really bad. And you did like that Elizabeth... the bad one. You were the perfect lover for me, mad passion, almost a little rapey at times, but it was exactly what I needed to tear me out of my shell."

He sees Victoria's jaw fall with the word *rapey*, but she tries to control it. Callum's head sinks into his hands. He can only imagine what she is thinking. He knows she is remembering the woman breaking the glass behind Callum's head at *The Orange Peel* and screaming that Callum was a rapist. Victoria reaches a hand robotically to sooth Callum's leg. He thinks he may throw up.

"Anyway, I was mostly careful, but one of your little swimmers founds its way through and I discovered I was pregnant last fall. I had an abortion scheduled when you told Jeremy about us." She refolds her sleeves looking a little bored with this part of the dialog.

"Elizabeth, why in the hell didn't you tell me that you were pregnant?" he asks, unable to comprehend that she would do this to him.

"Really Callum? What would have been the point? You were impulsive and exciting but nothing more than an arrogant shell of armor. There was no getting close to you. Your skills in the kitchen could only be matched by your skills in the bedroom." She turns to Victoria, "Sorry, but that was it."

He shakes his head, looking confused, still not understanding how she could do this to him. To their baby.

"I didn't want a life with you, Callum. I certainly didn't want a baby with you. When you told Jeremy about our affair, I was going to lose everything. Jeremy and I were still sleeping together, here and there. A child was the last thing I wanted, but it was an opportunity to keep things together with Jeremy."

"You are a fucking monster." He grasps the arms of his chair as he would like to grasp her neck.

"Be that as it may, it worked. I don't think he really even cared if the baby might be yours. He wanted a reason to fix things between us. Until the baby popped out, looking like a miniaturized replica of you. As time went by, his hair blonded up and his eyes got more and more blue and Jeremy couldn't handle it. The good news is, he left me, and he didn't want the restaurant. The restaurant is mine. I bought him out and …"

"You did all this to keep a restaurant?" Victoria really does want to understand, she just can't believe it.

"As I said, I'd come out sounding a bit of a monster," Elizabeth agrees.

Callum has heard enough. "So now what?"

She says it fast, anxious to get the words out. "I don't want him. I want you to take him."

Callum stands up and sits back down again. Then he stands up once more.

"You want to desert your child?" He starts walking and doesn't stop except to call back over his shoulder, "You make me sick." He gets in the car and drives off, leaving Victoria and Elizabeth watching after him.

"That was an awful lot for him to take in," Victoria tries to keep a neutral tone when she feels anything but neutral. There is no discussion necessary for her. Callum will be back and somehow they have a new baby boy.

"He seems different now. Is he?" Elizabeth asks.

"He is."

Callum needs to get drunk. Christopher is an alcoholic. Randy is a single Dad. He has no drinking friends in Asheville. In London, he could walk into any one of a hundred restaurants and be welcomed by name and a swift pour of scotch. He wishes John was here. John is a great drinking buddy. They could down shots of bourbon and John would play guitar and they could sing U2 songs or that old American shit John likes. Damn it, that would be good right now. If the traffic was lighter, Callum might drive the six hours right back to Osprey Island. He checks the time and he's tempted, but he wouldn't get there until midnight at best. *Fuck.*

He decides to go it alone, buys a bottle of bourbon and takes it to the apartment above the school. He has outfitted it for a furnished rental. There is a new bed with linens, a small writing desk and chair and a newly retiled bathroom. The first two shots warm him from the inside out and he takes a long, hot shower to wash off the road and filth that came from Elizabeth's mouth. As the water beats his back, he wonders how much of what she said was right.

He could strangle her for the lies. For intending to abort his baby without a discussion and then using his son as a pawn to win nothing more than a fucking restaurant. She is disgusting. *How did I ever love her?* He wraps a white towel around his waist and takes another shot before clearing the mirror with his forearm. The beard makes him look different, but a beard can't change a man.

The knock at the door is firm, insistent. He makes wet footprints on the hardwood and pulls the glass nob. Victoria takes him in her arms and holds him hard.

"Callum." She is here and ready to help him heal.

"No more talk, Victoria. Please," he pulls away from her embrace. He pushes his wet hair back and unconsciously styles it with flick of the wrist. A white towel rests low on his hips. After months of a consistent fitness routine, his muscle definition is as good as it has ever been. He looks strong, like he could conquer the world. The outside is not reflecting what is happening on the inside.

He is disgusted that Victoria heard those words from Elizabeth. That he was unworthy as a husband and a father. He is ashamed and fears that Elizabeth is right. He pours another bourbon and drinks it down, offering Victoria one.

"You drink, I'll drive. Or come on home and we can both drink. Marina and Jessie went over to stay the night with Jenna. It's just us."

After four bourbons, Callum knows it isn't going to do the trick. There is a buzzing in his head that won't be silenced. Callum needs a release and liquor isn't giving it to him. He thinks about stripping Victoria down and taking her lovely, sweet body right here on the hard wood. He could kiss her top to bottom and lick every inch of her. He could hold her face and bury himself inside of her. She'd wrap her legs around his back and he'd glide in and out of her. He could make the sweetest love to her the world has ever known. He swallows hard, because he does love her, but none of those is what he needs.

Bending that woman over the chair with his hand around her throat while she begged for it and came again and again. Fucking the tour guide over the side of the boat while half the harbor watched. Cuffing Elizabeth wide open and leaving her there naked for an hour, not knowing if Jeremy might come home. Callum knew Jeremy was at a late meeting but Elizabeth had no idea. She begged to be freed and finally bartered for it, sucking him off as he kneeled over her and fucked her face. He feels himself starting to get hard. That is what he needs.

He sits at the edge of the bed, hating himself. His eyes start to tear and he pours another shot to stop it. *I am a fucking filthy, rapey pig*, he thinks and throws it back.

"Do you want to be alone?" Victoria asks.

He nods wordlessly.

"Callum, please."

"Please go Victoria." He holds the door open for her. She shouldn't be here. He can't be around her now. He can't live like this. He won't be able to control it. He loves her, but when he feels like this, he is the monster.

She ignores him and the open door. "I need a shower. Pour me a drink and give me five minutes. Maybe you'll feel differently in five minutes."

Damn if she doesn't go into the bathroom and leave the door cracked. He hears the water running and the zipper on her jeans and then she steps into the shower. He imagines her naked and touching herself under the streams of hot water. He imagines his hands on Victoria's neck or bent over the railing of that ship or... or... He can't control it. He needs it. It will stop this buzzing in his head.

He has a raging hard-on by the time he opens the shower door and steps inside. He doesn't kiss her or feel her smooth skin. He turns her to face the tile and presses himself into her back, saying three words.

"Yes or no?"

"Yes," she says clearly.

And he takes her fast and hard without any preamble. He pounds himself into her, using her hips to hold her still. This isn't making love, it is pure and simple, biological, animalistic fucking. He doesn't take long. This isn't about finesse. This is about getting off. He pulls out and comes over her ass. The buzzing finally stops. Victoria didn't make a sound throughout and has red handprints in her hips.

Callum falls to his knees. He knows it is over between them. The water beats into the back of his head. He kneels, defeated, undone once again by his own impulses. It was bound to happen eventually. The release he gets from taking what he wants is undeniable.

Victoria turns to face him. She lays a hand in his hair and then lifts his chin, forcing him to face her, forcing him to look into her eyes. His are full of shame and sorrow. Hers are not. Victoria leans back to the white tile with a smile and circles his neck with her leg. She pulls his mouth to her. "Yes or no?" she asks.

"Yes," he says and his heart fills with wonder, before bringing his tongue to touch her. He is brilliant with his mouth and tonight he is relentless, devouring her and burying his tongue deep inside of her. She comes louder than usual, with a shout of his name, and it is the sweetest sound he has ever heard.

She falls to her knees to meet him and he pulls her to his chest. He reaches up to stop the shower and they kneel for a few minutes, just feeling each other's skin and breathing together.

Finally, Victoria speaks. She holds him tight and speaks to his chest. "Callum, you are the gentlest man. You are the best lover I could ever imagine."

"Jesus Christ is there a fucking *but* coming?" He almost laughs with the horror of it.

"Just shut up and let me say this" She takes a moment to resume her words. His panic threatens a return. "What happened to me, happened a long time ago. I was a girl then. Now, I'm a full grown woman. I'm not afraid of you. You'd never hurt me. You'd never try to overpower me or fill me with hate. I trust you completely."

He is grateful for her words, but knows there is more to it. "Yet?"

"This is tough for me to say, Callum."

"Out with it Victoria. Please."

"I want what you had with Elizabeth. What we have is wonderful but rather polite at times. You treat me like a glass doll. You protect me by hiding a piece of yourself. You are holding back Callum. I want the rest of you too."

He stands and pulls her to her feet. He wraps her in a towel and then wraps one back around his waist. He feels better but worse too. He isn't sure what to feel and sits on the bed in confusion. "I don't know what any of this means."

Victoria lowers herself in front of Callum's knees. After the blow to his head and his heart from Elizabeth, after the shock of Marcus and Elizabeth's verbal abuse, Callum doesn't need loving or soothing or her gentle kiss. Callum needs to feel like he did before he came into their lives. Callum needs to push boundaries. She slides her hands under the towel to reach for him.

"No Victoria," he holds her hands still. "I don't ever want to make you feel the way you did before."

"I'll never feel that way with you Callum. And I want more."

"I don't know where your boundaries are Victoria. If I didn't love you, it wouldn't matter. I would push and push, sometimes too far. But I do love you and it does matter."

"I don't know where my boundaries are either, Callum. Help me find them."

"Victoria, what if I go too far?" he asks.

"Let me decide what is too far. Stop deciding for me. Now shut up, please." She opens his towels and he does shut up. She spreads his legs wide and kneels on the hardwood between his knees. She takes him into her mouth aggressively. He doesn't want gentle tonight and she knows it. She understands instinctively what he does wants, and she gives it to him. Before he starts to come, she takes him deeper into her mouth, her throat. But he doesn't. He lifts her from the floor and pushes her to the window, taking her from behind again. This time he is gentle and glides with her as if in a dream. It is dark outside and dark inside, so they have enough privacy. But it feels so good to fuck in front of the world.

"Use my hand Victoria."

Victoria guides his hand and rocks against his fingers, leaning back into Callum's chest. She notices him studying her reflection in the glass, so she lifts her other hand to caress her breast. He vocalizes his pleasure and this encourages her on. She can put on quite a show. She wants more and he'll give her more. He'll give her the fuck of her life for the rest of her life. He comes with a force that lets her know for sure this was exactly what he needed.

Afterwards, he falls asleep within moments. The drive, the bourbon, the shock and the emotion, he is finished. Victoria lays down beside him, breathless and wraps herself around this man she loves and she sleeps too.

Hours later when she awakes, he is gone, but the smell of bacon entices her downstairs. She wraps his shirt around herself and walks into the kitchen. He has pasta boiling in a pot and pancetta frying in a pan.

"Carbonara?" he asks, testing the pasta.

"Yes. I'm starving." She sits at one of the stools by the counter. "We'll see a lawyer tomorrow. She wants us to sign papers and then he'll be ours. She is going back to England, to the restaurant, as soon as possible."

He uses tongs to lift the pasta from the water and lay it in the sauce. "Can you tolerate this Victoria?"

"Can you tolerate being a father to Marina?" she asks, without missing a beat.

"Of course I can. That isn't even a consideration."

"Exactly."

"Victoria. I'm not sure I'm fit for any of this. Suddenly I'm not sure I'm fit for you anymore."

"Everything Elizabeth said about you is wrong. Everything. If she had told you she was pregnant, you would have been the perfect father and perfect husband to her and the baby. You mean everything to me and Marina. We thank god every day she found you on the mountain. Elizabeth blew it Callum. The loss is all hers."

Callum frowns and shakes his head. "Victoria, everything she said about me was right. I was a different man in England. I was a shallow, arrogant, impulsive, shell of a man. It is all true."

She reaches for his hand and pulls him to her. "Well I am thankful for that or else you would never have found you way to us. You have been on a journey Callum and now you're home. Do you have any regrets?"

He thinks this over for a moment. "Elizabeth is vile and she was perfect for me back then. That is my only regret."

"Well I am perfect for you now," Victoria says with absolute certainty.

"Are you? After all that upstairs, are you still?" His heart is suspended between beats waiting for her answer.

She pulls him close and wraps her legs around his waist. She is wearing his shirt and she missed a few buttons as always. When he reaches for her, he sees it is just the shirt, nothing underneath. This is not her usual style and his body responds immediately.

"Now more than ever. Now I think you are truly with me Callum. All of you. No more holding back, no more fear. I have all of you now."

She pulls him to her and kisses him deeply. His hands pull her bare ass closer. Until he stops and pulls his mouth from hers. He can't believe this is happening.

"What Callum? What is it?" she asks, seeing his stricken face.

"I'm spent. I am literally worn out. I need some fucking food or I'll drop at your feet. I can't believe I'm not going to make love to you right here in this kitchen."

She laughs and hugs him again.

He turns back to the stove and plates the pasta. "When is she going?"

"She already had an attorney draw up the papers. She was ready for this before we even got to town. We have to be there tomorrow at ten o'clock. She'll be on a plane by six."

"We are having a baby then? You and me?" he asks, still incredulous.

"We are. And look at me, no stretch marks."

Her mouth finds his again. "Callum?" she asks taking her mouth from his.

"Hmm?"

"Don't rent the apartment out. We can come here from time to time, can't we? At home, we have the kids and all of the day to day. Here, things feel different, a little magical."

"You are everything to me," he says with wet eyes and holds onto her for dear life.

Her own tears flow then. He doesn't question her. There is plenty to cry about, happy tears, sad tears, tears of change.

"I love you. I love you," he tells her neck while she lets her tears go. "I love you."

Thirteen

And their family grew. Marina is mostly unphased by the prospect of having a little brother, but she has one demand. She doesn't want little Marcus to grow up thinking Victoria is his biological mother. She has had enough of life with secrets and she personally asks Elizabeth to be a part of Marcus' life in some way. Victoria encourages her to be honest and the experience seems cathartic to Marina. Like Callum, Marina has her share of anger at missing out on years with her sister and brother.

After hearing Marina's story, Elizabeth can't refuse. Though she tries to hide it, there is humanity in her. Her second visit is much better than her first. When she realizes she isn't going to be crucified, she lessens her defenses and her aggression. Callum is leery at first, worrying that she would leave the baby and come back a month later or a year later to reclaim him. All of her assurance and the signed legal documents give him enough peace of mind. They agree to occasional visits, emails and photos, befitting of distant relations.

Elizabeth has papers drawn up so Callum can change Marcus' name, but it doesn't feel right. Callum liked Jeremy's father well enough and it just seems wrong to take a name away from a nearly three-month-old baby.

So Callum becomes a daddy and, once again, Victoria becomes a mommy. Callum takes to parenting with the intensity of an athlete training for the Olympics. He checks out parenting books on tape from the library so he can absorb the content faster. He takes classes at the hospital for new parents in diaper changing and bathing and what to expect when you don't know a damn thing. He joins baby and me classes and rocks Marcus to sleep every night. After a few weeks Victoria suggests letting him cry it out a bit.

"Crying it out is for babies who didn't switch parents and countries at three months. He's going to be so fucked up!"

"He's doing fine Callum. He is as happy as a baby boy could be."

But Callum won't hear of it. Callum sets up a nursery corner at the cooking school and schedules a grand opening for the third week in September. Victoria encourages him to teach daytime classes to bored housewives, but he won't. He wants to connect the more vulnerable population in Asheville with those who can help. Also, his time with Marina brought him to the realization that he is good with kids. He enjoys teaching them and talking to them and learning to understand them. Being a kid fucking sucked for him, but from the suck, came an ability to connect.

Victoria keeps a few shifts at the hospital, more because she enjoys the work than she needs the money. George left them well cared for. The house is paid off, there are rental properties and investments. Elizabeth paid out Callum for his share of their home in London and he still has plenty of money from the buyout of *Mise en Place*. The investment in *Townsend Culinary School* is relatively small.

By the end of August, with summer winding down, they are settling into a nice routine. Victoria cleans out her teenage bedroom and personally paints it powder blue for Marcus. Cleaning out that space is a relief and giving it over to the Marcus makes her feel like she is doing something tangible to welcome him into their lives. This second time parenting a baby is peaches and cream for Victoria. Having another person around to share diapers and feedings and bath time is amazingly easy compared to doing it all herself, while worrying about money and trying to make a future. Mothering Marcus is just about loving him. And it is so easy to love him.

"Will you set the table, Marina?" Callum asks a few nights before school starts. He makes the usual cooking time small talk. "Do you have everything you need? Gym clothes? Backpack?" he asks.

This year is the start of high school for Marina. Callum can't believe how fast this time has passed. Since he met her, she has grown inches and now mascara and blue pencil line her eyes. Victoria allowed a few blonde streaks in her chin length hair. To Callum, she looks too old.

She gives him a grudging nod.

"Do you need a pep talk Marina? I have a good one prepared about the joys of growing up and…" he starts.

"Nope. Thanks." She cuts him off and spreads a red checked tablecloth silently. She reaches for plates and silver and lays the table carelessly.

"Is something bothering you Marina? You don't seem yourself." He knows there has been a lot of adjusting these past months.

She mumbles, "I can't believe I have to go to school without Jessie. We'll never see each other."

Victoria walks into the kitchen holding Marcus and sets him in the high chair.

"Let's talk about when you can see Jessie," Victoria says. "We can still have dinners and sleepovers, whatever you want."

Callum mixes a bowl of baby cereal and hands it to Victoria. She pulls a chair up close to Marcus and feeds him a spoonful. He takes in about half and the rest ends up on his chin.

"No." Marina slumps over her plate.

Callum places a bowl of pasta, a platter of chicken and a dressed salad on the table.

"Why not?" Victoria asks.

"Because it always has to be here or at Jenna's. George is gone now and you still haven't let me stay over at Jack and Jessie's."

Callum shoots Marina a look that says do not go there, but she goes there anyway.

"Why Mom? Why can't I stay in the house with Christopher and Grace?" she asks. Marcus slaps his hands in the air at nothing and blows bubbles with his cereal.

"Marina, can we do this later? Let's eat dinner. We'll work it through, I promise." Callum pleads, reaching to serve her some chicken. "I marinated this in lemon and the oregano from your garden."

"Mom?" Marina probes.

Victoria doesn't even turn to face her daughter. "Eat your dinner Marina."

Marina rolls her eyes and makes some vocalizations of grave displeasure. Callum keeps the conversation light, asking about field hockey tryouts. Marina made the junior varsity team and Victoria is hoping she meets lots of new friends. She spends most of her free time with her sister and Jenna. Before dinner is through, Victoria takes Marcus up for a bath. Callum decides not to protest. He knows she is avoiding further conversation with Marina. He is just as happy to have Marina to himself.

"What is going on with you?" he asks the angry faced teenager across the table.

"What could possibly be wrong, Callum," she says with more sarcasm than usual.

Callum tics off the list of what might be bringing this on. High school stress, new unexpected brother, impending wedding, George dying, not to mention a second family and knowing she missed years with them. It has been a hell of a year for her. He thinks it is none of those things though.

He remembers back to the night he showed Marina the engagement ring. She was very intent on letting the situation lie. She probably suspects, at least on some level, that she was right about the rape. Maybe she isn't using the word rape in her own mind, but she suspects something is off.

He has resisted bringing it up with Victoria. Why rock the boat? They are all doing so well despite a challenging few months, but he can't let that go. Marina needs a clear sense of right and wrong, especially now that she is in high school. But why is she questioning this now? In his vision of how all this would unfold, Marina has time to get to know her brother and sister before whatever comes next. He looks into her face, silently begging for her honesty.

"Marina," he speaks slowly, in a low voice. "I need to understand what has changed. Something is different." He takes her chin in his hand when she tries to turn from his gaze. "Tell me Marina. You have always been honest with me."

"Christopher drank," she finally says.

"Drank what?" A cold sweat rises up Callum's back.

"Liquor."

"How do you know?" *It is fucking over.*

"He goes to Alcoholics Anonymous meetings. He's an alcoholic. Right?" she asks.

"Yes, Christopher is an alcoholic Marina. He can never drink alcohol. It is an addiction. It is like a disease for him. What do you know?" *I will fucking end him.*

He hopes against hope she is wrong. Maybe it was a misunderstanding. Or misconstrued. Maybe they went to dinner and he ordered a virgin Pina Colada and she didn't understand the virgin. Maybe he drank a non-alcoholic beer. You can't tell the difference by the look of the bottle.

"Jessie told me he got drunk last night. Her Mom was screaming and he broke a lamp and went crazy." Callum's hands turn to fists under the table. His teeth grit into his jaw. *Christopher is a dead man.* A drunk Christopher raped Victoria. He gave sober Christopher a chance, but that is over.

Callum can't put words together. Marina needs comforting though. She wants to be reassured that she can trust her new father. But Callum can't put those words together for her. He rubs his eyes with the palms of his hands. They were making this work. Victoria gave it to Christopher on a silver platter. She let him keep his perfect life. She gave him a loving daughter. She gave him complete acceptance. All she did was hold back on the overnights, but she would have accepted that too eventually. *All in or all out, right? It's all gone to shit*, he thinks, and then there is a knock on the door.

He opens the door to Grace, Jack and Jessie with bags and backpacks on their shoulders. Grace's usual stylish, confident appearance is disheveled. Her hair is pulled from a ponytail, a crisp white shirt is untucked and torn, and her jeans are stained. She has chewed her usually long, manicured nails to the quick. Her swollen, red eyes tell the story.

"Callum. Can the kids stay here? I have to go. Christopher isn't well. He's sick. I need to go. I have to take care of Christopher. Can the kids stay?"

Callum stares for too long and realizes from the wide-eyed fearful look on both kids' faces that they are looking to him to do more than stare.

"Sure, of course. Kids, go on upstairs. Marina, take Jack and Jessie upstairs and show them the…the…watch a movie. Send your Mom down Marina, would you?" Callum fights to keep his voice calm, not showing any signs of the horror he is feeling inside, but he is about to become a murderer. He started this. He is responsible. He will end it.

The kids run the stairs, half in panic, half eager to get away from whatever is happening.

"Grace, what happened?" he asks.

Grace breathes his name, "Christopher," and watches Callum through blank, unseeing eyes. "He. He." Callum pulls her into his arms. "Christopher. He. He. He is sick. I need to go..." and then she finally let's go. Her legs give out and she stuffs her hand to her mouth to lower the volume of her sobbing. Callum supports her waist and she shudders in pain.

"He hit you?"

Callum doesn't know why, but he prays that Christopher just beat her. He could possibly manage a drunk beating his wife. Maybe counseling or anger management. That could work. Callum helps her to the couch and stands across from her watching her uselessly. It takes no more than five seconds, but a lifetime passes before Victoria comes down the stairs. She sets Marcus in his swing.

"Hey Grace. Hey there." Victoria sits by Grace's side and takes her hand, stroking the inside of her wrist to help calm her and regulate her breathing.

"Grace. Can we talk a minute?" Victoria asks in little more than a whisper. Grace's looks up as if she just notices Victoria.

"Hey there Grace. Are you breathing okay? I saw that your ribs were hurting you?"

She nods, holding a hand to her side.

"Did he rape you Victoria?" Grace asks. She doesn't really ask. Callum can see she knows now. She searches Victoria's eyes. "He raped you. I pretended he didn't, but I suspected. He was violent when he was drinking. I am so sorry Victoria. I thought he was okay. He was okay for twelve years."

"Did he rape you Grace?" Victoria asks. She needs to know for certain.

Grace shakes her head and tears flow. "He would have, but the kids came in and he stopped and he left in the damn car, as drunk as I've ever seen him. Oh god Victoria, I can't do this with him again. I'm done."

"Where is he, Grace?" Callum asks pulling keys from his pocket. "Where would he go?"

Callum holds his breath. No, he doesn't hold his breath. He can't breathe. It isn't the same. *Life as they all know it is over.* The realization is untimely, but he knows it is true. Marina will know everything.

"Grace? Honey we have to get you to a hospital." Victoria says, ignoring Callum.

"Can we just drive there? No police or ambulance or anything. I don't want to scare the kids any more than they are." Grace pleads.

"Grace, where the fuck is Christopher?" Callum keeps his voice low, but his rage is apparent.

Grace flinches at his tone but ignores his question. She wipes her nose with the back of her hand, and she and Victoria head to the door.

"Stop Victoria," he whispers. "I have to find Christopher?"

"Leave it for now Callum," she says. "Stay with the kids."

On cue, Marcus cries out from the swing and before Callum reaches him, Grace and Victoria are gone.

The children finally go to sleep or they are pretending to. Marcus takes his bottle down fast and Callum rocks his son for a long time. Marcus holds Callum's blue eyes with his own. Thinking of Grace and what this means for their families is too hard. Staring into the eyes of this sweet angel of a baby boy is the only distraction. He lets Marcus sleep in his arms for a long time. Callum kisses his son's forehead once, then again and lays Marcus down in his crib.

After pausing with an ear to the girl's room, Callum is convinced they are asleep. The girls kept to themselves this evening, lost in their tales of some tragedy they don't understand. He eavesdropped and heard talk about liquor and drunkenness and yelling and fighting. He pauses at Jack's room and hears Jack speaking quietly.

"No Daddy. She isn't here," Jack says in an urgent whisper.

Callum walks in after a quick knock. "Is that your Dad, darling?" he asks Jack. "Can I say hello?"

"Dad? Callum wants to say hi. Dad? He hung up." Jack says handing Callum his phone.

"Jack, when did you get a phone?" Callum asks this six-year-old boy, just starting first grade.

"Yesterday. Daddy got it for me," he says.

"For school? Not many first graders have a nice phone like this." Callum probes.

"My Dad got it for me because I go to camp in first grade. We're not supposed to bring phones, but Daddy says I can hide it."

"Well that sure is nice, Jack. Can I take it downstairs so it doesn't wake you?" Callum asks. He doesn't want Christopher calling again. "We'll make sure it is in your backpack for school tomorrow. Okay?"

Jack hands the phone over and high-fives Callum goodnight. When Callum checks the call history, he sees that Christopher has called Jack sixteen times in the three hours since they got here. *Fuck.*

Callum sits at the dining room table waiting for whatever comes next. He wants to pull out the bourbon and have one or two to settle himself down, but that hardly seems a solution with a house full of kids and a drunk rapist on the loose. Eventually, he hears a car pull in and goes to the front porch to meet Grace and Victoria. Except it isn't Victoria's car. It's Christopher's.

Callum walks up to the car to stop him. He doesn't want Christopher anywhere near the house and the kids. The first thing Christopher does is punch Callum in the mouth. He lands a good punch because Callum never expected it. In the moment that Callum rights himself, Christopher runs for the door. Callum catches him at the stairs and takes his legs out from under him with a sold tackle.

"You are not getting anywhere near those children."

"Callum, please," Christopher begs from his knees. He even holds his hand together in prayer. "Please let me get Jack. I'll go, but I need to take Jack with me?"

"Christopher. You are drunk. Get in the car, I'll take you home. Let's go. Get the fuck up." Callum tries to pull him to his feet, but Christopher pulls Callum to his knees.

"Callum. I have to save Jack."

"What are you talking about?" Callum asks.

"He can't go to the camp Callum. He can't go there. I won't let him."

"Why not? Why can't he?"

"It is a bad place Callum. He can't go there."

"Jessie went. Didn't she and she was fine?"

"No she didn't. She was sick. She couldn't go. Jack can't go either."

"Christopher, what the fuck is going on?" Callum asks.

271

Christopher gets back into his car and Callum reaches for the keys. The police car blocks the driveway anyway. Red and blue lights illuminate the yard. Marina and Jessie are watching from the doorway with little Jack standing between them as Christopher is cuffed, led to the police car and driven away.

Fourteen

"Can anyone get the door?" Callum yells from the kitchen. "Is there anyone hearing my voice? Anyone at all?" For a house full of people, it is awfully quiet. Callum presses the last bit of dry rub into the pile of baby back ribs he is seasoning.

"I got it," Grace hollers from the stairs.

"Where is everybody?" Callum calls, scrubbing his hands in the sink.

"They are next door getting the kids' stuff moved over. I'm still packing," Grace says and swings the door open.

"Victoria," Callum smiles at the sound of the familiar voice from the front porch. "My god you are even more beautiful than my brother let on. You don't happen to have a twin sister, do you?" Callum's brother, Eric, flirts old school but well.

Grace just laughs as Callum runs and lifts his brother off his feet for a good old American bear hug, with a spin. "Jesus Christ what have they done to you? A beard and a tee shirt? I had no idea *American* was so contagious? Callum, my god you do look well though."

Eric shakes his head at the changed man in front of him. Eric is just as tall as Callum and just as good looking. But his neat hair is dark and clipped close. "You looks so different. So happy."

Callum can't control the smile because what Eric sees is exactly what Callum feels. "Eric, I'd like to introduce…"

"Victoria, I am so pleased to meet you," Eric bows gallantly before taking her hand to his lips for a kiss.

"No, darling brother, this lovely lady is Grace, a very good friend, but not my soon to be wife."

"Are all women this lovely in Asheville? That wasn't the case at the airport." Eric shakes her hand trying to catch up on the who's who.

"We have been blessed with two lovely women in this house. Ah here comes my fiancé now."

Victoria walks the grass from the next house over, Mindy's former house, carrying Marcus on her hip.

"Dada," he says. With a full head of hair and a baby button-down shirt, he looks more like his daddy every day.

"My God, Callum," Eric says taking the baby from Victoria's arms. "What the hell took me so long to get here and meet this little guy? You really do have a baby?" Eric holds Marcus up for a good look. "Victoria, please forgive me. I'm in a state of shock right now. I promise to greet you properly in a moment." Eric hugs Marcus close, pressing his lips to baby cheeks. "He's a fucking angel."

"Callum, your brother is going to fit in just fine," Grace says. There may be some batting of eyelashes.

Before the afternoon is out, Eric has toured Victoria and Callum's home, Grace's new home next door, Callum's school and has the requisite lager in his hand, sitting in an Adirondack chair looking out over the mountain. The warm May sunshine and blue skies bring the first glimmer of summer.

"It is marvelous here," Eric says. "Aside from your beautiful fiancé, I can understand why you would make this your home."

"It is my home now. I'll never leave here," Callum admits.

"So let me get this all straight. You've not gone bigamist," Eric jokes.

Callum laughs. "Correct. If I had intentions of polygamy, I might have stayed in Utah."

"So Grace has had a tough time? Bad divorce?" Eric asks, testing the waters.

Callum doesn't tell Grace's story. He just tells what he needs to about Marina finding her father, Christopher's drinking and finally the divorce. "Things got rough there at the end. Grace wouldn't press charges. It is a terrible thing to drag the father of your children through the mud. She wanted to, but in the end she wouldn't do it. She'll always worry he'll come back and try to take the kids. He left with little more than the clothes on his back and I am certain we haven't seen the last of him. Grace had a state-of-the-art security system installed, as did we, but she'll always be looking over her shoulder."

"Where is the asshole?" Eric asks.

"We aren't exactly sure. First prison and then bail. He was in a rehab facility under an assumed name for a time, but he checked himself out. He sends the children postcards, the last was from out west. Montana. He seemed to be working construction. I just hope he has the good sense to stay away."

"And she has lived here with the kids for a time?" Eric asks.

"Since September," Callum remembers that night Grace knocked on their door in shock, ribs broken, her life destroyed, or so Callum thought.

"Losing their father was terrible on the children. Christopher is a complicated man, but he was a devoted father, even to Marina, for a short time. He was a classic Jekyll and Hyde. We decided the kids would be better off together. They are very close, even after only knowing each other a short time. Blood being thicker than water and all that. Eventually we decided to look for options to make the situation more permanent without turning into an episode of *Sister Wives*." Eric stares blank faced at the reference. "An American reality show, back to bigamy."

"So the house next door?"

"Yes. Grace offered a house swap to Mindy. Grace's house was a bit larger with an enormous yard so Mindy jumped at the chance. There have been painters and carpenters and new plumbing. Movers are coming tomorrow. Speaking of, what the hell are you doing here already? I was so excited to see you, I forgot you aren't due in for another week."

Eric pulls on his beer and looks at the swaying trees above. A gentle breeze dances along the leaves. "I wanted to get here before Mother. We haven't spent time together in far too long. I am sorry for that. I've been hiding a bit, running the continents so to speak."

"I'm thrilled to see you," Callum says. "Have you been well?"

"Mostly well. The world can be a very ugly place at times Callum. There is no shortage of sickness and violence. We physicians will never be short for work, unfortunately."

Callum senses Eric wants to keep the conversation light without getting into details.

"Am I an imposition coming early? I thought I'd call but just never did." Eric says suddenly. He shifts in his seat uncomfortably.

"Eric, what's wrong?" Callum says. The American ability to ask a direct question has infected him. "Something is wrong, isn't it?"

"No, not wrong, exactly. Just regretful. Seeing you with Marcus is a reminder. I need to settle down. I'm tired of living this chaos. I'm to a point where I can see I'm not fixing all of the world's problems on my own. I want a home. I want a fucking mailbox."

"Really?" Callum is amused. "The perfect prince wants a princess and a happily ever after? Maybe a few little royals as well?"

"Enjoy your mocking. I'm not to the best of it yet." Eric waits.

"News? Come on for fuck's sake. What is it?"

"What the hell do I want to be in England for? I have a new sister who I have hardly taken the time to know. I have a brother I've barely seen in ten years. I seem to have quite a few nieces and nephews all of the sudden. And Victoria and John, too. I need to know my own family."

"What are you saying Eric?" Callum can hardly believe his ears. *Eric, here in the states?* It is the best and most unbelievable news he has heard in a long time.

"I am saying this. Since I have expressed my determination to move to America to be nearer to my family, Mother too has decided to move to America." Eric gets it all out in one breath.

Callum nearly spits his beer. "You are joking," Callum says with eyes wide in terror. "You are absolutely fucking joking. Mother would never lower herself to live on American soil. Fucking never."

"It's true Callum. I'm so sorry. I wanted to get here and tell you first. I wanted you to have some time to get used to it before her arrival."

Callum just shakes his head and covers his eyes with both hands. "Fuck."

"So," Eric says, changing the subject. "The wedding will be out here?"

On the morning of the wedding, Callum wakes up early, slipping out of bed to let Victoria sleep. Her red hair streaming the white pillow still takes his breath away. Callum pulls on a sweatshirt and shorts. Marcus is sleeping soundly in his crib when Callum tiptoes past his room. Eric is staying down in George's old room for a few weeks until he decides where to settle in America. He is considering a tour of the states, not unlike Callum's, to visit cities up and down the coast. Eric wants to settle within a day's drive of his sister and brother.

When Callum walks by the front window, he sees Marina sitting on the porch swing. She stayed the night next door, so he is a little surprised to see her here. In the kitchen, he uses a press to make a pot of coffee. He looks out the window to make sure the enormous tent for the wedding fared well overnight. Tent, chairs and tables all look to be in good order. Florists, caterers, photographers will be here by noon. They have planned the most casual wedding they could, but these things tend to take on a life of their own.

Callum pours two cups of coffee and meets Marina on the porch.

"You are up with the roosters today," he says handing her a cup.

She takes the offered coffee and he sits at her side, careful not to spill.

"Thanks Callum," she says taking first sips. They sit and watch the sun make its way from behind the peaks. "Happy wedding day."

"Thank you so much, darling."

Marina looks very different than just a few months ago and a world of different from the little girl he met on the slopes. She has grown inches and has developed the muscle tone of an athlete. As a freshman, she made the varsity lacrosse team. She has found her niche in sports.

In September, after Christopher's breakdown and having to come to terms with the circumstances of her conception, Marina started running with Callum. First, they ran just a half mile. It took weeks to get her to run two miles straight, but she was up every day, dressed and ready to run before school. He never let her down. They ran their first 5k in November, a Turkey Trot. Over Easter in Osprey Island, they ran a 10k together.

Her long hair is knotted on top of her head and it makes Callum smile.

"What's funny?" she asks.

"You hair reminds me of the day we met. I was a monsterous ass that day. I don't think I've ever apologized for that," he remembers.

"You sure didn't like my hat," she says blowing on her coffee. "I loved that hat."

He smiles remembering. "Marina. Can we have a serious moment?" he asks. "Just a quick one?"

"Sure Callum. It is a big day. We might have more than one." She smiles out of the side of her mouth.

Callum has become much more of a sharer these last months. It may have something to do with the therapist he started seeing after Christopher left. They all needed some help to get through that time. Figuring out how to best support three devastated children and two incredibly strong women who were victimized by the same man, was difficult.

Callum watches the sun climb, silently collecting his thoughts. "Marina, you saved my life. I have told you this before and I'm going to say it again. If you hadn't taken me down that day in Park City and temporarily crippled me, I shudder to think where I would be right now. I think Elizabeth only left Marcus here because she was betting on your mother caring for him, not me. Christopher was going to break down eventually. Marina, because you were here, Jessie and Jack and even Grace had someplace safe to land when that happened."

After Christopher ran, during his days in rehab, he wrote a letter to Grace. He told her about his own abuse as a child while at camp. He never told a soul, not even his parents. He was six and the details were vague, but he was taken from his bunk at night and raped. His abuser threatened to kill Christopher's family if he ever told and instructed him to stuff his underwear with toilet paper until the bleeding stopped. Christopher lived in terror until he left the memory behind a wall of repression. Callum was sickened to think that his own mock attack of Christopher may have hastened the breakdown.

When Jessie was six and preparing for camp, she had a stomach bug and wasn't able to go. Callum couldn't help wondering if Christopher drugged her. Not enough to harm her, but maybe ipecac to induce vomiting to prohibit her from going. Preparing to send Jack sent him over the edge.

"Marina, you brought all of these people together and we are a family. And you are the heart and soul of this family."

A tear falls from Marina's eye, but she doesn't wipe it. They have all learned to fight the tears a little less.

"Callum," she says. "Back in Utah, mom and I were so alone. Even with everything that has happened, all the good and all the bad, I am really happy that we are here and all together. I am so happy you and Mom have each other." She scoots to his side and he covers her shoulders with his arm. "You are a great dad, Callum, to all of us."

Now it is his turn to share a tear. He never imagined that being a great dad would be the best compliment of his life.

"Everyone's up early today. Are we all a little excited?" Victoria asks from the doorway, coffee cup in hand.

"Yes, that reminds me!" Marina jumps to her feet and runs off the porch. "We have a surprise. Don't eat breakfast. Come over at ten o'clock, not earlier. Okay? Text me before you come." She runs a few steps toward

Grace's house, stops and turns back. "I love you both," she says, before running the rest of the way.

"Love you too Marina," they each call to her.

Victoria sits on the swing by Callum's side.

"Oh my God," Callum says, when Marina is out of sight. "My heart. It is so full, it might burst."

Victoria lays her head on his shoulder. "What do you think the surprise is?" she asks.

"Anna, John and the kids are hiding out over there. I saw them sneak in late last night. Probably my mother too. I think John is probably already cooking a very large breakfast."

"I bet Anna is making scones."

Callum nods in agreement. "Marcus is still sleeping?" he asks.

"He is a sleepy boy today."

"I have a thought. How about we go inside and we can enjoy one last morning in bed as singles."

"You read my mind perfectly," Victoria agrees.

"I was thinking this might be a banner day to start trying to make a baby together," Callum says.

Victoria laughs out loud. Babies were not the conversation she expected this morning.

"Is that funny?" Callum jokes. "Do you not want a baby with me?"

"Of course I do, Callum. Are you ready for another baby though?" she asks, but the answer is obvious.

He sets his coffee down onto the wood of the porch and pulls Victoria into his lap. "I am ready to take on anything as long as I am with you."

Callum slides a hand under her shirt and begins his campaign on her very smooth, quickly warming skin. Her lips on his are all the answer he needs. He leaves the coffee and carries her prematurely over the threshold.

"I love you in a way I never thought I could love, Victoria. You are the best thing that has ever happened to me," Callum whispers into her neck. "Before I knew you, I was broken and you fixed me."

"No Callum," she says seriously, holding his face in her hands. "You fixed me. You made me be a better mother for Marina. You made me do the right thing, even though it was so damn hard. You were right about everything. You saved us both."

He kisses her deeply and lays her on the bed.

"I'm having thoughts of undressing you and doing things to you with my mouth. I could do wonderful things to you with my mouth," he says just like he said that day in Park City.

"By all means, do wonderful things to me with your mouth. Then let's make a baby together."

Callum closes his eyes for a moment and takes a deep breath, feeling grateful for all he has. He remembers the day he landed in the states feeling alone and hopeless less than two years before. An entire life can change in just eighteen months. If he had met Victoria on that day, she would never have taken him seriously. To marry her and have a family with her is the dream Callum never dreamed.

"I read that women over thirty are more likely to have twins. What do you say, Victoria? Let's shoot for a matched set," Callum pulls off his sweatshirt.

"Callum," she laughs. "Knowing you, you could probably make it happen."

"Together, Victoria, we can make fucking magic." he says and indeed, they do.

-THE END-

Sunshine and Moonlight
continues with Book Three

Coming
To
Brooklyn

Acknowledgments

It is difficult to list everyone who has supported me through this second novel. Writing is all consuming sometimes. The energy pulls from other places and not always in a good way. Sometimes written words take the place of human interactions.

My daughters are incredibly indulgent. Having a Mom who wears heels to an office by day and sits for countless hours in yoga pants in front of a laptop writing novels by night (and weekends, snow days, sick days, vacation days, etc.) has to be weird. They have both always let me know that they are 100% okay with this and proud of me and that has been kind of awesome. I was struggling to name Victoria's daughter during the first draft (and NO she was not inspired by my girls in any way). My younger daughter came up with the perfect name...Marina. She also drove the thousand miles roundtrip to Asheville with me to take the cover photo. Time I spend with my girls is magical. I have to love my girls. It is a requirement. But I like them. They intellectually surpassed me about the age of eight. They are just amazing kids. They tolerate my social media nasty talk and agree to keep it to themselves if they read my books. However, I was at the pool this summer rereading *Circling The Shadows* and a neighbor said, "How funny, I saw your daughter reading that same book a few days ago." None of us is ready to discuss the fact that I write sex scenes. As far as they know I had intercourse twice in my life since I have two girls. End of story.

My family is kind of awesome. They don't always understand me, but they do always love me. They are insanely talented and funny and all vote the way I vote, thank goodness. (I write this on November 6, 2016, two days before a presidential election.) We all drink bourbon, thanks to my Kentucky sister. We love the beach, loud music, our kids, food and the list goes on and on. I truly appreciate each and every one of them. Special shout out to my Mom because she has been incredibly supportive of me during a very tumultuous time in my life, even though it was hard on her at first. It doesn't matter how old you are, feeling good with your Mom makes life so much better. LOVE YOU MOMMA!

This has been a big year of change for me. I have made a few new really good friends and have been lucky enough to keep some I have known for many years. My friends are more important to me than ever. Occasionally you need a good friend to move you into a new apartment on a 95 degree day or empty mouse traps or cut your hair for free or just call you during a dog walk and make you laugh endlessly. You know who you are and what you mean to me. I love you all.

Thank you to the cities of Asheville, North Carolina and Park City, Utah. These cities are absolutely beautiful and fun, with amazing music, restaurants, sites, shopping, and full of wonderful people.

Not to be missed... thanks to my Starbucks baristas, bartenders, gastroenterologist, pharmacist, Ulises, bank lady, "special store" lady, Radiohead, Civil Twilight, Foo Fighters, strangers on social media who feel more like friends, my IT Director who taught me how to put windshield washer fluid in my car without laughing at me, and everyone else I should list by name and I'll regret not adding later.

Bottom line – thank you all. I am grateful...